Taking VENGEANCE

VENGEANCE SERIES

KAYLEA CROSS

AUTHOR'S NOTE

This one's for all my Valkyrie fans. It's always so much fun to get this crew back together and see them in action. Hope you enjoy the ride!

Happy reading,

Kaylea

CHAPTER ONE

Her instincts had served her well over the years. In fact, they were the main reason she was still alive today. And right now, they were screaming at her that this might signal more danger was on the way.

Amber leaned back in her office chair, drumming her fingers on the armrests as she stared at her custom laptop. Lady Ada was so much more to her than just a computer.

The machine was a part of her. A near perfect creation that Amber had nurtured and kept improving from the moment she'd received the individual components and begun the building process from scratch several years ago.

Lady Ada was also never wrong. And right now she was telling Amber they had a serious problem brewing.

Amber shoved the rolling chair back on the rug, stood and strode from her highly secure office into the downstairs hallway of the two-story house she shared with her husband. Large picture windows at the back of the house overlooked the lush green lawn and the acres of Montana pastureland beyond it, anchored in the distance by the majestic, jagged peaks of the Rockies.

Beneath her bare feet, the rhythmic thump of bass and drums vibrated up through the floor long before she reached the door to the basement. The dark, gritty beat of an old Depeche Mode song hit her when she pulled it open and jogged down the staircase into what they'd made into their home gym.

At the bottom, she paused. Jesse stood in the middle of the mat-covered floor, facing away from her as he went to town on the heavy bag suspended from the ceiling. Sweat glistened on his golden-toned skin and dampened his short, dark brown hair, highlighting every bunch and ripple of muscle across his back and shoulders with each punch he threw.

Watching him here was a reminder that like her, he was deadly. That he had been trained to kill with his bare hands in addition to a variety of weapons, and that until recently he'd made his living as a hired killer.

Now those same skilled, deadly hands protected her. Supported her. Made her tingle and shiver all over when they caressed her.

He was her partner. Her lover. The only man who had won her respect, trust and heart.

A wave of desire rolled over her as she watched him deliver a rapid combo of powerful blows to the bag, the sheer, masculine power of him momentarily taking her breath away.

He knew she was watching. Would have known the moment she opened the door at the top of the stairs, or maybe even before that, even with the music up loud enough to vibrate the floor. Because Jesse's awareness was as finely honed as hers.

Reminding herself why she'd come down here, she pushed those thoughts firmly away and stepped forward. He met her gaze in the mirrors on the opposite wall and stopped, wiping a forearm across his sweaty forehead as he turned to face her, his pecs and abs flexing with each rapid breath.

She hit a button on the wall to kill the music, and suddenly Jesse's elevated breathing was the only sound in the silent room. "Need you to come look at something."

He held her stare as he removed his boxing gloves. Assessing her. "Something wrong?"

"Maybe."

Unwrapping his hands and wrists, he snagged a towel from a bench and prowled toward her, all sexy male grace and power. If she hadn't been so worried about the current situation, she would have dragged him off to the shower in the next room to enjoy running her soapy hands all over that chiseled body, and then following them with her mouth.

Instead, she turned and jogged back up to the main floor and headed straight into her office. Lady Ada was continuing her latest scan as Amber sat back down in the chair to review what was showing on screen.

Jesse moved in behind her, quiet as a stalking panther and splayed a big, tanned hand on the desk to the left of her keyboard. He leaned in over her shoulder with the towel now draped around his neck, filling her nose with a mix of spice, sweat, and something all him that made her want to rub her face against his neck.

"What am I looking at?" he asked in that deep, dark voice that could easily distract her if she let it.

"It's something I've been monitoring for a while now." She'd always kept tabs on her remaining Valkyrie sisters, and still did in case of this exact situation, to ensure they all stayed safe. God knew they'd all been through more than enough shit already.

"It started shortly after Kiyomi and Marcus's wedding," she added. This past Christmas Eve, to be exact. Already seven months ago now. "Lady Ada picked up the first hint of trouble on one of her routine scans and there've been a few other hints since then, but I've noticed a marked uptick in unusual activity over the past few weeks."

She closed one screen and brought up another, turning her head to watch Jesse's reaction.

His dark eyebrows pulled together instantly as he scanned the intel, his expression hardening. "All your names are listed."

"I know." All eight Valkyries identified by name—or at least the names they'd been known by while they were still involved with the Program. That was worrisome in itself. No one should have access to that information anymore.

"Someone's been watching all of us," she continued. "Possibly trying to locate us, I'm still not sure. And I can't say for sure yet whether whoever is behind this poses a real threat or not. But as you can see from the number of hits Lady Ada has come back with, this person seems to be most interested in one of us in particular."

Staring at the data, Jesse raised his free hand and absently rubbed at his chin, the scar on the right side visible through the dark stubble. "Yeah, shit. Any idea why?"

"No. And before you ask, no, I haven't alerted the others, because I don't want to cause undue concern while everyone is trying to move on and find their footing." Trying to forge actual lives for themselves after decades of being government pawns and having to constantly look over their shoulders every time they ventured out of their homes.

They'd more than earned that right. All of them had. Just as they'd all earned the money they'd taken back in the fall during the joint op to end the Architect.

Now she was worried that this new development might threaten all of that. Everything they'd fought for—their futures.

Their freedom.

She expelled a long breath and looked up at Jesse, thinking of all they'd been through and how far they'd come together. Initially he'd been sent to hunt her down. Now he would protect and defend her with his last breath.

She would never take that for granted. Or his insight. She valued his opinion on security matters. "What do you think?" She was wired to be paranoid. She and the others had been trained to be suspicious of everything and every-one, and to notice the smallest detail, no matter how insignificant it seemed.

More than that, aside even from her computer know-how and skills as an assassin, first and foremost she'd been trained not to trust anyone. Ever. To never let anyone in. As a result, she'd been alone most of her life, with no one to turn to or rely on.

Her sister and Jesse had changed all of that forever,

along with her other Valkyrie sisters. Now she couldn't imagine her life without them. That was why she was determined to stay on top of this emerging evidence, and head off any threat before it surfaced.

Jesse straightened, face somber as their eyes met. "Better call her and let her know what's up."

～

Friends forever. No matter what happens.

Kiyomi pulled away from the memory and surfaced slowly in the present, that long ago silenced voice startlingly clear in her mind as she allowed herself to return to her surroundings. The beautiful, private walled garden set back from the manor house of Laidlaw Hall. A paradise of flowers, fruit trees and humming insects nestled in the rolling Cotswolds landscape.

But even her formidable mental discipline couldn't stop the inevitable barrage of images that followed.

Horror. Darkness. Blood. A face she'd once loved, savagely beaten until the features were almost unrecognizable. Except by her.

Kiyomi would always have recognized that face.

She released a deep breath and focused on her body even as the sharp talons of grief dug into her, using all five senses to ground herself as she'd been practicing. Shifting her awareness to the solid feel of the earth beneath her where she lay stretched out on her back on a patch of sun-warmed grass. The sweet scent of roses and lavender carried on the breeze. Soft, trilling birdsong mixing with the rustle of leaves. The distinctive *kak-kak* of a jackdaw nearby.

Sometimes it was easy to keep the ugly memories at bay. Sometimes they stayed put beneath her consciousness.

Today wasn't one of those days.

She fought the last of the ghostly images away through sheer force of will and consciously slowed her breathing and heart rate. *You're okay. That's all in the past, it can't hurt you anymore.*

Maybe someday that would be true.

Opening her eyes, she blinked up at the canopy of leaves arching above her. Golden afternoon sunshine filtered through the branches, the leaves having faded from the acid green of spring into the deeper green of English mid-summer. A warm breeze washed over her, rippling the ornamental grasses where she lay inside the walled garden, making the roses and daylilies nod.

She wiped her damp cheeks with the heels of her hands and released another long breath, glad for the privacy this place gave her. Giving into tears was still embarrassing and seemed pointless, but her therapist insisted it was a sign that she was healing. All part of the unthawing process after believing herself to be numb and impervious to emotion for most of her life.

The faint crunch of footsteps on the gravel path to the left, beyond the far side of the stone wall, drew her attention. She glanced over in time to see Marcus step through the ivy-smothered archway framing the doorway cut into the stone, his wooden cane in his left hand, and his loyal Anatolian shepherd Karas at his side.

She didn't move, just watched him come, conscious of a lightening in her soul as he approached in faded jeans that clung to his hips and thighs, and a snug T-shirt that molded to the powerful muscles in his chest and shoulders.

7

In another couple months he would switch out the T-shirts for cable knit sweaters and sheepskin-lined jackets he favored when the weather turned cool. On him, both looks were equally sexy.

He stopped next to her and sat down, failing to hide a flinch at the pain in his left hip, the scars pulling around his eye. His injuries had healed as much as they ever would a long time ago, but the scar tissue, muscle and nerve damage were a permanent reminder of his horrific captivity in Syria.

Just as the scars on her back would always remind her of the same.

He stretched out beside her on his back, tucked one arm behind his head, and captured her hand in his. Karas lay between their outstretched legs, muzzle resting on her paws. She was still a daddy's girl for certain, but sometimes followed Kiyomi around now instead of him.

Marcus ran his deep brown gaze over her face. "Penny for your thoughts, love?" he said in his deep, Yorkshire accent she adored.

She gave him a wry smile. "You sure you want to know?"

"Positive."

That made her smile a little, and she was struck again by how perfectly this place suited him, even though living at Laidlaw Hall was an entirely different world from the blue-collar life he'd grown up with in Yorkshire.

He'd told her that he'd only rarely come here to visit sometimes on summer holiday with his mother as a child. It hadn't been until he was medically discharged from the military that he'd suddenly inherited the massive property from a great uncle he'd barely known. Yet Marcus had accepted the responsibility and massive workload that came with it, to preserve this piece of his ancestral legacy.

She couldn't imagine him living anywhere else. "Just practicing my meditation. And remembering a friend," she murmured.

"Good thoughts, I hope?"

Mostly. "Yes." Bittersweet ones.

"Who were you thinking of?"

"Julia."

Flashes of memory from the stolen times they had spent together during the second, intense phase of the program without their trainers knowing. Sharing food, forbidden outside of strictly scheduled mealtimes during their training. Talking about hopes and dreams they'd both known were impossible back then, even before they'd been permanently separated into different specialties.

Kiyomi had been fortunate to survive her career as a Valkyrie, and finally win her freedom. Julia had not. Instead, her best and only friend back then had suffered at the hands of inhuman monsters before being dumped in a Moscow alley to die.

"Ah." Marcus rubbed his thumb over the back of her hand, watching her, the dappled sunlight highlighting the puckered and pitted scarring on the left side of his face and neck.

He was still the handsomest man she'd ever known. His scars, the suffering he'd endured and the courage it had taken to overcome it all, had transformed him into the man he was. The only man who could have broken down her walls and captured her ice-encased heart.

She could smell the sweet, dusty scent of hay and horses on him, indicating he'd just come from the barn. She must have been out here longer than she'd realized. "Just get back from the northeast pasture?"

"Aye. Karas took a shift guarding the neighbor's flock again."

"Always on duty. Good girl." She reached down to pet the dog's soft head and received a wet lick on the back of her hand in reply.

"This is three days in a row you've come out here," Marcus said, taking in the garden. "Seems a good spot for thinking."

Yes. This was her very own secret garden, a magical place where healing was possible.

Turning onto her side, she came up on one elbow, resting her head in her hand to gaze down at her husband. "It's peaceful here. And it reminds me of Eden." A Valkyrie trained as a saboteur, and an expert with poisons. She would know every plant here, every one of their toxic properties. Now she was back in the States with Zack, tending her own poison garden. They were all scattered apart again.

Marcus met her gaze again. "You miss them."

Yes. And it was a strange feeling for someone who had lived a solitary life as an intimate assassin. "Sometimes." She ran her fingertips down the side of his face, across the scars partially hidden by his thick, dark stubble. "But every day I wake up and pinch myself to make sure this is still real." That *he* was real, along with the life they were making together in this beautiful, historic place his ancestors had owned for over five hundred years.

He caught her hand, kissed her fingers, and reached up to slide his hand into the back of her hair. "It's real, love," he said quietly, and drew her down for a slow, thorough kiss.

Kiyomi let her mind go blank and melted into him, opening up her senses until there was nothing but him and the rising tide of longing and arousal he created. He made her come alive. She'd been dead inside until him.

A ringtone went off, disturbing the quiet. Not hers. She never brought her phone with her during therapy homework.

He leaned back to fish his phone out of his pocket, glanced at it. "It's Amber."

Her interest sharpened. Amber and Jesse had pulled her out of hell that day in Syria and saved her life. She would never forget it. "Go ahead."

"Amber. How are you?" He paused. "One second." He put the phone on speaker. "Go ahead."

"Hey, Kiyomi. Listen, something's come up, and I need to tell you about it."

At her friend's somber tone, she met Marcus's gaze. "What's wrong?"

"I'm not sure yet. But we're being monitored. All of us."

She sat up, instantly on alert, the peace of the garden forgotten. "Monitored how?"

"Right now, it's a low threat level. Seeking behavior that tells me whoever is looking isn't sure where we are. But the problem is, we've all been identified somehow."

Marcus's jaw flexed, anger sparking in his eyes. "Can you tell where the intel leak came from?"

He was right. It had to be a leak. There was no other explanation for how anyone would have found out their identities otherwise.

"Not yet. Whoever this is, they're clever, and good at hiding their tracks. So far I can't even pinpoint *where* they are."

Unease slid through her. Amber was one of the most talented and gifted hackers in the world. If someone was looking for them and she couldn't crack this, there was definitely cause for concern. "What do they want, any idea?"

"Not sure. There's been nothing specific so far, but I'm keeping on top of it. Also, you need to be aware that whoever this is, they seem to have a particular interest in you."

An invisible fist grabbed her stomach. "Meaning what?"

"There are almost four times as many searches for you than for any of the rest of us. I don't know why."

Marcus stilled, his expression taut. "Looking for her location?"

"Looking for anything on her at all. Though as far as I can tell, the person hasn't found anything to compromise your safety."

Yet. "What about our marriage certificate?" She'd used a different surname that she'd adopted for all her new IDs, but kept Kiyomi as a first name because she refused to give that part of her up. But if someone had found that record and realized it was her, it would lead them straight here to Laidlaw Hall.

"I scrubbed it from public record as soon as it was

issued," Amber replied. "The only way anyone could get it now is if they accessed the original through the parish—which they would have to do in person—and so far, no one has. So far, there's no credible threat. I just wanted to alert you about what's going on."

It still made her uneasy as hell. "Thanks. We appreciate it. How are you and Megan?" Her sister.

"We're both fine. Miss you guys though."

After they ended the call a minute later, Marcus brought her hand to his lips and kissed the center of her palm. "She'll stay on top of it. If there's any danger, she'll let us know straight away and we'll go to ground somewhere."

Kiyomi nodded and tried to downplay it. She didn't want him worrying about her. "I'm not worried. Amber's watching, and I feel safe here with you."

But a frisson of unease wound through her anyway.

The danger should have ended with the Architect's death last fall. They'd all gone through so much. Too much, and she couldn't bear the thought of losing anyone from the family she'd only just found.

Reading the concern in her husband's eyes, she put on an easy smile and got to her feet. "Let's go inside," she said, holding out a hand.

He took it, allowed her to help him up and immediately braced his weight on his cane while Karas popped up beside him, tail wagging. They walked hand in hand up the pea gravel pathway toward the old Georgian manor house, its warm, golden Cotswold stone glowing in the sunlight that glinted off the windows.

Thoughts raced through her mind with each step.

Trying to figure out who could be targeting them now. What thread they might have failed to tie up last fall. Anything they could have possibly missed last time.

She came up blank, and that was almost worse. Hard as it was to accept, they were being hunted again.

CHAPTER TWO

I vy set down her coffee cup on the desk and paused to stretch her back before resuming her work at the keyboard. Every day for months now she'd been working on this same project. Conducting her research. Looking for any sign of weakness she could exploit. Any tiny slip.

So far they hadn't disappointed her by making it easy.

Three monitors were set up in front of her at different heights, allowing her to process information more quickly and weed out the chaff. She focused on the middle screen, where all the current files were displayed, containing all the relevant information she'd found so far.

Eight of them, one on each surviving Valkyrie. Eight deadly female operatives who posed a threat to her.

They'd done a good job of trying to wipe their identities from the record. Most people wouldn't know who they were now, and sure as hell wouldn't have the capability of finding anything on them at all.

But she wasn't like most people.

The intel she'd compiled thus far had taken countless hours to find, using the best computer that money and her skills could get her. She had earned the right to finally do something for herself. Something that mattered to *her*.

This was it.

Once upon a time she'd been naïve enough to break her number one rule and risk trusting others, and had nearly paid for that mistake with her life. As far as the rest of the world was concerned, she had ceased to exist that night. Because of that, in many ways the woman staring back at her in the mirror now was still a stranger to her as well.

She scanned the latest search results displayed on the first monitor, struggling to ignore her rising frustration and impatience. In spite of all her work, she hadn't yet found anything that would help her locate the Valkyries. Still nothing solid on Kiyomi.

She twisted the bracelet on her left wrist as she thought, toying with the cool, smooth jet bead that bore the image of a cherry blossom. It was the only token she'd kept from her former life, before the betrayal. To remind her of the past, and act as a symbol of her motivation to track the remaining Valkyries down.

All she needed was one solid thread to tug on. One tiny filament, even. From there it was only a matter of pulling on it until she had what she wanted. Patience and perseverance were the key.

Her black and white cat Mr. Whiskers meowed and jumped onto her lap to butt her chin with his head. "You're hungry, huh?" she murmured, still staring at the screen as she scratched behind his ears and finished reading the results of the scan.

There had to be something here. She was getting close, she could feel it.

The cat persisted, so she got up and fed him and warmed up her coffee from the pot on the kitchen counter before going back to her desk in the second bedroom she used as an office.

Mr. Whiskers was her first pet, and she loved him to pieces. She'd wanted a cat her entire life and had never been able to have one until recently. In Paris last year she'd heard his tiny mews while walking down a back alley, and discovered him trapped in a Dumpster with his dead littermates.

There was no way she could have left him there. She had been abandoned and preyed upon as a child, and if she hadn't rescued him, she was convinced he would have died. He was her best friend. Her only friend, a source of the unconditional love and acceptance she'd been denied her entire life.

Through the cracked-open window, the sound of a wedding procession making its way up Great Queen Street drifted in from outside. The flat's location was one of the reasons she'd snapped up this place as soon as she'd seen the listing come up, despite the high cost of the rent.

Nestled right in the heart of Covent Garden, it was the only place she'd ever been able to choose and set up with the intent to stay for at least several months. She loved its quirky, antique charm with the squeaky wood floors and the old beams in the ceilings, loved the vibrant neighborhood with all the shops, cafés and restaurants, and the theater district was only a short walk away.

Here she could venture out into the streets and disappear into the crowd. Here she could be anyone she wanted.

But she wouldn't be free until she'd finished this one, final mission.

A soft ding from the computer alerted her to a new hit. She leaned forward, eyes on the third monitor where she brought up a new story about the suspected crimes of a dead female former CIA officer. The article didn't mention the woman's name, but Ivy knew exactly who it was.

She had followed the story about Jane Allen's death last fall during a high-security prison transfer here in England with great interest. The US and British governments had both rushed to cover it all up with a cover story, but in this digital age, no one could ever cover up the truth entirely.

Ivy had immediately started digging, had kept going until she'd compiled enough evidence to be satisfied that her suspicions were correct. That transport van hadn't been destroyed in a freak accident.

The Valkyries had executed the so-called "Architect." Ivy applauded them for it. But they remained a potential threat to her, and she was going to find every last one of them.

She sat back, tapping her fingers on her desk. All eight women had disappeared since then. Not a surprise given their training and how highly skilled each of them were. They were to be admired—and feared.

Above all, they were not to be trusted. They were elite killers, every last one of them, and the bonds of loyalty that supposedly linked them all meant nothing in their world.

Having been targeted by their kind once before, Ivy knew that all too well.

Lost in thought, lulled by the rhythmic tapping of her

fingers on the wooden surface, she considered her options. Of the remaining eight, Amber was still the best choice as a target for what Ivy had in mind. They shared certain… similarities that could be used to her advantage.

And she just happened to have some information that Amber and another Valkyrie would be personally interested in.

After stretching her fingers, she quickly opened a specialized, private messaging program on the first monitor and began typing out a message, her fingers flying on the keyboard. When she was done she sat back to read it through several times, tweaking the wording in a few spots.

With a few shortcut commands, her custom program encrypted it. The message itself was already coded, but the encryption added another layer of protection on the off chance it was intercepted by anyone other than Amber.

When everything was ready, she hit send.

Mr. Whiskers jumped up into her lap again, purring like an engine while he rubbed his face against her neck. She smiled, stroking his thick, soft fur.

He was the only living being that had ever truly loved her back. She'd thought someone had loved her once, a long time ago, but she'd been wrong. The lesson had gutted her, and almost cost her life.

"And now we wait," she murmured as nerves and anticipation fizzed in the pit of her stomach. She'd just taken a huge risk, but there was no other option at this point.

This was a test, and Amber was one of the only people in the world who could pass it.

If she did, then it would only be a matter of time before

the thread Ivy needed to find would appear. After that, she would keep unraveling everything until she found their locations. Only then could she finally make her move.

∼

Just after breakfast Megan strode into the barn to find Ty in the middle of brushing his horse, muscles flexing across his back and arms under the T-shirt stretched across his lean torso. He glanced up at her and raised his eyebrows, continuing with his smooth strokes. "What's up?"

"Amber just texted. Said she needs to talk to us in person right away." When her sister said something like that, Megan dropped everything.

He lowered the brush, watching her with those alert, slate blue eyes. "Why, did something happen?"

"Must have." She opened the stall door where her horse Houdini was waiting. The mare wasn't as big or as bomb-proof as her beloved Rollo, who she'd had to leave back at Laidlaw Hall, but the horse was a talented escape artist, and Megan enjoyed that quirk in her personality. "Come on, girl. Time for a ride."

By the time she'd put the bridle on Houdini and mounted bareback to ride out of the cool shadows into the hot July morning sun, Ty was already waiting outside the paddock gate atop his gelding, highlights shining in the golden brown hair he'd recently grown out.

Normally, she would pause to admire the sexy view, but right now she was too amped up inside. Tightening the leather thong beneath her chin to hold her hat on as she joined him, she grasped the reins and leaned forward. "Hyah!"

Both horses leapt forward, hitting a canter within seconds, and then opening up into a gallop. Ty was right with her as they raced across the gently undulating Montana pastureland, so different to the rolling, patchwork Cotswolds hills she'd ridden across with Marcus while she'd lived there.

Her life was here now, with Ty on this three-hundred-acre horse ranch they shared with her sister and brother-in-law. Amber and Jesse's timber-framed house sat just under a mile away to the east, perched atop a slight rise in the terrain.

When the house came into view they slowed the horses to a trot, allowing them to cool down a bit as they approached. After clipping leads onto the bridles at a water barrel placed where the pasture met the edge of the back lawn, Amber hopped the white-painted rail fence and strode across the long expanse of manicured grass on her way to the patio doors.

She knocked once and punched in the security code before walking in. "Amber? Jess? We're here."

Jesse appeared around the corner and stepped into the large chef's kitchen, his deep golden skin tanned bronze by the prairie sun, and nodded at them. "Come on back. She's in the office."

Amber must have found something big.

Megan exchanged a look with Ty, then followed Jesse down the hall to Amber's private lair. No surprise, her sister was stationed in front of Lady Ada, her chocolate-brown hair pulled up in a messy bun held in place by a pen stuck through it.

"Hey," Megan said when her sister glanced over at them, struck again by how alike they looked. Slightly

21

different coloring, Amber with darker hair and green eyes, but similar features that immediately marked them as sisters.

Even now it was still surreal to think of all that had happened to them, and everything that had led to now. They'd been separated when they were young, recruited into the top secret Valkyrie Program and sent to different training facilities on opposite sides of the country. Soon after that, they'd both been told the other had died.

Lies. One of many that had warped and twisted their lives.

Amber had almost destroyed the remaining Valkyries because of other lies. If Megan and two of the others hadn't succeeded in finally capturing Amber on that op in Vienna, they never would have found each other, much less known the other was still alive.

Hatred hardened like a diamond inside her at the thought of all the years they'd been denied together. At the sheer toll in human suffering their psychotic aunt had caused when she'd started everything. The bitch was dead now, and Megan hoped she was burning in hell. "What's going on? Your message sounded urgent."

"Come take a look at this." Amber rolled her chair aside, allowing Megan to come stand at the desk and view the center monitor.

Ty positioned himself just behind her, looking over her shoulder. And he smelled damn good, too, but now was not the time for distractions. "Who's this from?" she asked, reading the message. It looked sort of like an email, but clearly wasn't.

"No idea."

Megan stopped reading to blink at her in surprise.

Amber was a wizard with all things technical and electronic. She could crack anything. "None?"

"No," she said in a flat tone, crossing her arms. "Lady Ada found it early this morning, otherwise I wouldn't ever have known it existed. That alone tells me whoever sent it set this up *expecting* me to find it. The encryption on it was cutting edge. And even after I'd cracked that, I still had to run it through a bunch of my other programs because it was all in code."

"Wow." Megan scanned it again. The short paragraph read like an anonymous tip, about a kidnapping ring currently operating in the UK. Preying on women and possibly teenage girls.

"What do you make of it?" Ty asked Amber.

"I'm thinking it could be the same person who's been trying to find us all. And they have at least some solid info on us, because guess who else was named in this message besides me?"

Megan and Ty both looked at her expectantly.

"Kiyomi."

Cold spread through Megan as the significance of that registered. "So then...whoever sent this is somehow familiar with our recent activities."

A few months ago Amber had begun doing pro bono work for organizations and law enforcement agencies specializing in hunting down human traffickers. Kiyomi had privately—and anonymously—been assisting and funding organizations dedicated to fighting the exploitation of orphaned girls across the globe, with an eye on starting her own foundation.

"Exactly." Amber spun her swiveling chair around to

face them. "Whoever sent this knows too damn much already, and I can't find them."

Unease began to take hold. Megan already hadn't liked the feel of this before, when Amber had told her the other day that someone was relentlessly searching for them. This new bit was way worse.

"Any truth to the tip?" Ty asked.

"Yes."

At that low response they all looked at Jesse, leaning against the doorframe with his ripped arms crossed over his broad chest. "Several news agencies in the UK have reported a possible kidnapping ring working there over the past few weeks. Seven women have gone missing so far, and one eighteen-year-old. I talked to Marcus about it an hour ago, and he confirmed everything we were able to find."

Megan nodded, boiling it all down in her head. "All that aside, bottom line is, we're dealing with a serious security breach."

"Yep," Amber answered, green eyes hard. "And I still can't get a lead on whoever this 'source' is."

Her constant companion, anxiety, began to bubble in the pit of her stomach. "What if it's a trap?"

Amber stared at her with that same fixed expression. "Chances are good it is. What do you want to do about it?"

There was only one answer to give. "I think we need to bring the Valkyries out of retirement."

CHAPTER THREE

Arms folded across his chest, Marcus leaned against the bookcase on the back wall of his study and listened to the conversation happening. A few feet in front of him, Kiyomi was seated at his desk in his favorite leather chair, on a secure video chat with some of the Valkyries.

So far, he didn't like what he was hearing.

Finding out that someone was relentlessly searching for Kiyomi was bad enough. What Amber had just disclosed prior to the meeting disturbed him even more.

"Any word yet on whether the cops think the missing women's cases are linked?" Chloe asked.

As usual, the explosives expert was chomping away on some gum, her blond hair peeking out from under one of the baseball caps she favored. He couldn't read her T-shirt, but he would bet Laidlaw Hall that whatever it said was full of some sarcastic cheek.

"Not officially," Kiyomi answered. "However, everything Marcus and I have found on the cases so far suggests that the majority of them are probably linked in some way. Given the timeline, the backgrounds of the women and the area where most of them were taken, there's a high likelihood we're dealing with a professional kidnapping ring." Her voice and expression were totally calm, giving nothing away about her feelings on the matter.

That didn't mean shit, however. She had been trained to be calm in any situation, including capture and torture. The kidnappings and possible trafficking involved here infuriated her on the deepest level. Yet she acted like this new threat against her didn't bother her.

Well, it sure as hell was bothering *him*.

There should be no further threat against her or any of the others. Amber had taken elaborate steps to scrub their identities and pasts from all government records, aided by former NSA agent Alex Rycroft, their unofficial government ally in their fight for freedom. Only a handful of people outside of this video chat should even know of their existence at this point, much less their names, intel on prior ops, or current interests and activities.

So even if Kiyomi might look calm, he knew his wife better than that. She might still be a mystery to him in some ways, but she couldn't fool him with this. There was no way this hadn't shaken her on a deep level. It was driving him bloody mad that she was trying to hide it from him.

"I've spliced together some local news coverage on the investigation over here," she continued, and started a video feed for the others.

Marcus shifted his attention from his wife to the stories she'd edited together, detailing the recent disappearances, and the police force's frustration with having no solid leads.

Over the past seven weeks, eight women had gone missing from the Birmingham area. All different ages, different ethnic backgrounds, none of them subscribing to a specific "type." The likelihood that they were all victims of this same kidnapping ring was high.

But what made these cases odd was that the women weren't the usual, easy targets kidnappers usually preyed upon. These women couldn't easily fall through the cracks, without anyone noticing their absence for days or weeks.

They weren't sex workers or addicts. None of them were homeless.

These victims had jobs. Homes. Families and friends who stayed in frequent contact. A couple of them were even married or living with someone.

"Police are warning women in the area to take extra caution if they go out alone, especially if they go to a place that doesn't have a lot of people in it," the female reporter from Birmingham continued. "We have several uncon-firmed reports about an unmarked silver minivan being linked to two of the cases. Police have so far denied this claim."

The kidnappings had caused a lot of fear within the community. It was all over the newspapers and media outlets. Women were being targeted in a specific way, then snatched off the street on their way home from work or the gym, sometimes in broad daylight. Marcus's intel sources had confirmed that the police had no leads yet.

"No demands for ransom or anything?" Eden asked. The toxins expert pushed her dark, spiral curls away from her face, her fiancé Zack seated beside her.

"No," Kiyomi answered. "These women have all disappeared without a trace."

"There's always a trace," Amber said darkly. "All we have to do is find one, and I'll start with this." Clicking started in the background as she worked her black magic on the keyboard while her sister, Ty and Jesse looked on from behind her in the room. "Which brings me to the real reason we called this emergency meeting."

The decrypted message she'd been sent earlier appeared on screen, along with a live feed of whatever Lady Ada was working on at the moment. "Everything I've been able to find so far on the cases backs up what Kiyomi and Marcus have said. The only pattern or similarities to these women that I can see are their general location, and they mostly seem to range in age from early twenties to late thirties."

She paused and looked into the camera. "My working theory is that whoever sent me this message knew enough about Kiyomi and me to guess that we would be personally invested enough in the story to start digging on our own. But there's more."

More clicking, then other images began popping up. Mug shots and security photos of various men.

"Including a list of men potentially involved in the kidnapping ring," she finished, sitting back while a slideshow of images played.

"Stop," Kiyomi blurted suddenly.

Marcus's gaze snapped to her, his whole body tensing as a taut silence blanketed the room.

"Stop where?" Amber asked, peering at her intently through the screen. "What did you see?"

"The pictures you just showed. Go through them again, more slowly."

While Amber did, Marcus divided his attention between Kiyomi and the images flashing on screen. Something was wrong. She'd recognized one of the men.

"*Him*," she said, and Amber stopped on the mug shot of a thirty-something, dark-haired bloke with tats on his neck.

Marcus's jaw tensed but he remained where he was, fighting his instinctive reaction to go to her. She wouldn't want comfort or concern right now, especially not in front of the others, and his position behind and slightly to the side of her didn't allow him to watch her reaction. Instead, he studied her profile, her body language, looking for clues as to what was going on inside her.

Her spine was stiff, her hands knotted into fists on the desk. Both uncharacteristic, outward displays of emotional distress. And her gaze was riveted to the image of the dark-haired man on screen, her lips compressed into a tight line.

"What's his name?" Her voice was low, and hard as the look on her face.

"Luka Tarasov," Amber said, watching her.

The name meant nothing to him, but it clearly meant something to his wife. And Marcus was suddenly desperate to know why.

KIYOMI STARED AT the man's picture, pure hatred melting the icy shock that had hit her when she'd first seen his image flash across the screen.

Luka Tarasov. So that was his real name.

"How do you know him?" Megan asked quietly.

"How did you get this?" Kiyomi demanded of Amber instead of answering.

"Our anonymous source sent it with the others, thirty minutes before this meeting," Amber said. "And if you know him, you need to tell us all how right now."

Drawing a slow, steadying breath, Kiyomi consciously relaxed her shoulders and uncurled her fists. She was keenly aware of Marcus watching her along with everyone else, could sense his concern. "He killed Julia."

A shocked silence answered her as the others looked from one of Amber's computer screens to the next, taking in all the intel Amber had gathered.

"Julia Green, you mean? Valkyrie hacker?" Amber asked, frowning.

She nodded grimly, her stomach muscles pulled tight. "Tarasov had an alias when I searched for him. He's a dual Russian/British citizen, and former Bratva." And the son of a bitch was somehow still alive.

Sadness flooded her, that old grief rising to the surface. "Tarasov and his goons tortured her, then dumped her in a back alley in Moscow and left her to die." She fought a new wave of fury as the raw memory exploded to life in her mind once again.

"What happened?" Zack asked, moving in closer beside Eden, his expression intense.

Her fellow Valkyries already knew the story because she'd told them about it at Laidlaw Hall last year. But the guys deserved to know too.

She drew a deep breath. "You remember who Zoya and Hannah were?"

The men all nodded, and Jesse spoke. "The Valkyries

who set up Amber to die in Rome, after she helped them steal a shit ton of money from a Russian rival of Zoya's boyfriend."

"Because I was an idiot," Amber muttered in disgust.

"No. Because they betrayed your trust." Jesse bent and kissed the top of her head.

Kiyomi sat back in the chair and pulled in another breath, inhaling the scent of leather, books, and wood smoke from the fireplace. Marcus hadn't moved, but she could feel him just there behind her. Could feel his stare, his growing anger, and knew there was going to be a reckoning between them after this meeting wrapped up.

"The boyfriend's name was Stanislav," she said. "Tarasov was his 2IC. They needed an incredibly skilled hacker for the job, so they located Julia and tried to recruit her."

"How do you know, were you in contact with her at the time?" Trinity asked. She was their unofficial group leader, the mother figure who had started the chain of events that had reunited them all in the first place.

And a former intimate assassin, like Kiyomi. The rarest kind of Valkyrie. No one understood her like Trin did, and that gave them a special bond.

"Yes. She and I became close during our initial training, and kept in touch periodically even when we became operational." Even though that had been expressly against the rules. "She told me about Zoya and Hannah, said something felt off about the job, so she turned them down and they recruited Amber instead."

When the others all continued to watch her in silence, she continued. "Julia kept tabs on them after that, sending me updates and occasional files for safekeeping.

31

Somehow Hannah found out what she was doing, and told Zoya. They were afraid Julia would expose them, so they turned on her, using Zoya's boyfriend and his pals as the muscle."

"Ah, shit," Heath breathed, settling his arm around Chloe's shoulders.

Yeah. They were animals, not men. "When I didn't hear from her for over a week, I knew something was wrong and started looking for her. I finally got a solid lead to follow, but by the time I got to Moscow it was too late. Stanislav's Bratva buddies had already tortured and dumped her. When I found her in the alley she was already dying. The death certificate I uncovered later stated that she was pronounced dead on arrival at the hospital, and could not be identified. Hannah and Zoya had already planted a cover story, so the media reported her as an unknown prostitute, killed by a rough John."

The words were bitter in her mouth. Her friend had been a straight arrow who took pride in her work taking down corrupt criminals around the world. Knowing she had suffered so much was still like acid eating at Kiyomi's soul.

"Anyway, they're all dead now," she finished, anger still pulsing through her.

Stanislav and Zoya had been killed by Amber. Kiyomi had set Hannah up to be captured and executed by Fayez Rahman, never dreaming she too would wind up his captive and almost die. If not for Amber and Jesse, she would have died in that makeshift prison.

"All except for Tarasov," she added.

Heath let out a low whistle and rubbed a hand over his bristly jaw. "Damn. Okay, so whoever sent you these files already knew all of that, and is trying to twist the screws on you and Amber."

"Yep," Amber said. "This person absolutely knew Tarasov was still alive, and knew about the connection between him and Julia."

"So what're we gonna do about all this?" Chloe demanded, brown eyes narrowed in anger as she chomped on her gum. "He had Julia killed, might even have tortured her personally, and now he's involved in a kidnapping and possible trafficking ring?" She snorted. "Motherfucker has to die." She glanced at the other video squares on the display. "Come on, guys. Bitchilantes ride or die, and I say we end this asshole. He can't get away with what he's done, and he might still be a threat to us. Time for a little Valkyrie justice."

Heath closed his eyes a second and shook his head. "Oh, man, here we go."

"We can't just sit back and do nothing," Amber agreed. "It's too dangerous to leave alone, and Tarasov is sitting at the middle of all this."

"How do you know it's not a trap?" Ty asked. "How do you know this mystery person isn't working with Tarasov to target you all, knowing you'll go after him?"

"For that matter, how do you know it's not Tarasov himself behind everything?" Zack countered.

"We don't," Amber said. "But I don't see that we have a choice at this point. Whoever sent this intel isn't going to back down now. We need to be proactive, and Tarasov's the obvious starting point. If it's a trap, we'll be ready."

"Cool," Chloe said over the rumble of male voices in the background.

None of the guys looked happy about this, and Kiyomi

knew without looking that Marcus's face would be dark as a thundercloud right now.

"So we're all heading to London then? We'll meet up at the Hall?" Chloe's was by far the most enthusiastic response, her expression equal parts excitement and eagerness.

Amber looked at her sister, then Jesse, and faced the camera again. "Your call, Kiyomi, and Marcus. Tarasov is—"

"Mine," Kiyomi said, her voice low. Deadly as the steely determination forming in her gut.

"Kiyomi." Marcus stepped up next to her, reached a hand toward her shoulder.

She shook her head and twisted away, refusing to look at him, meeting the gaze of each and every one of her Valkyrie sisters in turn instead. Making her stance clear. Staking her claim.

Tarasov was hers to kill. Only they truly understood what this meant to her.

"Does he know who you are?" Megan asked with a worried frown. "Will he recognize you?"

"No. We never crossed paths. And the only reason I didn't hunt him down before was that he'd been reported dead in a shootout with a rival Bratva sect."

She could feel the weight of Marcus's stare drilling into her. He wouldn't want her to do this. He would argue with her, try to stop her from going through with it. But it was already too late for that. Tarasov was a dead man walking, and she would be the one to end him. "He's. *Mine.*"

"Leave him to the police, or MI5," Marcus said in a

hard voice, "and focus on whoever's bloody locked onto you from the other end of that computer."

"No. We can't." They couldn't leave this to the cops now. There was too much at stake, their safety included. "They'll take forever to get anything done, let alone find anything. The women being held need rescue *now*, and any delay will result in more being taken. On top of that, the cops are bound to screw it up at some critical point, and I'm not going to risk allowing Tarasov getting off on a technicality down the line." She shook her head. "No way."

Tarasov was still alive for a reason. He was a slimy, cunning bastard. The instant he even *thought* someone was onto him, he would slither away, go to ground in whatever hole he'd crawled out of, and their chance of ending him would be over.

No way. Not fucking happening.

"Marcus?" Amber asked.

"Doesn't bloody matter what I think, does it?" he snapped, his fury beating at her in invisible waves. "She's already made her choice."

He stalked from the room, cane thumping in anger. Karas jumped up from her bed by the cold fireplace and hurried after him, her nails clicking on the worn flagstones on the way out the door.

Kiyomi pushed aside the twinge of guilt and hurt as he walked out. She would go to him later, once he'd cooled off. But she already knew they were never going to see eye to eye on this one.

"You sure about this?" Amber asked her while the others stared at her.

"I'm sure."

"Okay, then." A small smile lifted the corners of her lips. "Guess we'll see you tomorrow night."

"Yeah!" Chloe cried, pumping her fist in the air. "Let's *do* this."

Shutting off the video, Kiyomi sat alone in the empty room and thought of Julia. Of her sunny smile. The sound of her laugh. And she thought of the horrific distortion of her friend's beaten face as she lay dying in the cold that hellish night.

I will avenge you, my friend, she vowed, goosebumps erupting all over her body as she rose from the desk.

Tarasov would die for what he'd done, by her hand. It was her responsibility, and no one was going to stop her— including the man she loved.

CHAPTER FOUR

S prawled out on his stomach on the bed, Heath cracked an eye open when the mattress shook after what felt like four seconds after he'd dozed off.

Chloe was perched next to him on her knees, stark naked, staring down at him with excited brown eyes. "Are you sleeping?"

He sighed. "Not anymore."

She bounced in place impatiently, making her perfect breasts jiggle as they peeked through the long blond waves falling around her shoulders. "How can you be sleeping right now?"

He was a guy. Sex did that to him. Good sex mellowed him out. *Great* sex that finished with a spectacular orgasm put him straight into nap mode.

Not her. For reasons he would never understand, finding release somehow wound her up even higher, giving her a burst of added energy. And Chloe definitely did not need added energy.

"I'm not, I was just resting my eyes," he protested. That video call with the others was to blame for this.

She ripped the covers back and swatted his bare ass, her brown eyes gleaming with an excitement he could practically feel pulsing from her. "This is going to be *epic*," she gushed, showing no sign at all that only five minutes ago she'd been gripping his hair and crying out his name as she came apart under him.

It was impressive, really. She'd come so hard she should be unconscious next to him right now.

"All of us back together again to avenge one of our fallen sisters and take down a kidnapping ring at the same time." She bounced again, giving him a tantalizing peek of tight pink nipples through the curtain of her hair. "Bring it."

Giving up any hope of a nap, much less resting his eyes for a few minutes, Heath flopped over onto his back and put his hands behind his head to stare up at her. "How are you not tired right now? Seriously."

She cocked her head. "How could I be tired? I just had a great orgasm *and* we're going to be meeting up with the others to plan a mission. I'm stoked."

"A *possible* mission." He really hoped it wouldn't come to that. Though where the Valkyries were concerned, there was a good chance it would. Trouble seemed to find them. And when it did, Chloe was guaranteed to get in the middle of it.

She flicked his comment away with a dismissive wave of a hand. "Whatever. I can't wait."

Yeah, well, excuse him if he wasn't as excited by the idea. Knowing Chloe might be exposed to more danger triggered each and every one of his protective instincts.

He suspected that of all the guys, he and Marcus were firmly in the same camp right now. And that things had to be pretty strained at Laidlaw Hall at the moment, judging by the way Marcus had exited the room before the meeting ended.

"God, it's been way too long since I've been able to do anything useful with myself," Chloe went on with a faraway look on her face, then gave him a saucy grin. "We'll save those women, then Tarasov and his goons won't know what hit them."

Heath sighed, trying to think of how to handle this situation in a supportive and loving way. She'd been bored and a little down these past few months, still struggling to adjust to a quieter, tamer lifestyle here in Virginia. Together they'd put out feelers within the military and security contracting world about looking for above board jobs requiring her unique skill set.

Needless to say, pickings had been slim, and what sporadic work they *had* found, hadn't fulfilled her. After spending years doing assassinations and covert demolitions on strategic targets, who could blame her?

On one level, he understood. They both had unique skill sets that didn't often translate into the civilian world. He'd been out of Pararescue for a while now too, and he missed it like hell.

Still didn't mean he wanted to see her put herself in danger ever again. He was still getting over the last time.

Damn, he loved her though. Fiercely. Forever. "What am I gonna do with you, firecracker?" he murmured, reaching out to trace the curve of one perfect breast with his fingertips. The nickname suited her perfectly.

"I thought you knew by now," she teased, cocking her head.

He'd just shown her without words how he felt about it right after the meeting, by channeling it into sex. Dominant, forceful sex where he'd demanded her submission, and then shown her exactly how good it could be when she complied.

Getting Chloe to submit to anything was a challenge. And he knew her well enough to realize that getting her to change her mind about this upcoming mission was futile.

Outside of the bedroom, sometimes he felt totally clueless as to what to do with her. But he'd known what he was getting into when he fell in love with her. So as much as he hated her being drawn back into a world of danger that seemed unique to the Valkyries, he would suck it up and support her however he could.

"What?" she asked when he kept watching her silently.

"Is this because you're bored?" He had to ask. Because that was at least part of it.

She lost the teasing look. "No, it's about justice. For Julia, and the kidnapped women. And to make sure we protect ourselves and our futures."

Maybe. But she was definitely pumped about the prospect of conducting an op again and being in the action, and that's what had him worried.

He slid his hand down her ribs, gripped the taut curve of her waist. They were opposites in so many ways, including temperament. But they also balanced each other out in so many others, and he couldn't imagine his life without her. "You know I love you. I just hate that someone's been looking for all of you, and that you're moving ahead with this based on intel specifically spoon fed to you by an unknown and potentially dangerous source."

Her expression softened. She crawled forward, stretching her lithe, sleek body out on top of him to stack her hands on his chest and rest her chin on the backs of them. "I love you too. And we're going to be careful."

He raised an eyebrow at her. "Careful isn't really your strong suit."

She huffed out a laugh. "Luckily, this is a group effort. I'll abide by the group's decisions, and answer to whoever is overseeing my part if we go operational. And besides, you'll be there to watch my back anyway if it does."

He would. Because there was no way in hell he would ever have let her do something like this without him there to help protect her.

He lifted a hand to push a honey-blond wave away from her face, concern eating at him. "I keep thinking it has to be someone within the government. Someone we all missed last time."

"Doubt it. But whoever it is, they need to be dealt with once and for all." She bent and nuzzled his chest, planted little kisses along with the stroke of her tongue, looking up at him with a naughty glint in her big brown eyes. Trying to distract him and get him out of his head. "Still feel like resting your eyes?"

He curled his fingers into her hair. Squeezed, a powerful blend of tenderness and protectiveness rushing through him. "No."

How could it be so damn hot to know what she was capable of operationally, and yet thinking about her actually using those skills simultaneously turned his gut to a solid block of ice?

"Don't worry," she said with a grin. "Amber and Trin are going to be on top of this and whatever happens going forward."

She pushed up to drop a kiss on his mouth, then climbed off him, smacking his bare ass when he turned onto his side to watch her. "Now go pack. Trin's going to call Briar right now, and have her pick us up at Heathrow. So get moving—we're leaving for the airport in an hour."

He admired the sight of her perfect ass sauntering to the bathroom, unable to shake his lingering unease. They'd all been lucky to survive everything that had happened before, and for some reason stepping back into that world felt too much like tempting fate.

~

"So how's the job going?" Trinity asked on the other end of the phone.

Briar DeLuca grunted, glanced around to make sure no one was watching, and ducked into an empty office at MI6 headquarters in London. She didn't want anyone else wandering by to overhear this conversation.

"Honestly?" she said when the door shut behind her. "I'm bored to freaking tears." She'd taken this short contract job and come over here as a favor to Alex Rycroft. After only three days, she was already regretting it.

Trin laughed. "Tough being relegated to a desk job, huh?"

"Yes, awful." She was a sniper. One of the best in the world. She wasn't cut out for investigative work and all the paperwork that came with it. "I only took this contract because it's short, and because I like Alex."

"Bet you're missing Rosie, huh."

The mention of her little daughter made her heart twist. Rosie had been on her mind constantly. "God, you have no idea. I don't know why I thought I was ready to leave her for a few days." Maybe she'd been testing herself. If so, now she knew the answer. She wanted to be home with her kid.

"I'm sorry about that, and sorrier still, because I'm probably about to make that worse."

Briar frowned as her friend told her about the meeting the others had just held. She listened intently, remaining silent until Trin finished.

Hell. Someone out there was trying to track them, and might be setting them up with the intel handed to them on a suspicious platter.

She pushed out a long breath, thinking. She'd been counting down the hours she had left here, was due to fly home in three days. Now…

"Listen, none of us will hold it against you if you decide to sit this one out," Trin added. "You're a mom now, and that changes everything."

Briar rubbed the back of her neck. It *did* change everything. Rosie was the single most important thing in her world. Besides, the team had more than enough operatives to do this without her, and she had Rosie waiting for her at home.

Yet…what if this threat followed her home? What if she sat this one out, and something went wrong? She wasn't sure she could live with herself.

"What did Brody say?" she finally asked. Trin's

husband was leader of one of the FBI's Hostage Rescue Team sniper teams. Briar's husband Matt was his commander.

"He's…not thrilled that we're considering going operational again, but I didn't expect him to be," Trinity answered. "I think mostly it's a timing issue for him."

"Why, is Blue Team being deployed somewhere?" Matt hadn't said anything to her.

"No. Anyway, I'll tell him not to say anything to Matt until after you talk to him. Everyone's flying to London tonight. Can you pick Chloe, Heath and me up, and take us up to the Hall? Come talk with the others there, then decide."

It was a reasonable request. "Does Alex know about all this?"

"Some. We're trying not to involve him any more than we have to."

In other words, he was still mostly in the dark, and in that case, Briar wasn't going to say anything to him. But she definitely needed to find out more before she made her decision on being involved farther.

"I'll pick you guys up tomorrow and take you to the Hall. And I'm going to talk to Matt as soon as I get off the phone with you—but I'm reading him in. I won't keep a secret like this from him." Secrets killed a marriage. Secrets like this ended them.

"No, of course not. See you tomorrow."

A minute later Briar stared down at her phone screen as it rang, waiting for Matt to pick up. It had only been twenty-six hours since their last video call when she'd gotten to see Rosie, but it felt more like twenty-six days. The five-hour time difference between London and

Virginia, combined with Rosie's new sleep schedule was playing hell on Briar's ability to talk to her daughter while she was awake.

Matt picked up. He was in their kitchen with his phone camera angled to capture his face, and Rosie in her high chair behind him. "Hey, good timing. She just woke up from her nap."

Briar's heart swelled at the sight. Her husband was ridiculously hot, yet her gaze went straight past him to their daughter. "Rosie! Hi, stinker. How's my sweet girl today?"

"Rosie, who's this?" Matt turned the phone around and held it in front of their daughter.

Rosie stopped eating the cut-up fruit he had put on her tray and stared at the screen.

"Hi, baby," Briar said brightly, missing her something fierce. She couldn't believe their daughter was going to be two in a couple more months.

Rosie stared at her for a second, then broke into a big, toothy grin. "Hi, Mama," she said in her little voice, reaching her dimpled hands out toward the phone.

A giant lump lodged in Briar's throat. She swallowed, overcome by the rush of emotion. She'd felt things she hadn't even known she was capable of since Rosie was born. "Are you eating your snack?"

Rosie nodded and shoved a piece of strawberry into her mouth, staring at Briar. "Where are you, Mama?"

"I'm in a big city across the ocean called London. Where Paddington the bear is from." She'd read Rosie a story about him before the trip. And right now she'd never felt so far away and homesick in her life.

"She didn't eat much this morning," Matt said from

45

somewhere behind the phone, keeping Rosie centered in the shot. "Had a bit of a rough night, but grandma handled her like a champ, and half of that molar's through now."

Matt's mom had flown out from California to help with Rosie while Briar was away, taking care of her while Matt was at work. "Oh, those mean old teefers," Briar said, wishing she was there to pull Rosie out of the high chair and smooch those round, rosy cheeks over and over.

"Our girl's tough. Right, sweetheart?" he asked Rosie, who grinned at him in adoration. He turned away and focused the camera on him as he crossed to the counter. "Anyway, how are things there?"

"Okay."

A grin tugged at his mouth, his green eyes twinkling. "Bored stiff already?"

"Mama, miss you," Rosie said from out of view, and Briar thought her heart would explode. Her daughter was putting more and more words together all the time.

"Miss you too, baby."

"Just three more sleeps, Rosie cheeks. Then mama will be home again," Matt said.

She winced. "Yeah, about that… Something's come up."

At her serious tone his smile faded. "What's going on?"

She told him, and by the time she'd finished his face was somber. "I'm going to pick up Trin and a couple others at the airport in the morning and drive them out to Laidlaw Hall. I promised I'd stick around long enough to hear what the plan is, but that's all."

Matt held her gaze through the screen, and her chest ached as she stared back at him. Most husbands would have told her to forget it and insisted she come home. Or even tell her she couldn't take part in the op.

Fortunately for them both, Matt understood that Valkyries didn't respond well to threats and ultimatums. He trusted her judgment, saw her and treated her as an equal.

"Okay," he said slowly. "You'll update me when you know more?" His deep voice was calm. Quiet. And it only made her miss him more. He was her rock.

"Of course I will." She expelled a hard breath, torn. "Matt, what if we *are* being targeted again? I can't come home and potentially put Rosie in danger until I know it's safe."

"Find out the latest when you meet up with the others tomorrow. You don't have to decide anything yet."

"If things turn operational, you know what that means." His role as HRT commander made this even more complicated for them both. She couldn't tell him anything, because if something went wrong and people in the government found out he'd known about it beforehand, it was bye-bye to his security clearance and career.

He nodded once. "I know." No arguments. No complaints.

She swallowed, her whole chest hurting now. His understanding, his faith in her judgment and abilities, meant everything. "God, I love you," she whispered roughly.

Sometimes that little voice in the back of her head occasionally popped up to tell her she didn't deserve him. But it only happened rarely now. And she never doubted his love for her.

"Love you too. We both do, right, Rosie cheeks?" He

walked over and scooped Rosie up, holding her in the crook of one muscular arm as they both grinned at the camera. "Say bye to Mama."

"Bye, Mama." Rosie waved her little hand.

Briar had to blink fast to hold back a rush of tears. "Bye, baby. See you soon." She looked at Matt, wishing she could magically transport herself home for even just a few minutes to be able to hold Rosie, and feel his arms around her. "Talk to you tomorrow."

After she ended the call she canceled her return flight, just in case. A weight settled in her chest as she left the empty office and headed down the hallway, only to stop when her phone rang and Rycroft's number appeared.

Oh, this wasn't gonna be good. But she answered anyway.

"Why did you just cancel your return flight?" he said without preamble.

He must have previously set up an alert on her to have found out so fast, she thought with a mental eye roll. She wasn't sure how much he knew, and wasn't going to give him anything just in case. "I'm extending my trip by a few days. Thought I'd go see Kiyomi and Marcus before I come back."

"Uh huh." His tone said he didn't believe it for a moment. "And it has nothing to do with all the rest of you suddenly booking flights to London within the past few hours, right?"

Hell, he must have alerts set up on all of them, still sharp as ever in unofficial retirement. "It's just a reunion."

He snorted. "That would almost be funny if it wasn't so damn insulting." A pause followed, and when she didn't say anything more, he continued. "I've been getting

48

updates from Amber. I know what's going on. What I don't know is what you're all planning to do about it."

She didn't know. And didn't want him involved any deeper, just in case. Plausible deniability would protect him.

"Briar." His tone was far less patient this time. "What are you guys planning?"

Trying to pretend she didn't know what he was talking about was stupid at this point, not to mention highly insulting to the both of them. So she told him straight. "I don't know yet. We're meeting tomorrow at Laidlaw Hall."

He grunted. "Well, you tell the others that they better think long and hard on this one, because I'm not in the same position I was last fall. There's only so much I can do in terms of damage control now, if you catch my meaning."

The lead weight in her chest spread into her stomach, his message clear. If they went operational on this, they were going to be on their own, and would have to accept whatever consequences it brought. Rycroft wouldn't be able to run interference on their behalf and mitigate the fallout. "I'll tell them."

"Briar."

"Yeah?" she asked as she headed for the stairwell that would lead to the building's lobby.

"Be careful. We still don't know what we're dealing with here."

Yeah, that's what bothered her the most.

CHAPTER FIVE

T rinity was in the UK.

Ivy leaned back in her chair, fingers resting on the keyboard as she studied her monitor and the customs records she'd hacked into. It was real. Trinity's flight had landed less than two hours ago, and Briar had already been here for several days already.

She started checking for the others, sure this signaled that the Valkyries were gathering. Within ten minutes, she was looking at the passport picture of Chloe Wilson, whose flight from a different DC airport had landed an hour after Trinity's.

Goosebumps broke out across her arms.

It was working. They had taken the initial bait she'd sent, and Ivy was willing to bet that more Valkyries would be entering the UK very soon. Amber for sure. Maybe others.

She'd love to know where they were going. The likelihood of her finding that out was almost zero, however.

They were too good at covering their tracks, and would be extra cautious as they gathered together to…what?

Excitement fizzed in her veins as she anticipated watching what they did from here. There were several ways she could play this. But only a few that would be satisfying.

"What to do, what to do," she mused as Mr. Whiskers rubbed against her calf. "Can't overplay my hand. Gotta take this slow and careful," she told him. "Amber and the team she's assembling are smart."

Smarter than any other target she'd gone up against before, and that made her dangerous. Knowing at least some of the surviving Valkyries were working together again on this made Ivy more paranoid. This was risky. Life-and-death risky.

She pulled up her carefully curated files, went through them and selected a few key pieces of intel. Enough to lead the Valkyries down the path she wanted, without giving away her…personal involvement with Tarasov.

Amber and at least some of the others had already swallowed the first bait. Ivy would keep feeding them exactly what she wanted them to know, and nothing else. Until they were all in.

Hook, line, and sinker.

～

This was not even remotely close to how Brody had imagined spending the rare and incredibly precious time off from his job as Hostage Rescue Team sniper team leader he'd requested two months ago.

"You talked to Rycroft about this yet?" he asked Trinity as they got into their rental car parked out front of Laidlaw Hall for the drive to the private range Marcus had arranged for them to use.

He'd come here with her because he wanted to know everything about the threat facing her and the other Valkyries, and what was being done about it. But he was treading a fine line. He couldn't be involved in any of the plans Trinity and the others made. Not if he wanted to keep his job or ever work with an elite unit again.

"No."

Yeah, he hadn't thought so. And when Rycroft found out what they'd been up to here, he wasn't going to be happy.

The golden limestone manor house loomed large in the rearview mirror as he drove down the crushed gravel driveway. Marcus had to feel like he'd been invaded right now, because the manor house was full to bursting with people, every bedroom occupied and even a few storage rooms pressed into service.

"So you're not going to?" he asked. If things kept progressing the way there were and Trin and Amber decided to pull the trigger on this thing, it could get awkward with Rycroft fast.

The guy had done a lot to help them in the past. Stuck his neck out and risked his security status along with his reputation in the intelligence community by assisting them on ops that resided firmly in the gray area, and then smoothing everything over after. If they went ahead with something like this behind his back, he wasn't going to be happy about being left in the dark.

"I don't want to say anything until I know for sure. No

point in putting him in an awkward position if nothing's going to happen."

He nodded, but already had his own view of what was going on here. The odds of nothing happening when eight Valkyries and their former military partners had gathered here ready to go, were pretty much nil.

They passed the gatehouse where Megan and Ty were staying, and turned left onto the quiet, two-lane road running along the front of the estate. It was pretty countryside. Softly rolling hills in every shade of green imaginable, made up of fields bordered by ancient hedgerows and dotted with copses of trees. In some ways it reminded him of his family's horse farm in the Shenandoah.

The range Marcus had secured for them was located in between some farmers fields down in the valley a few miles northeast of Stow-on-the-Wold. When they arrived, the others were already waiting.

"Thought you guys would never get here," Briar said, striding toward them.

Another couple was already set up on the range with a sniper rifle. The blonde turned to them with a half-smile. "Hey. Good to see you."

"Georgia." Brody nodded at her, then focused on her husband, standing next to her. "Bautista. Been a long time."

The former cartel enforcer dipped his head and held out a hand. His reputation as a stone cold killer preceded him, and even though he'd gone straight a few years ago, he was still a menacing bastard. "Colebrook." Then he looked at Trinity, and his hard features softened into a half-smile. "Mrs. Colebrook."

"Hi." Trinity reached up for a hug. Bautista returned it, then she hugged Georgia too.

Brody couldn't help but grin. There was a shitload of history between these four, not all of it good.

Trinity, Briar and Georgia had been close early on in their training, before being separated and eventually turned on one another. Bautista had gotten involved in the mix not long after that and fallen hard for Georgia, and then Brody had met Trin that fateful night when he'd found himself staring down the barrel of her pistol.

Life had never been dull since. And even though they were all on the same side now, everything that had led them to this moment still seemed incredible.

"So? We gonna shoot, or what?" Briar asked impatiently, bouncing up and down on the balls of her feet.

Trin laughed. "You remind me of Chloe right now. About to burst with pent-up energy."

Briar grunted. "I've been stuck behind a desk all week, I'm across the damn ocean from my kid and husband, and it's been way too long since I shot anything. I'm ready to put some rounds downrange. Anyone wanna join me, or you wanna hug it out some more?"

"I'll spot you. Then hug you after," Trin said, walking over to one of the two M110s set up and ready to go.

Georgia tossed a sharp-edged smile at her husband. "You wanna shoot?"

"I'm good. Promised Chloe we'd throw some knives for a bit later. You go ahead, I'll spot you until she gets here."

Both Georgia and Briar wasted no time in getting set up behind their weapons, lying prone on the mats laid out.

Soon the reports of the powerful rifles echoed across the field. Marcus had said the farmers on either side were used to it and wouldn't bother coming to investigate, since he and Kiyomi came here to shoot occasionally.

Brody watched both women shoot for a while, admiring their technique and skill. They were both damn impressive shooters, as good as him or any of the guys on his sniper team.

It also gave him a chance to admire his wife in action. He didn't often get to see Trin use her training anymore, and seeing her now as she expertly spotted Briar was yet another reminder of how damn sexy and incredible his wife was.

His *wife*. He still loved how that sounded, how it felt. It had taken a long time to get her to say yes, but they'd finally been married in May, back at his family home in the Shenandoah. And marrying him wasn't all she'd said yes to.

After a while Trin got up and sauntered back to him with that sexy walk that called attention to every luscious curve on her body, her smile and the sparkle in her eyes telling him just how much she'd needed this. He'd been hesitant to fly here at first, with good reason, but now he was glad he'd come.

Even if the others went ahead with the op and she decided not to be part of it, coming here to at least spend this time with the others had definitely been the right decision. Valkyries would never truly assimilate into a regular life. The way Brody saw it, all of them getting together at least once a year was necessary for their mental and emotional wellbeing.

He caught Trin by the waist and tugged her around in front of him, pulling her back tight to his chest as he wrapped his arms around her from behind. "When are you gonna tell them?" he murmured against her ear in between shots.

"Soon," she answered.

He was leaving that up to her. It was her call. "Sweetheart… You know I can't stay." Not only because of his job. But because something even more important could be put in jeopardy by what was about to happen. He needed to be back stateside to ensure that didn't happen.

"I know." She squeezed his forearm. "But I'm glad I had you here with me for at least a little while."

❧

The sudden yet necessary departure of her husband left Trinity with a bittersweet ache in her chest, but with Laidlaw Hall full to bursting with other people she loved, she couldn't help but smile. Though it had only been seven months since they'd all last been together, with them all living so far apart now it felt much longer.

"Hey, you," Chloe said, coming over with a plate of snacks in her hand, wearing a T-shirt that read: *Explosives expert. I'm a blast at demos.*

It seemed she was always eating. Had to keep her hands busy, or at least some part of her busy, or she would explode. "I don't have to ask how you are, I can see how pumped you are to be here."

Chloe grinned. "I'm sooo ready to get back in the field."

Trin chuckled. "Poor Heath." His nickname of fire-cracker for her couldn't be more perfect.

"What? He'd be bored without me. I make his life interesting."

She put her arm around Chloe's waist and squeezed her. "I don't doubt that for a second, babe."

"Where's Brody?" Chloe glanced around the room.

"He had to fly out."

"Oh. Work emergency?"

"Security issue." At least that wasn't a complete lie.

"Okay, let's get this meeting started," Amber called out from the front of the library where she had the big screen set up along with Lady Ada.

"Here we go," Trin murmured, releasing Chloe as everyone gathered around on the plush velvet and leather furniture.

It was her favorite room in the house, light and bright and airy, with pale green paint, a big, white marble fire-place on the end wall, and shelves upon shelves stuffed with books. The combination of wood smoke, leather and the vanilla-scent of old paper was divine.

Amber scanned the group with a half-smile. "Thank you all for coming on such short notice, and for Marcus and Kiyomi for having all of us."

Trinity glanced their way. Things were definitely not all sunshine and roses with those two right now.

Marcus stood in the doorway, leaning a shoulder against the jamb, arms crossed over his chest. Kiyomi was seated next to Megan and Ty on one of the couches. There was a noticeable tension between them, and it wasn't hard for Trinity to guess its cause.

"There have been no major developments on the intel I

gave you all yesterday," Amber continued. "I've done a little more digging into the background of the suspects involved. Looks like they're all in the UK right now, and they're keeping a low profile."

"What about who sent you everything?" Georgia asked, perched on Bautista's knee on the chaise in the corner.

"Still nothing. I've put everything I have into it, and nada so far."

A resounding silence answered her. Everyone understood how bad that was given Amber's skills.

Amber slid her hands into the back pocket of her jeans, looked up at the screen where everything of importance was displayed, then surveyed the room. "The kidnapping ring is real, and Tarasov is definitely involved. Probably calling the shots from behind the scenes. So far I've found one offshore bank account with recent deposits of a few hundred thousand each. From buyers."

"So what, some guy contacts Tarasov and buys a woman his guys have kidnapped?" Megan said with a curl of her lip.

"Worse. Looks like he's taking custom orders for women. Maybe even specific women."

"Wait." Heath looked disgusted. "You mean people contact Tarasov with a freaking human shopping list, and his guys target women based on that?"

"That's exactly what I'm saying. So far they've been taken in a specific area, but unless he's stupid he'll branch out elsewhere. Right now, this is a testing ground for him."

A chorus of outraged murmurs followed the announcement.

"It's been a challenge to try and find who the buyers

are though," Amber said. "I'm still trying to find the original sources for the money."

"Kiyomi, you're positive Tarasov's to blame for Julia?" Eden asked, seated across the room from her.

Kiyomi's dark gaze slid to her and Zack, and she nodded. "One hundred percent."

"We have to take the bastard out," Chloe said, shoving to her feet. Already standing, Heath curled an arm around her and drew her into his side.

"It's worth a deeper look to see if we're right," Trinity said, drawing everyone's attention. "And then we can see whether it's a setup."

"How do we know this isn't Tarasov pulling strings behind the scenes, feeding us tidbits to draw us out into the open?" Heath asked.

"We don't," Trinity answered. "So we have to keep that in mind as we plan our response."

"We could set up a sting where one or more of us acts as bait, and see exactly who's involved," Briar said. "We could find Tarasov that way, and like Trin said, we'd find out if whoever's feeding us the intel is clean or not."

Amber nodded. "I could create a fake buyer profile and feed him specifics on what kind of girl I want, matching one of us. Then we dangle the bait and wait to see what happens."

Low conversation broke out all over the room. Trinity noticed Marcus watching Kiyomi from the doorway, his jaw taut.

She felt for him. As an intimate assassin, Kiyomi was the obvious choice to send as bait for this kind of operation. And Kiyomi had already made it clear she intended to kill Tarasov. If this went ahead, she would once again be in the thick of the danger.

Trinity pulled her attention away from Kiyomi and let out a soft breath as her Valkyrie sisters and their partners discussed everything amongst themselves, torn. It was clear things were turning in a decidedly tactical direction, and from here everything would move fast.

She'd wanted to wait to do this, but...

"I have something I need to tell you all," she said over the conversations going on.

Everyone stopped to look at her.

She released a breath. "I'm sorry, but I'm going to have to sit this one out. Brody and I are expecting an important call any day now, and..." When everyone kept staring, she sighed and just said it. "We're adopting a baby sometime in the next few weeks."

Excited gasps met her words, but she hurried on before anyone could speak. "The birth mom is nearing her due date, so we could get the call any time. I want to stay and be part of this, to help, but if we get that call..." She shook her head. "I can't stay."

"Of course you can't," Briar said, jumping up and coming over to throw her arms around her in a big hug. "I can't *believe* you didn't say anything to me about this before."

"Sorry. I wanted to." She squeezed her friend tight, tears pricking the backs of her eyes.

She'd wanted to be a mother for so long, and the choice to have a baby of her own had been taken from her years ago. Adoption was her only chance. "You know how these things are. I've heard all kinds of stories about birth moms changing their mind at the last minute, so I didn't want to jinx anything, just in case."

"No jinxes. Everything's gonna be fine," Briar insisted with a delighted smile, then sobered. "Is this why Brody left so suddenly?"

"Yes, but don't say anything to Matt," Trinity said. "He requested the time off weeks ago, and Matt thinks it's just for a holiday."

More Valkyries had gathered around them, waiting for their turn to hug her. "Is it a boy or a girl?" Megan demanded.

"A boy."

"Ohhh!" More gushing, more hugs, and Trinity found herself perilously close to tears.

This was her family. Brody and his dad and siblings had accepted her into the Colebrook clan, but these women... These women were blood to her.

"We're so happy for you guys," Eden said, her pretty golden eyes misty.

"Thanks. We're happy too." The whole adoption process would have taken a lot longer without Rycroft pulling strings for them and eliminating some of the red tape.

Trinity was nervous and excited about becoming a mother. But she'd also missed these women so damn much, and felt bad for not fighting shoulder to shoulder with them on this. She knew she was making the right choice, however. Her priorities had shifted the moment their adoption was pending, and her child came first now.

She doled out more hugs, finishing up with Heath, and gave a laugh. "Okay, sorry, I totally hijacked the meeting, and we need to get back down to business. Amber, you've got the floor."

"Okay, well, first thing we need is to track down someone on the suspect list, intercept him and access his phone." She tapped her chin, perusing the audience as she pretended to seem uncertain. "Hmm, if only we had someone who was good at stealing stuff."

Megan's grin was cocky as hell. "Put me in, coach."

CHAPTER SIX

Something was definitely up. A *reunion*? Come on.

Alex snorted to himself as he stepped into his home office and shut the door. It was early but Grace was up too, already puttering around in the kitchen, and their daughter was still asleep. Time for him to sneak in a little more work.

He opened his email, scanned the contents of all the alerts he'd set up so he could try to keep some semblance of tabs on the remaining Valkyries. "Well, would you look at that," he deadpanned. All eight of them, and all their partners except for Matt DeLuca had arrived in the UK throughout yesterday morning London time.

What were they up to, and why were they hiding it from him? It was driving him insane that he didn't know what was going on, that no one was updating him.

Maybe it wasn't his place to oversee them anymore officially, but he didn't give a shit. Somebody better tell him what the hell was happening, otherwise how could he step in if needed?

Picking up his encrypted phone, he dialed Trinity. The call went straight to voicemail.

So he called again. And again. And again.

Pick up, he finally texted, growing more annoyed by the second. All of them in the UK together? It couldn't be good.

A million possibilities flooded his brain. Everything from taking down an international crime syndicate, to assassinating a suspected war criminal. Or maybe a terrorist cell. With these women, it could be anything.

His phone rang as he angrily typed out another text. An unknown number showed on the display. "Hello," he answered, his voice clipped.

"It's me," Trinity said. "What's the matter?"

"You tell me. And this line's secure, by the way."

He could hear voices in the background. Lots of them. "Just a sec, it's too noisy in here." The background noise faded as she presumably left the room. "That's better."

Was it? He had to unclamp his jaw to speak. "What's going on? I know you're all together there." Amber had leaked little tidbits of intel to him over a secure network, but not enough for him to piece everything together, and he no longer had a team of analysts under him.

"Together where?"

"Somewhere in England," he growled. "Probably at Laidlaw Hall." Okay, so he was a control freak. But that's exactly why he'd been so good at his job. This semi-retirement bullshit was wearing thin already. He itched to be in the middle of things again.

"Yeah, everyone's here. But nothing's going on. We just talked about the situation."

He wasn't buying it. "Are you guys in danger? Did you receive a credible threat?" He couldn't shake the suspicion, and he'd grown to care about these incredible women. Probably more than was wise, but he couldn't help it.

"There's no credible threat at the moment."

That they knew of, she meant. Or maybe Trin was hiding more from him than he realized. "I want a video call. Now. With you, Amber and Briar."

She sighed as if he was being ridiculous. "Fine. Hang on a sec."

Just over a minute later she called back using a video link, and three Valkyries appeared on screen in Marcus's study at Laidlaw Hall. *Knew it.*

"Hi, Alex," Amber said with a friendly smile, waving. "What's up?"

He grunted, glaring at them all. He'd lost more damn sleep over them over the course of the last twelve months than he had in the first two sleep-deprived years as a parent. "I want to know what you're planning. I don't want to be directly involved, but I'm also not gonna leave you all hanging in the wind if it goes sideways."

"Awww," they all chorused, giving him identical, adoring smiles that tugged at the heartstrings he didn't like people outside of his family to know about. Then again, in a way these women were like extended family to him.

"Don't aww me." He folded his arms, raised an eyebrow. "Am I going to have to clean up a big-ass mess again like last time?"

Last fall they'd blown up Jane Allen, aka "The Architect" while she was riding in the back of a van during a prison transport that was supposed to have been top secret

65

and high security—and then claimed it had been a freak accident. The political, legal and bureaucratic aftermath of that one had been a nightmare.

"Because in case you weren't aware, I keep trying to retire, and you guys are making it really goddamn hard."

"We are well aware, which is why you're on a need-to-know basis," Briar said. "And besides, we don't know what you're talking about."

Then he got it.

It wasn't that they didn't trust him. They knew he was in a sort of limbo, career-wise, and didn't want to involve him in anything incriminating or that would cause him any problems. Dammit to hell, how was he supposed to stay mad now?

"Okay, then hypothetically speaking, if anything should happen—and I'm not saying it will, because history has shown what peaceful and model citizens all of you are —" he added sarcastically, "I'm here."

"We know," Briar said. "And we appreciate it."

None of them said anything more. He studied the three of them, and thought of the other five somewhere else in the manor house.

They were the most infuriating people he'd ever dealt with, and he'd dealt with a lot of infuriating people over the course of his military and intelligence careers. But damn, he had such a soft spot for each and every one of these women. Against all odds they'd survived a reprehensible government program that had stripped them of everything and forced them to endure years of danger and unimaginable hardships, and had finally won their freedom with Jane's death.

"If it makes you feel any better, we're all being extremely well-behaved so far. Even Chloe," Amber added with a bright smile that did nothing to dispel the level of his unease.

"Yeah, but that's mostly because Heath's here to watch her," Trinity added. "She and Bautista got in some knife practice earlier."

Alex shook his head, a surge of fondness making him fight a grin. "I know this is a lot to ask, but for the love of God, be careful. And...at least *try* to stay out of trouble." That was like asking for the moon where they were concerned, but it still needed to be said.

"We will," Trin said. "Love you, Alex."

"Yeah, love you," Amber added, and the three of them blew him a freaking kiss before signing off.

He set his phone down on the desk, shaking his head at himself in disgust. They'd just played him, stroked his ego and manipulated him into backing down, and he'd let them. Folded like a cheap-ass tent. Becoming a husband and father had made him turn soft.

A tap came at the door, and Grace poked her head in. "Hi." She stepped into the room wearing a short, peach silk robe held together with a flimsy tie at the front, giving him a tantalizing outline of her breasts and leaving her legs bare from mid-thigh.

Glancing from his phone to his face, she raised her eyebrows. "Everything okay?"

Probably not, but there was nothing more he could do about it at the moment. "Yeah."

"Who were you talking to?"

"The Valkyries."

Her eyes lit with amusement as she crossed the room to him, her mere presence reducing all the static buzzing around in his head. Without her, he would still be an obsessive workaholic. Grace, and everything they'd been through together, had taught him what was truly important in life—family, and friends who had become family. It was the reason he'd decided to step back from his job and phase into retirement.

"Really. And what's up with them?" she asked.

"I don't know. But something."

Trying to smother a grin and failing miserably, Grace slid into his lap and looped her arms around his neck. "I love that you care so much about them."

He grunted. "Remember how much dark hair I still had when we met? Now look at me. They've aged me prematurely," he grumbled.

She made a soft, purring sound and stroked her fingers through his hair, the scrape of her nails on his scalp sending tingles down his spine. "I should thank them, then. Because now you're a silver fox."

He chuckled at that, stroking a hand up her back as he gazed up at her. "God, I hope they stay out of trouble this time."

"But they probably won't."

"No." And he was worried that he wouldn't be able to protect them this time. "Guess I'm going to have to make an unscheduled trip to London in the near future."

～

Luka set his cutlery down on the fine china plate bearing the dinner his private chef had made for him, and glanced at his chiming work phone. An expensive, heavily encrypted piece of tech he changed weekly to mitigate the risk of being tracked.

A new order had just come in. From a previous client he'd worked with once before.

The specs given this time were impressively detailed and exact.

Biracial female—half Black, half white—mid-thirties. Five-six to five-ten, hundred-thirty to hundred-sixty pounds. And hot, which went without saying.

The guy definitely knew what he wanted, and had the money to back up the request. Luka typed back a response. *Might take a while to find a target that matches.*

Fine. Would rather wait and get what I want.

Okay with him. *Any specific area you had in mind?* This buyer was specific enough with everything else that he might have a preference for that. If not, it didn't matter. Two of his guys were on call twenty-four-seven, ready to head out and scout for potential targets wherever he sent him.

Moseley area, Birmingham. Saw a woman there the other day I'd be interested in. He attached a picture.

Though unexpected, singling out a particular woman made Luka's life that much easier. He'd already expanded his area of operations into London, but he had to be careful not to go too big to soon. Eventually he would branch out wider, maybe somewhere outside the UK. *Got it. Will get someone on this and get back to you.*

Pulling up another text, he scrolled through a list of pictures one of his guys had sent this afternoon. Potential targets for another client who wanted a thirty-something blonde MILF with big tits.

He dismissed the first three women after only a quick glance. Not hot enough. Numbers four to seven were better. But number eight… He'd do her.

He called Will. "Number eight from that batch. Where is she?"

"Hampstead. Commutes into the financial district for work. She's an investment banker in London."

So she worked *and* lived in London. That would make it easier to track her. "Family status?"

"Living with a guy, but doesn't wear a ring. Not sure if they're married."

They'd have to do careful surveillance to figure out the easiest time to grab her. "Got a pick-up location in mind?" London was one of the most heavily surveilled cities on earth, making it hard to pull off a kidnapping without leaving video or photo evidence. As a result they didn't take many targets from there, but the money offered in this case made the risk worthwhile.

It was crazy how much some men were willing to pay to buy the embodiment of their fantasies, and Luka was already on his way to being a rich man because of it. Turned out that old adage about whatever doesn't kill you makes you stronger was real.

His life had gone to shit for a while after the Julia Green job. He'd been destitute. For months and months he'd scrambled to get from one day to the next, never knowing where he would lay his head at night, or where his next meal was coming from.

Then he'd met Elena. He'd fallen hard for her. Would have done anything and killed anyone for her. Then she had betrayed him and crushed his soul last year, nearly getting him killed in the process. For a while the pain of it, the heartbreak of losing her had made him want to die.

Now he understood that she had done him a huge favor. She'd taught him the truth. Women could never be trusted. They were all liars and manipulators, and no man in his right mind would ever give his heart to one.

But he'd gotten his revenge.

Elena had been his first capture and sale. Since then, he'd used everything he'd learned from her and the underground criminal world to build his new business. Making a killing off buying and selling women in the skin trade, and so far the cops hadn't come near him. Another few months of work here, then he'd go somewhere else and set up shop there. Somewhere warm this time. Maybe the Balkans.

"She takes an art class every Tuesday night after work," Will said. "The studio's in a good spot for us. Narrow alley with two entrances. Fairly dark there at night, and not a lot of traffic around."

Two days from now. Perfect. "Keep me posted. And we just got another job in Birmingham. I need you to start on this tomorrow. Specific target requested this time. I'll send you the info."

Slipping his phone into his pants pocket, he stood and walked for the dining room doorway. His bodyguard fell in step with him as he entered the hall. "Where are we going?" the man asked in Russian.

"The warehouse. Got a new shipment in I need to inspect. How's your father doing today?"

The bodyguard's expression softened. "He's getting surgery tomorrow, thanks to you. We're all incredibly grateful."

Luka waved the thanks away, uncomfortable. For the

few people he trusted and displayed unwavering loyalty to him, he was protective and generous. Finding people like that was rare, and more valuable than diamonds. This business was risky, and he had many rivals along with a list of enemies he'd earned along the way.

Paying for private surgery to remove a cancerous bowel lesion for the family member of his most trusted employee was nothing compared to what he got in return. "I'll keep him and your family in my prayers."

Yeah, he still prayed. Although he was pretty sure God had stopped listening to a sinner like him long ago.

If this new woman being kept at the warehouse met all the criteria his client wanted and passed the physical inspection Luka did personally with each target, he would set up the meeting location for the transfer. After that, it was only a matter of waiting for the wire transfer to go through with payment in full.

As soon as his men delivered the product, the transaction was complete. He didn't know what happened to the women after that, and he didn't care. As soon as one job was completed, it was right on to the next one.

～

Things were moving faster now, like a runaway freight train gathering momentum as it sped down the track. Soon there would be no stopping it.

The Valkyries were all somewhere in the UK, Ivy just didn't know where yet, and wasting time and energy trying to track them down at this stage was pointless. She still had the advantage, however, because she held the power to draw them out of hiding.

She was privy to Tarasov's plans. Knew his tastes in everything from food and cars to art and women. Knew how difficult it was for a man in his position to hold onto the power he'd managed to accumulate, and how tenuous his hold on it was.

She even knew about the women he'd trafficked, though he didn't realize it. Because she'd made it her business to know.

Absently scratching Mr. Whiskers as he stood on the side of her desk eating his dinner, Ivy studied the data she'd compiled, considering her options. It was ten o'clock at night on a Friday. Most people her age would be out doing something fun with friends or curling up with their significant other.

Since Ivy had neither, she was here in front of her computer. This was her life, because she'd never known anything different and would never have a sense of normal. But if this plan worked, it would change all that forever. And that tantalizing prospect made all the risk and the threat level she faced worth it.

"Option two it is," she murmured to herself, snipping little bits of intel from her files. After arranging everything the way she wanted it into a message, she put it through her encryption program before sending it through the usual channel.

She grabbed her mug of overly salty ramen noodles and slurped some up with her chopsticks, anticipation humming in her veins. Everything depended on how the team responded to this latest intel. If things went according to any of the possible scenarios she had already thought of and mapped out, it was only a matter of time before she got what she wanted.

A soft beep sounded, an icon appearing on screen to show that the encrypted message had been received.

Your move, Amber.

Their mental chess game was now well underway. With each successive move, Ivy came another step closer to checkmate.

CHAPTER SEVEN

W ill stared at his phone, pretending to be scrolling through something, when in reality most of his attention was on what was happening around him. Like the number of people walking by the end of the alley he was standing in, and the number of vehicles either parked nearby or driving past him.

The alley itself was a narrow, one-way lane that fed from a short, quiet road lined with cafés and shops into another, even quieter one in this trendy Hampstead neighborhood. The art class was ending soon. Within the next few minutes, he would know whether this op was a go or not.

This morning Luka had given the order to proceed with capturing the target discussed on their previous phone call. It was Will's job to scout potential targets, and then, once a target was verified, to track her and plan the actual op itself. His martial arts background made it fairly easy to subdue the women. That's why Luka had recruited him from the dojo in the first place.

It wasn't something he'd ever imagined he'd wind up doing. But the money was too good to pass up, and if his conscience pricked him now and then, the lifestyle he was able to afford now instead of living trapped in a slum made it more than worthwhile.

The workplace accident he'd suffered two years ago, and with only disability pay during the lengthy rehab after his surgeries had left him practically destitute. This new gig was only meant to be temporary until he could get out of debt and make enough to get himself a nice flat, but he would miss the money when it was over.

For him, this was just business. He couldn't let his emotions get involved. Couldn't let himself care about what happened to the women involved. Once the target was captured, she was taken directly to their transition facility near Birmingham and held for no more than four hours after that, to minimize the risk of anyone finding out.

Will was only with a target from the time of capture to about ten minutes after arrival at the facility. He never spoke to the women. Never looked at them once they were in the van. That made it easier for him to distance himself from it all, then put it out of his mind when he went home at night.

The door to the art studio partway down the alley opened. He kept his head still, moving only his eyes as he looked at who exited. Two women, both brunettes. Not his mark.

Three more women left a minute later, followed by a middle-aged couple. The women passed him, while the couple headed the other way up the alley. The door opened again, and he caught a flash of pale yellow out of the corner of his eye. When the person followed the couple, he turned his head to look.

There she was, the blonde. And she was by herself, which would make this a whole lot easier. The couple ahead of her wouldn't be an issue. He'd just call out to her, wait for her to stop so he could engage her in conversation and keep walking toward her, giving the couple more time to disappear around the corner. Asking for directions usually worked, and allowed him to stay close to her as they walked.

Will pushed away from the brick wall he'd been leaning against and followed her, texting one of the guys he was working this job with.

Got her. Heading north up the alley.

The van wasn't far away, maybe three or four blocks from here in an area with minimal CCTV cameras. Receiving a thumbs up in reply, he lowered his phone and followed the blonde away from the studio.

As his former recon had shown, this tiny nook in Hampstead was especially quiet this time of night. The couple ahead of the blonde turned right at the end of the alley and disappeared from view.

He would stop her before she reached the end, and lead her to the left. The van was on its way. The driver would follow him, waiting for his signal before approaching.

Alerted to his presence behind her, the blonde glanced over her shoulder at him. He pretended to look at his phone and put on a frown for good measure, trying to appear confused. She faced forward and kept walking, maintaining her pace.

He increased his, lengthening his strides. Just before she reached the end of the alley he opened his mouth to call out to her, but stopped when a woman suddenly came around the corner and headed toward them on the sidewalk.

Damn.

Tamping down his irritation, he edged closer to the brick building to his right, preparing to let the brunette pass him on the sidewalk. His gaze stayed locked on his prey.

He had to capture the blonde tonight. The client had already paid the money and was on his way to the transition center. If Will didn't bring her in within the specified time window, the deal was off. And then he would not only be out a sizeable commission, he would be in serious shit with Luka as well. Maybe even out of a job entirely—or worse, if Luka thought he might talk.

Will was smart enough to know he never wanted to get on the wrong side of Luka Tarasov.

Shoving that disturbing thought aside, he kept going. The brunette smiled at the blonde and turned her body slightly to pass her, busy reading something on her phone.

Will slowed when they got close to each other. She wasn't paying attention, and his focus was now divided between her and the blonde.

Head down, the brunette kept on coming at her hurried pace. He was forced to slow again, clamping his jaw in frustration as he watched the blonde near the end of the alley.

Bloody hell. He was practically stopped with his back inches from the brick wall behind him to avoid impact when the brunette got close, and she had no clue she was about to run into him.

"Hey," he said.

She glanced up, her eyes widening when she realized she was about to collide with him, and stumbled. She tripped over her own damn feet and bounced into him.

He cursed, tried to shove her aside but she'd already gripped his forearm to steady herself and managed to knock both their phones loose in the process.

He hissed in a breath when his phone clattered a few feet down the sidewalk, then dove for it. It had incredibly sensitive information on it. He couldn't risk anyone else seeing it.

But the damn woman was closer.

"I'm so sorry," she exclaimed, scooping both phones up before he could reach his, and handed it over to him.

He snatched it from her. "Watch where you're bloody well going," he snapped, sidestepping her to look for the blonde.

A spurt of panic hit him when he saw she was already turning the corner, headed to the right. Away from where he needed her to go, and toward the closest underground station instead.

Shit!

Without giving the brunette another glance, he broke into a run, determined to lure the blonde in the opposite direction she'd just gone.

If she got on the tube, it was over. Even if he managed to follow her home without being detected, her neighborhood was too busy to attempt a kidnapping on the street, and they weren't going to risk breaking into her flat. He liked the money, but not enough to risk getting himself arrested.

When he turned the corner, his heart sank. She was

half a block up now, and there were too many people around for him to grab her.

Unwilling to give up just yet, he kept following, struggling to come up with a different plan to salvage this. Except the number of cameras and people around made it impossible.

Finally, he stopped, anger pumping through him as he watched the blonde cross the street and approach the entrance to the underground.

Fuming, dreading what Luka would do when he found out, he spun around and put his phone to his ear as he stalked back the way he'd come. That bloody idiot brunette had cost him this entire operation. "Abort," he growled when the man picked up. "She's gone."

And now he'd have to face the consequences of his first failed target acquisition.

THE ASSHOLE WASN'T paying any attention to her at all as he ran up the alley after the blonde.

It always surprised Megan how oblivious most criminals were. Heaver didn't have a damn clue that she'd just tagged his phone with a nearly invisible electronic device, and that everything on it was now being transmitted to headquarters.

Finding and tracking him here to this alley hadn't been easy, but Amber was a tech goddess for a reason. They'd taken a risk in using the intel breadcrumbs fed to them by their shadowy source, but it had panned out. Amber had used every tool available to make this happen, putting together enough intel for Megan and Ty to find Heaver two days ago and follow him to this spot.

Amber had also started the next phase already by posing as a buyer specifically interested in Eden, sending Tarasov a picture of her and giving her location. Now that Megan had tagged Heaver's phone, Amber's job would be a lot easier. It should just be a matter of planting Eden in the previously specified area and waiting for Tarasov's crew to ID her to get that ball rolling for the next phase.

Except Megan wasn't done with phase one yet.

She waited until Heaver disappeared from view before doubling back and following him, the sheathed blade strapped tight to her calf under the leg of her jeans. She had a loaded syringe in her "purse" from Eden in case things got messy.

Not three seconds passed before Ty's voice came through her earpiece. "Where you going?" He was tracking her via her phone from a car a block over.

"He's following the target." She kept her voice at a murmur so as not to be overheard. "I'm going to make sure she's safe."

No way would Megan desert her when this bastard and his pals were tracking her. The trafficking ring worked with tight time windows. As long as the woman got away from him right now, she should be safe and in the clear.

"Okay, but don't take any chances if he sees you. I'll follow as close as I can."

I can take care of myself. "Roger that," she said instead, knowing better than to argue about her ability to protect herself. Of anyone, Ty was the most intimately familiar with her skills. They both knew she could more than handle this asshole if he tried anything.

Near the end of the alley she turned her reversible jacket inside out and put on the hat she'd shoved into her

81

bag earlier to change her appearance. Even though she'd literally run into him moments ago, she doubted he'd been paying close enough attention to her to recognize her with the changes.

Rounding the corner, she took in the situation within seconds. Heaver was partway up the next block with his back to her, staring after the blonde, who was now angling toward the underground station. Suddenly he stopped and looked back.

Avoiding eye contact, Megan immediately crossed the street at an angle and hurried on. He wasn't moving, and judging from the expression on his face as he looked around, he was pissed that his prey had escaped.

She kept going anyway, positioning herself between him and the blonde just in case he decided to make a last-ditch attempt to grab her. Besides, from what Amber and some of the others had been able to piece together, a few of his buddies were no doubt somewhere close by in a van, waiting for the signal to intercept.

Heaver spun around and stalked back the way he'd come, his expression livid. Megan didn't trust him or the assholes he was working with not to keep pursuing the woman, so she tailed the blonde down into the underground anyway, staying close to her while they waited for the next train to arrive at the platform.

There was no sign of Heaver, and no one else was watching the blonde. But Megan was seeing this through.

She stepped aboard the train and kept watch, getting off with the woman two stops later and following her to a brick, Victorian-era building that had been converted into flats. She waited until the woman was safely inside, then scanned her surroundings to ensure no one had followed before checking in with Ty.

Clear. "She's home safe. Where are you?"

"Right behind you."

A dark gray compact appeared around the corner ahead and pulled up to the curb beside her. The passenger door popped open before she could reach it, and there was Ty.

"Hey, dimples," he murmured as she climbed in, leaning over to cup the back of her neck and kiss her.

Her pulse skipped, triumph and adrenaline mixing with arousal. It was so hot to know he was armed right now, especially since it was illegal here, and that he'd been watching her back this entire time.

"Hi," she answered when he straightened a few moments later, a little breathless. "They won't get her now."

"Nope. But we'll get *them*."

Damn right, they would. And on that note...

She took out her phone and called her sister as Ty drove them away from the building. "You got it?" she asked Amber. By now the little device she'd stuck to Heaver's phone should have spewed its contents onto Lady Ada.

"Oh yeah. Working perfectly. Idiot didn't even bother permanently deleting photos of all the women they've targeted, or pictures of himself."

Good. With any luck they might even be able to find where the missing women were and give them a chance of survival. Maybe even prevent any other women from being kidnapped. "Perfect. Looking forward to finding out what else is on there. See you soon."

"So, where to now?" Ty asked, smoothly merging into the traffic pouring out of London onto the motorway.

She reached for his free hand and curled hers around it. "Home." The gatehouse at Laidlaw Hall, where they'd first lived together before heading back to the States.

The first part of this mission was complete, and phase two was about to begin. She couldn't wait to deliver some Valkyrie justice to the assholes responsible for all this suffering.

CHAPTER EIGHT

E den let her hand brush over the tufted tops of the
purple fountain grasses as she wandered along
the border planted nearest to the south side of the
high-walled garden, enjoying the peace and tranquility
while it lasted. This gorgeous spot was something right out
of a fairytale.

All around the perimeter of the garden, the golden
stone walls absorbed the heat of the summer sun, making it
the perfect spot for the beautifully espaliered fruit trees
growing along it. There were apple, cherry, pear, peach
and plum trees, their carefully pruned branches anchored
to the stone.

"Thought I might find you here."

She glanced up and smiled at Zack as he strode
through the door set in the opposite wall. "Isn't it incredible? I'd forgotten how gorgeous it all was."

Aside from spending time with her fellow Valkyries,
the gardens were what Eden had missed most about this
beautiful place. Plants had long been a passion of hers. She

knew every single one in here by both their common and Latin name, knew all their properties and toxicity levels—and how to make the best use of that.

Zack stopped in front of her and closed his big hands around her hips. She stared up into his gorgeous gray eyes, a smile curving her lips as she looped her arms around his neck. After a long, heartrending journey, they had found their way back to each other and were all the stronger for it.

"Miss me?" she teased.

"Yes, and you left your phone inside so I had to come find you in person." He leaned in and kissed her, bringing one hand up to tangle in the back of her curls as he pulled her flush to the front of his body and proceeded to make every thought disappear with the slow, thorough possession of her mouth.

Then he straightened suddenly, leaving her clinging to his broad shoulders and hungry for more. "Amber just called everyone to a meeting."

"So she found something juicy." Four hours ago, Amber had taken all the intel from Will Heaver's phone and put it through her insanely powerful laptop. Eden was eager to find out what she'd uncovered.

"Must have." Lacing his fingers through hers, Zack started for the open doorway in the garden wall.

The others were all gathered in the library again when they arrived. Standing at the back of the room, Eden leaned into Zack, his strong arm around her waist.

"Good, everyone's here," Amber said when she saw them. "This likely won't come as a surprise to anyone, but Will Heaver's phone turned out to be a gold mine of infor-mation, and better yet, he has no clue we have any of it. I was able to retrieve almost all of what he tried to delete, and Lady Ada found a lot of leads for us to follow up on."

She paused a beat. "Unfortunately, it's going to take us longer to track the missing women. Tarasov moves fast. From time of capture to delivery at their holding facility appears to be only a few hours, and in most cases they're done one at a time with no doubling up. After the client has the woman picked up, tracking them becomes a nightmare. They could be anywhere in the world by now."

A rush of anger hit Eden. She'd seen a lot of things over the years of performing clandestine missions. But this disgusting, horrifically callous and entitled mindsets of these men, who thought they could just pay to have a woman who matched their sick fantasies pulled right off the street because they were nothing more than objects to them, was pure, twisted evil.

Amber faced the screen set up above the large fireplace behind her and started the presentation. "So far, Jesse, Trin and I have identified who we think are the major players involved in the kidnapping ring, but as of now there's been nothing more on the origin of the tips we received from our anonymous source. In the meantime, we can deal with the other potential threat—Tarasov and his crew."

She pulled up a satellite image of what appeared to be an industrial area. "Here's where we think they're holding the captured women, at least temporarily."

The camera zoomed in on a long, rectangular building, and Amber continued. "Mostly warehouses and storage facilities in this area, along with some shipping companies. This is our target building." She circled it in red, then detailed the surrounding area and talked about the security measures they'd found so far.

Not surprisingly, Tarasov was using a small crew at the holding facility. The turnover was quick, and sporadic. They brought the women in, held them for a brief period, and released them to the buyer. No schedule, no set shifts or patrols, nothing that would make it easy for law enforcement to plan a raid.

"We're going to have to rely on recon right up until the moment of the op for this one," Amber continued. "Next, we've got Tarasov's lair."

She pulled up a live feed of an upscale, terraced house and gave a rundown of the floor plan and likely security measures. "And, finally, the pick-up crew. Heaver leads that team. Small rap sheet of petty crime, and he's a triple black belt in two different disciplines. He usually works these jobs with two other guys waiting in a vehicle for his signal. He intercepts the victim, and the others swoop in to make her disappear."

Eden studied the men's pictures on screen, hating them all on sight.

"Basically, to make this happen we're looking at a three-pronged attack, involving three simultaneous ops. Starting with Heaver and his crew. And for that, we're gonna need someone to pose as bait. Eden, you're up."

"I'm ready," she announced. Zack's hand tightened on her waist but he didn't argue. The wheels for this had already been set in motion the moment Amber sent Tarasov Eden's picture and specified her as a target.

Trinity glanced at Kiyomi. "You're still a go for Tarasov?"

"Yes," she said without hesitation.

Eden shifted her attention to Marcus, who stood hovering in the doorway. His expression was dark and he looked about to crack a molar his jaw was clenched so hard.

She felt a pang of sympathy for him. It wasn't easy, loving one of them and coping with the danger involved, and Kiyomi's demons ran deep.

"All right," Trinity said to the room. "Amber and I will divide you into teams, and then we can start breaking everything down."

Amber motioned for Eden and Zack to come up front and waited for them before speaking. "To make the bait angle work, we need to pretty much hand them everything on a platter. I'm going to send them a specific address where the fake client I'm posing as has spotted you."

Eden nodded, totally on board. "Then it'll be just a matter of putting me in Heaver's path, and monitoring their communications?"

"Exactly. And the money. I'm interested to see what the fee is for a return customer. I'll say I'll pay extra for you if it's a tight turnaround. You'll go to Birmingham tonight. Heaver will start tracking you at the address I send. Once Tarasov green lights the kidnapping, we'll know the date and place, and then we can coordinate your part with the other two teams and plan the joint op as a whole."

Kiyomi came over to them, Marcus right behind her. Still with the disapproving look on his face, but standing near enough to hear exactly what was said. "What else have you got on Tarasov's location?" Kiyomi asked.

Amber pulled up the exterior shot of his place on her laptop. "I've got the blueprints and specs on the kind of security system he's got." Everything popped up on screen a second later.

Kiyomi studied it, and Marcus moved in closer. Karas left his side to poke her nose at Eden. She stroked the top of the dog's soft head as she watched and listened to the conversation.

"He'll have a safe room of some sort in the basement," Kiyomi said. "How much security does he normally have with him?"

"Enough," Trinity answered. "He's cagey, rarely leaves his place. Electronic security for sure on the exterior and interior, and from what we can tell, he's usually got between one and three bodyguards around him at all times. Maybe even while he's inside."

Kiyomi nodded, appearing totally unfazed by the news. She'd dealt with many men like him over the years, alone. This time she would have trained teammates with her. "Who's my backup?"

"Marcus and Chloe," Trin answered. "That work?" she asked them.

Kiyomi murmured an affirmative, and Marcus gave a curt nod, none too happy, but accepting that this was happening and determined to help protect his wife.

"I heard my name." Chloe stepped up between Marcus and Kiyomi and put her arms around them both, either oblivious of the tension between the couple, or ignoring it. "Hey, teammates." She peered up at the schematic for Tarasov's place. "Oooh, the prime asshole." She looked at Trinity expectantly. "What do I get to do?"

Trinity's mouth quirked. "I'm almost afraid to say it, but you'll need to create a diversion."

Chloe let go of Marcus and yanked her fist in toward her hip. "*Yes.*"

"A small one," Marcus added with a warning look.

Chloe didn't so much as glance at him, too busy staring at the blueprint, her excitement palpable. "What's this building here?" She pointed to a shorter building across the street and down two doors.

"Used to be an old bakery before it was converted into a garage," Trinity said.

Her face lit up. "So it's vacant?"

"Except for some of Tarasov's car collection, yes."

"Perfect." She chewed on her gum, didn't look up when Heath appeared behind her.

"Uh oh. I'm well acquainted with *that* look," he muttered, and perused the images. "Hoping this goes without saying, firecracker, but you can*not* blow up a building in the middle of an occupied neighborhood."

She shot him an insulted look and went back to studying. "I wouldn't blow up an entire *building*. Although that would be cool," she mused to herself.

Eden shared an amused look with Zack, glad their part of this mission was simpler and wouldn't involve any explosives. Explosions drew attention. She wanted hers to be a surprise attack. Quick, clean, and most of all, unexpected.

"Hey, can you mix me up some custom sedatives, and maybe some sodium thiopental?" Kiyomi asked her.

Eden raised her eyebrows. "You want truth serum? I thought you were doing a hit." When Kiyomi had said she wanted Tarasov, everyone assumed she'd meant he wouldn't survive to go to jail.

Kiyomi shot a glance at Marcus, who was watching her closely, then looked at Eden again. "I want to find out what he knows first. He's former Bratva. He won't talk, even under torture. But I bet you could mix something to loosen his tongue at least a little."

Oh, she absolutely could. "All I need are the chemicals."

Kiyomi nodded. "Gimme a list, and I'll get them for you." She glanced at Marcus again, her expression veiled. "We'd better see about dinner."

Chloe's face lit up, all her attention on Kiyomi and Marcus as they turned away. "Dinner? Good, because I'm starving." She trailed after them, following them out of the room and presumably toward the kitchen.

"Is it just me, or is Chloe totally clueless as to what's going on with those two?" Zack mused.

"At least the mention of dinner took her mind off blowing stuff up for a little while."

He looked at her, gray eyes brimming with amusement. "Your friends are weird."

"Yeah." Eden looped her arm around his waist and shook her head, a fond smile curving her mouth. "God, I've missed all my badass babes."

CHAPTER NINE

Marcus strode for the kitchen after Kiyomi, the tap of his cane mixing with the click of Karas's nails on the old flagstones. Chloe was right behind him, chattering away like a magpie, and Heath behind her.

"What are we having? A roast? You make the best roast beef I've ever had. I've tried a couple in the States since we got back, and they're not even half as good. If you are making one, can you do Yorkshire puddings like you did on Bonfire Night? Maybe an extra pan or two this time. Heath stole two of mine that night, and I still haven't forgiven him for it."

"You mean I was forced to nab two from your plate before they were all gone, because you'd already eaten three and the pans were empty before they got to me," Heath said.

"Lies," Chloe argued.

Marcus pulled in a deep breath and kept walking, praying for patience. God, what he wouldn't give for an hour of privacy and peace and quiet in his own home right now. He liked everyone well enough, but having the whole group together under his roof while working up to a mission he already hated was a lot to take.

Being furious with his wife wasn't helping his mood any either.

He stared after her as she entered the kitchen. What was she thinking, wanting to be the one to target Tarasov?

The few times he'd tried to start a conversation with her in private, she'd refused to talk about it and walked out of the room. Leaving him to simmer in his own angry juices and pushing his frustration level to the breaking point.

Anxiety had become a constant grinding in the pit of his stomach these past few days, his fear for her a living thing inside him. A fear that had nothing to do with his belief in her abilities, and everything to do with the level of danger she would be facing once again.

They'd all been through so much already. Too much, especially Kiyomi. He'd naively thought that kind of danger was done.

With the Architect's death, Kiyomi's past, that old life full of danger and violence and death was supposed to be over now. Forever. Yet here he was, forced to once again watch the woman who held his beating heart in her hands put her life at risk—and for revenge.

That made it worse. He intended to speak privately to both Amber and Trinity about it before the night was through. The way things stood at the moment, there were far too many risks and holes in the plan right now.

He couldn't stop his wife from doing this—though God knew he would love to—but he at least wanted to be satisfied that she was in the least amount of danger possible when she did.

The scent of rich tomato sauce redolent with Italian seasoning wafted down the hall. He and Kiyomi had made a big batch of it together this morning, working with a brittle silence standing between them like a wall.

Feeding a crowd this size was a job in itself, and all of them had to pitch in. Given the sensitivity of the intel and mission prep happening around here, he hadn't wanted his cook around, so he'd given her a paid week off to afford them maximum privacy. Until he was certain that the threat looming over them was neutralized, he wasn't taking any chances.

"Ten more minutes on the lasagnas," Kiyomi announced from in front of the oven, bent over at the waist to peer inside one of the cobalt blue Aga doors.

His gaze strayed to the perfect shape of her ass outlined in her snug jeans before he could stop himself, and when he realized what he was doing he berated himself. That pose was anything but coincidental.

She was manipulating him. Not in a sneaky or under-handed way, but trying to coax him out of his mood by distracting him with her body and the promise of sex.

It had been days since they'd last enjoyed each other. That wasn't helping improve his mood any.

A low, distant rumble drew his attention to the deep windows above the sink. Dark clouds had rolled in throughout the afternoon, blotting out the bits of blue sky that had been there this morning. The wind had picked up, shaking the trimmed yew hedges surrounding the formal knot garden and stripping petals from the rose trees planted amongst the neatly-clipped boxwood rows.

Karas shifted next to him and licked her lips nervously, her ears going back as she moved closer, pressing against his leg. "It's all right, lass," he murmured, reaching down to stroke her head in reassurance.

"Oooh, looks like we might get a thunderstorm," Chloe said, coming up beside him to scan the darkening horizon. "I *love* thunderstorms."

Shocking. He managed not to roll his eyes as he grabbed a couple large bowls from one of the cupboards and thrust them at her. "Here. Make yourself useful and help me get the salads together. I just had the knives sharpened," he added, knowing that would hook her.

"Ooh," she said in delight, already reaching for the large butcher block on the counter.

Dinner was noisy but fast, the lasagna served with two different kinds of salad and toasted cheese bread on the side. Kiyomi sat halfway down the table from him, laughing about something with a few of her fellow Valkyries. She drew his eye without even trying, the happy sound of her laughter increasing the heaviness in his chest.

He kept glancing at her amidst his conversation with Ty and Jesse. The woman meant everything to him. Did she understand that?

He couldn't seem to settle down. Couldn't get his secret fears under control.

As he and the lads helped clear up, a brilliant flash of light lit up the dark sky out the kitchen windows. Thunder rumbled, closer now. The storm was almost here, its seething energy perfectly matching the building chaos inside him.

This wasn't like him. He needed to get away. Needed

time and space to get himself back under control before he did or said something he would no doubt regret.

He left the others to finish up and went out through the back door, pausing on the crushed gravel path to pull in a deep breath. The air smelled like impending rain, a heavy, taut quality to it.

Thunder cracked, rolling like a wave above them. Karas whimpered and ducked her head, looking up at him nervously. The horses would need to be checked. "It's all right," he told her, and started for the stable.

The first drops of rain hit him halfway there. Fat drops that splattered when they hit the ground. Intermittent at first. Then, seconds later, the clouds unleashed their watery load in a deluge.

He hurried through the rain and stepped inside the shelter of the stable, leaving the door partially open while the sweet scent of hay and horses surrounded him. In their stalls the horses blew anxiously from their nostrils, their shod hooves clattering on the floor with their nervous shifting.

He ran a hand over his wet face and then through his soaked hair as he flipped on the lights and went to check each horse. Rollo was the first one to greet him, sticking his large head over his stall door, his ears perked and an almost eager expression on his face.

"She's not here, mate," he said, meaning Megan, who had bonded strongly with Rollo early on when she'd lived here. "Afraid you'll have to make due with me."

"Yes, I am."

He spun around to see Megan striding in through the partially-open door, her coat glistening with rain. She pushed her hood back and grinned, coming over to stroke

Rollo's head. "Hey, handsome boy. You're not afraid of a little thunder."

"He's missed you," Marcus murmured, watching as Rollo's eyes half-closed under Megan's touch. The horse loved Kiyomi, but he was besotted with Megan.

"I've missed him too. I love my horse back home too, but no horse could ever replace Rollo." She turned her head and met his gaze. "Missed you more, though."

His cynical heart squeezed. "Why would you miss a crippled old sod like me," he muttered, though he was touched. They'd spoken regularly since she and Ty had returned to the States, but he thought of her often.

She'd changed the trajectory of his life. If she hadn't come to stay here when she had, he would have merely gone on surviving instead of living. And without her, he never would have met Kiyomi.

Megan cocked her head a little and measured him with warm hazel eyes. "Guess I'm sentimental. I miss riding Rollo at dawn and shooting arrows at the targets you used to hide along the trails for me before the sun came up. But mostly, I miss the quiet times we had here, when it was just the two of us."

He glanced away, a pang hitting him. She had saved more than his physical body when she'd pulled him out of his prison. Over the months that followed, she had done the impossible and made him want to live again. He owed her everything for that.

"Aye." He cleared his throat. "Did you come out to check on Rollo, then?"

"No. Came to check on you."

He shot her a frown. "No need for that."

She leaned against the stall door and watched him with

a knowing expression, rubbing Rollo's sleek neck. "You've been like a lion with a thorn in its paw since the rest of us got here."

"No, I haven't."

"Okay," she said easily. Too easily, and went back to giving Rollo a fuss.

Marcus pivoted and continued down the center corridor between the rows of stalls, checking on the other horses. The thunder made most of them nervous, but they calmed slightly when he approached.

"Have you tried talking to her about it?"

He stopped walking, his shoulders bunching up. Damn. He should have known she wouldn't let this go. "About what?"

"You know exactly about what."

He grabbed a brush from the bucket hanging on the opposite wall and entered the stall at the end to run a soothing hand down a nervous mare's neck. "No point. She won't listen."

"She might."

"No." He ran the brush down the mare's back and over her flank in a firm sweep. Kiyomi was a strong, determined woman, and when she set her mind on something, not even one of Chloe's explosive devices could move her. "I hate that she's doing this," he finally admitted. That was the crux of it.

"I know. But do you understand why?"

"Aye. Vengeance. Justice." Didn't matter what she called it, it wasn't reason enough to place her life and their future in jeopardy.

"Maybe it's something more than that."

He heaved out an irritated sigh, annoyed that she was

pushing and digging instead of letting it alone. "And what would that be?"

"You."

He stilled, didn't respond for a few moments, her words hitting too close to home.

His gaze strayed to his cane, propped against the corner of the stall. Mocking him. "I don't want to see her get hurt again." Or worse—and it kept him up at night. "I couldn't stand it. It's bad enough every time I see the scars on her shoulder…"

He clenched his jaw, thrust back in time to that terrible moment when he'd lined up the shot in that field. When he'd been forced to do the unthinkable and shoot her to have any chance of saving her life.

It haunted him still. Always would. It was an ever-present reminder of how close he had come to losing her forever, and he never wanted either of them to go through anything like it again.

"I know," Megan said softly, and he didn't argue, because aye, she likely did understand. "But just talk to her. Don't leave things like this. You'll regret it if anything happens."

An arrow of fear buried itself in his heart at her words. At the thought of something going wrong, and losing Kiyomi. He'd survived being wounded. Being taken hostage and held in captivity. He'd survived torture and the long, endless road during recovery.

He wouldn't survive losing Kiyomi. There was no way he could ever bear that amount of pain. Without her, life wouldn't be worth living. He would eat a bullet to end his suffering.

Megan's footsteps faded away behind him, lost under

another rumble of thunder. The mare shied, ears back, prancing nervously. "Shhh," he soothed, stroking her neck. "It's all right. There's a good lass."

When she'd calmed more, he grabbed his cane, exited her stall and went across the corridor into the tack room to put away the brush, deep in thought. He wanted to mend things with Kiyomi, but he didn't know how.

She wouldn't listen to his concerns, wouldn't stand down or stand aside through what was coming no matter what he said, not even if he begged. And he would never be okay with her putting herself in danger again.

Over the drum of the rain on the roof and the rush of it hitting the path outside, he heard footsteps approaching. He glanced toward the door, expecting to see Megan returning, and stilled when a jagged bolt of lightning backlit the familiar figure standing in the open stable doorway.

Kiyomi stepped inside wearing a long, black leather trench coat that came to her knees, and a pair of high-heeled boots that disappeared beneath the hem. She paused near the first stall to push her rain-soaked hood back, and their gazes locked across the length of the stable.

His pulse accelerated, his awareness of her heightened as she started toward him with her innately sensual gait, those liquid, dark eyes on his. There was nothing hesitant about her. She was pure, sensual confidence as she came toward him.

Every thought in his head vanished, his entire body reacting to the hungry way she was looking at him. As if she wanted to strip him right here and devour him whole.

He straightened, all his muscles going taut. She had always tested his control, but this time it was different.

Frustration mixed with longing and a dark, raw possessive-ness with every step she took, slowly erasing the distance between them. She knew she was playing with fire, and wanted them both to burn.

"They more settled now?" she asked, pausing just outside the tack room door.

"Aye." He turned away to tidy a few things lying around, hating what was happening between them. How tangled his thoughts and emotions were. He craved the closeness and peace he'd had with her just a few days ago, back when she was safe and everything in their world had made sense to him.

"Are you planning to ignore me until this is all over?"

He stilled, setting his jaw as he reined in the sudden rise in his temper. Having a go at her now wouldn't do anything but drive her away. Megan's words played over and over in his head. She was right. He couldn't live with more regrets. Not when they involved his wife. "I'm not ignoring you."

A long sigh came from behind him. "Marcus. Will you look at me?"

He turned to face her and raised an eyebrow, waiting. "Well? Why did you come out here?"

"To talk."

"Fine, then talk."

She gave him a curious look, as if she was trying to figure out what he was thinking and couldn't quite read him. They rarely argued, so that wasn't a surprise. "I know you don't approve of any of this."

"Not true. I approve of taking down the kidnapping ring, and Tarasov with it. But there are plenty of other ways to do that by tipping off the police and feeding them everything they need to know without any of you being directly involved."

She watched him for a moment, eyes dark and mysterious as a midnight sky. "Why do you think I asked Eden to mix me those sedatives?"

"To make him talk. You said as much to the others."

"No. It's because I would be willing to capture him instead of killing him."

Marcus stared at her, sure he had misheard. "Come again?"

"I'll dose him, interrogate him to get what we need, then knock him out and hand him over."

He frowned, suspicious. It was only a partial concession on her part, but she'd never backed down from something she wanted before, even if it endangered her life. "Why the change of heart?"

She lowered her gaze, staring at the ground. "You."

"What about me?" He'd made his feelings on the matter plain enough before. Letting Tarasov live would take away the worry that Kiyomi would be caught and face a murder charge.

Her gaze lifted to his, and she started toward him again. Sensual, sinuous grace concealing the lethal weapon she was. "I know you're worried."

Of course, he was bloody worried. "You're my *wife*."

"Yes, but it's not just because you're afraid something would go wrong on my end." She stopped within arm's reach, her gaze delving deep into his. "It's because you're afraid you won't be able to protect me if it does, because of your leg."

His insides constricted, her instinct dead on. A sodding bull's eye in the painful wound that would never heal.

103

He'd served in one of the most elite military units in the world. He had the training, discipline and experience to still be an operator. But the injuries he'd sustained in Syria meant he would never be that man again. The plain, brutal truth was, he could well be a liability to the team on an op. And it would kill him to be unable to protect her if something went wrong.

"What about you?" he countered, nodding at her left shoulder. "You're not at a hundred percent this time either."

"I know." A little smile played about her lips as she edged forward and reached up to place her hands on his shoulders.

Her nearness threatened his control, her luscious scent intoxicating him. He grasped her hips through the trench coat, holding her away from him. "Then don't do this. Don't let your need for revenge cloud your judgment. Let someone else handle Tarasov."

Her smile vanished, and a flare of anger flashed in her eyes. "No." Her voice was calm. Her tone final. "He's mine."

"God dammit," he exploded, releasing her and stepping back a pace to glare at her. "We've already been through this, once when you went after Rahman, and then again during the attack here. How can you be so selfish, to put me—us—through this again? Expect me to sit back and watch you risk your life again?"

"Marcus, stop," she warned, shaking her head. "I don't want to fight."

"Then bloody listen to me!"

"I *have* listened. But I don't want to talk about this anymore."

Holding his gaze, her hands moved to the top button on her coat. His whole body tensed, twin spears of arousal and anger hitting him as he realized what she was about to do.

He shook his head, jaw bunching. "Don't." His voice was low, rough.

Not like this. He wouldn't touch her when he was like this, so close to losing control. Not after everything she'd suffered at the hands of men before him.

He backed up another step, his hip butting up against the wall.

She didn't stop, her hungry stare magnifying the turmoil inside him. Testing him. Pushing him, when he was already riding the edge.

Yet for the life of him, he couldn't tear his eyes away as her fingers slipped the first button free, then immediately moved to the next. And the next. Exposing a thin strip of golden-toned skin as she went. Until she reached the last one and the halves of the coat finally parted to reveal her naked body beneath.

Air hissed between his teeth in a painful rush, all his anger and frustration and fear colliding with a towering wave of desire. His body was pulled as tight as a tripwire, lust coiling low in his gut, blending with a dark possessiveness that made his heart pound.

He didn't dare touch her. Didn't dare unleash what was happening inside him.

She stepped closer, eyes on his, and deliberately pulled the edges of the coat back, thrusting her perfect breasts out.

Marcus sucked in a sharp breath, his already hard cock pulsing. Aching for her. She was so close he could smell her. A light, sensual blend of floral and spice. And that bold look in her liquid dark eyes.

Challenging him. No, *daring* him to take what he wanted.

Watching him, she lifted a hand and slowly drew the pad of her index finger down the side of his beard-roughened cheek. Down his throat to the V above the neckline of his shirt. Over his right pec, skimming the nipple on her way to his shoulder and down his arm to grasp his hand.

His pulse thudded, his breathing harsh in the enclosed space of the tack room. Thunder growled again in the distance, the drumming rain echoing through the stable. But he was only aware of her, and this seething, crackling energy between them about to break.

Kiyomi curled her fingers around his hand. He didn't dare move, hardly dared to breathe, his cock as rigid as the rest of him as he stared at their joined hands. Watched her bring them toward her, and he was powerless to resist.

He held his breath, his body coiled and ready to spring.

The second his palm curled around that perfect breast, the last thread tethering him to his control snapped.

Unleashing the demons tormenting him, he grabbed her and spun them around, lifting her off the floor to pin her against the wall, her bare mound pressed to the ridge of his trapped erection and her bare breasts poised inches away from his mouth. His wife at his mercy.

She stilled, a tiny gasp escaping her at the abrupt movement, but then she wound her bare legs around his thighs, her pupils dilating. Becoming pools of naked want as her tongue came out to drag across her tempting lower lip.

Something dark and territorial expanded in his gut as

he pinned her there, ignoring the ache in his hip. She'd driven him to this, made him insane with need and frustration.

She'd started this fire. Now they would both burn in the flames.

"You're *mine*, Kiyomi," he growled, and captured that tempting mouth with his.

CHAPTER TEN

K iyomi gasped into his mouth, caught off guard by the abrupt move, even as a thrill ripped through her at the dominant way he handled her. He was always so careful with her, especially during sex, and he'd never let her feel the full extent of his strength before.

He broke the kiss to stare at her, breathing hard, the muscles in his jaw standing out.

Arousal pumped through her body at the primal desire she read on his face. Felt it in the bite of his hands on her hips and in the taut, bunched muscles across his shoulders as he held her against the wall, the fabric of her long trench protecting her back from the rough wood.

Through the layer of cloth, she felt the thick, hard length of his erection pressing against her bare folds. His body was rigid, nostrils flared, and volcanic heat burned in his dark eyes.

She pulled in a breath and deliberately softened. Submitting to him and this charged moment. "Don't stop," she whispered, her clit throbbing and her nipples beading tight.

His molten gaze dropped to them, standing at attention just inches from his face. Abruptly he shifted his grip to wrap a muscular arm under her ass, lifting her against the wall as his other hand came up to cup her breast as he bent his head toward her.

She clenched her fingers around the tops of his rock-hard shoulders and arched her back, a soft moan spilling from her when his hot, wet mouth closed over the rigid peak. Pleasure spiraled down to her core.

Instead of fighting it as she would have months ago, she gave into it and let it flow through her. Something that was much easier now than when they'd first gotten together. He would never hurt or humiliate her. Her trust in him had allowed her to open herself up, let herself be vulnerable and actually *feel*.

Marcus switched to the other nipple and lowered her feet to the ground, his hands gripping her hips tight as he dropped to one knee before her. She could feel the heat of his stare on her sex. He took hold of the back of her leg and lifted it, wrapping it over his shoulder to expose her flushed, slick folds, his gaze searing her.

She had only enough time to draw in a breath before the velvet warmth of his mouth closed over her, his tongue flicking at the swollen bud of her clit.

"Marcus," she whispered, knotting her fingers in his short hair. The kneeling position was hard on his injured hip. It had to hurt, but he gave no indication of it and stayed right where he was, his hands holding her still while his tongue stroked across the taut bundle of nerves over and over, giving her exactly the right pressure and friction.

He was an expert at bringing her pleasure, knew every secret of her body.

She rolled her hips, rocking against his tongue. It felt so damn good, the urgency of it, the bite of his fingers into her flesh contrasted with the warm, velvet strokes of his tongue heightening everything. Her core contracted, her bones beginning to melt as ecstasy spiraled up, up—

He stopped as abruptly as he'd begun and shoved to his feet, a pained grimace twisting his face an instant before his mouth came back down on hers. She opened instantly, twining her tongue with his, her hands greedily shoving his T-shirt up.

He tore it over his head and grabbed her shoulders, spinning her around to bend her over an English saddle draped over a sawhorse near the wall.

Yesss...

She wanted him inside her. Wanted to feel him stretching and filling her as he took them both over the edge.

She tossed the back of her trench to one side, threw her hair over her shoulder and looked back at him as the rasp of a zipper lowering filtered through the echo of the pounding rain. His face was set, his eyes blazing as he freed himself, his eyes on the glistening flesh between her thighs.

She set her palms on the seat of the saddle to brace her arms and widened her stance. Tempting him. Daring him, her clit throbbing and her body on fire.

There was no time to touch him. No time to enjoy the view behind her as he stepped up close and seized a fistful of her hair.

She sucked in a breath, surprised, but his grip was

assertive, not painful. And when he pressed his bearded face into the curve of her neck to suck on a sensitive spot that sent a shiver through her, she felt the hard warmth of him pressing against her folds.

"Is this what you wanted?" he rasped out, his tongue gliding over that same spot while he kept hold of her hair, the authoritative position and the tantalizing pressure of him lodged at her entrance sending another wave of heat through her. "Is this what you wanted to happen when you came in here wearing that and started pushing me?"

"Yes," she whispered, pushing her hips toward him. Growing desperate to feel him inside her.

He made a low, rough sound that was almost a reprimand, the hand in her hair squeezing as he pressed his hips forward, lodging the thick head of his cock inside her. Before she could even process the sensation, he dropped his other hand around her to slide between her legs, fingers tightening on either side of her clit.

Her breathing faltered, belly and thigh muscles quivering against the strain, the tantalizing pressure of his fingers and cock teasing all her most sensitive nerve endings, without giving her the friction she needed to get off.

"*Marcus.*" Her voice was breathless, pleading.

"Ask me for it," he said in a delicious, deep voice that made her shiver. She'd always sensed this dominant edge inside him. It made her even wetter, her body tightening around him. Dying for more. "Ask me for it nicely."

Her mind rebelled at being told what to do, even by him, but she craved the pleasure he could deliver, and there was no shame in surrendering to this. In surrendering to him. And she desperately wanted the release waiting coiled deep inside her.

She licked her lips and allowed herself to slip into a submissive mindset, excited to see where it took them. "Please," she whispered, putting the edge of a whimper into it.

He made a low, rough sound somewhere between a groan and a growl. "Please what?" He tightened his fingers and dragged them up and down either side of her clit, all the while holding her in place while refusing to thrust deeper, giving her just enough stimulation to keep her at a simmer. "Say it."

It took all her will to stay still instead of pressing back toward him and take over from the bottom the way she longed to. She could feel the wild, dominant energy pulsing from him. He needed this. They both did.

Licking her lips, she remained still, waiting. Frantic for more. He'd never shown her this side of him. How long would he make her wait?

"Please make me come," she whispered in a rush, breathing fast.

He growled against her neck and drove deep, his fingers sliding along her clit in a way that lit up every nerve ending. Her eyes squeezed shut at the sudden lash of sensation, her lips parting on a soft cry of pleasure. Of surrender.

"No," he bit out, stopping his fingers to merely cradle her most sensitive spot while he withdrew from her body almost completely before surging back inside.

Slow, full thrusts that made her feel every hard inch of him, cradling her clit but not giving her anything else. She hissed out a breath and dug her fingers into the leather of the saddle, his low, erotic groans punctuating each thrust making her crazy as he enjoyed her but refused to let her come. Reminding her that he was the one in control. That she belonged to him.

She cursed in her head, fought to stay still when her entire body demanded she take over. She trembled with a mix of anticipation and the most exquisite frustration she'd ever felt, but she'd be lying if she said what he was doing didn't turn her the hell on.

Just when her control began to fray he shifted, releasing his grip on her hair to hold her hip, more low sounds of masculine pleasure vibrating in her ears as he thrust slow and deep again and again. The change in grip and his steady motion tipped her hips forward, rubbing her clit against his cradling fingers.

She sucked in a breath, her head dropping forward as tingles of ecstasy shot everywhere, making her legs quiver. She wanted to come so badly, could feel it building, building...

As if he sensed it, he stroked his fingers softly over her clit, the motion almost lazy.

God, yes. More.

She pressed her lips together to hold back a cry. Her heart was racing, her breathing unsteady, the high-heeled boots making her legs wobble. This was the sweetest torture, and while she desperately wanted the orgasm building within her, a tiny part of her wanted it to keep going.

"You came out here to seduce me, thinking you could manipulate me into forgetting everything else." His voice was a deep, dark rasp against her ear as he stroked her swollen clit again, harder this time. Making her shiver with

113

longing. "But I won't forget, love, because you're mine. Mine to take care of. Mine to pleasure. *Mine*."

The utter possessiveness behind his words thrilled her as much as they turned her on. This time there was no controlling the whimper that rolled from her throat as he hit the most perfect spots, inside and out. Her control suddenly shattered, making her babble mindlessly.

There was no pulling back from the pleasure. No escape or even the urge to shut it out.

"Don't stop, don't stop, don't stop," she blurted, uncaring that she was begging him, focused only on the intensity of this moment together.

His breathing turned harsher, his grip on her hip tightening as he surged a little faster. Harder, the tender, swirling caress of his fingers enough to wring erotic moans from her throat.

The orgasm that he'd been keeping frustratingly out of reach suddenly began to gather low in her belly. A storm about to break.

When it finally did, she threw her head back and shouted to the ceiling, bucking in his hold, greedy for more friction, more pleasure. Milking every ounce of it from him that she could.

Locking his arm around her waist, he drove deep one last time and stiffened, frozen in place as his guttural growl of release sounded in her ear and he pulsed inside her.

Dazed, trembling muscles melting like butter in a hot pan, Kiyomi leaned forward, all but collapsing on top of the saddle. Mind blank, body floating.

Marcus groaned and let go of her to brace himself on the saddle as well, breathing hard. A soft kiss landed on her shoulder, then he eased from her body, his hand smoothing down her spine as the back of her trench slid back to cover her damp skin.

Awareness of her surroundings suddenly returned. The rain pouring down on the roof and outside the open stable door. Horses blowing and shifting around in their stalls.

She heard the rustle of denim and the rasp of a zipper, then a rush of cool air surrounded her as he stepped away. Legs unsteady, she pushed upright and started to turn around, but Marcus caught her, pulling her back to his chest, and slid to the ground with a pained grunt.

She twisted sideways across his lap, pushing her hair out of her face to look up at him. His jaw was set, but there was no anger in his eyes anymore. "Leg hurting?"

He nodded. "Aye. Damn thing," he muttered, and gathered her to his chest, wrapping those big, strong arms around her. Enveloping her in his warmth and love as he sighed against her hair.

"You still mad?" she whispered. He seemed a lot mellower now.

"Aye." But there was no heat in his tone, and he stroked her hair and pressed his lips to her temple. When she murmured in pleasure he caught her chin in his fingers and tilted her face up to rain tender kisses all over it.

She relaxed into him with a sigh, rubbing her cheek against his bare chest. Secure in his embrace, and in the knowledge that he would love her no matter what. That there was nothing she could ever do that would make him stop.

She felt the same way about him, but it still awed her. Throughout her life, her body had been a weapon. A means to an end, nothing more.

Until Marcus, she had never known pleasure under a

man's hands. She'd been frozen inside. If not for him, she would have remained that way for however much time she had left.

He had saved her. And, she hoped she had saved him in return.

She kissed the spot over his heart, basking in the closeness between them. "That was... Where has that been all this time?"

A deep, grudging chuckle rumbled in his chest. "You drove me to it."

"Mmm, and I'm not sorry."

His arms tightened around her, squeezing. "I can see that."

The rain on the roof was so soothing. She was more relaxed than she had been in days. "We should probably head back inside," she murmured regretfully, in no hurry to move anytime soon. "Everyone will wonder where we are."

"Bloody houseguests," he muttered.

She tilted her head back to look at him. "Unless you want to stay out here a while longer to show me who's boss again?"

One side of his mouth lifted. "Not much of a punishment if you're already wanting more, is it?"

No. But she was already wondering what naughty things she could do to make him give her another demonstration in the near future.

CHAPTER ELEVEN

Trinity muttered to herself under her breath as she read through her notes for what felt like the fiftieth time. After all of them working around the clock to get everything ready, the day of the op was finally here.

She'd been up since four to review everything again, make sure it was all nailed down perfectly and to ensure that none of them had missed anything. Lives depended on it, and she felt even more responsible for everyone's safety because she was still struggling with her guilt about staying behind here at Laidlaw Hall, safe and cozy while everyone else was out putting themselves in danger.

Amber walked into the breakfast room carrying two mugs of fragrant coffee and set one down in front of her before taking the next chair over. "Thanks," Trinity murmured without looking up.

"Everything okay?" Amber took a sip of her coffee and opened up Lady Ada.

"Yeah. Just want to be sure I'm on top of everything."

She also missed Brody, but couldn't tell him about anything that was going on.

Amber snorted softly. "You know you are. But let's go over everything from the top anyway."

There was something more than the impending ops bothering her though. "Anything more from our mysterious source?"

Amber shook her head, the end of her brown ponytail swishing across her shoulders. "Not a damn thing."

What did it mean? Trinity was convinced they were all still being hunted. As a precaution they'd all done everything in their power to mitigate the possible risk in case this whole thing was a trap.

Honestly, she would have felt better if they had found evidence for it. Because as careful as they'd been, and no matter how well they were all trained, nothing ever went exactly as planned during an op.

She felt a bit easier after reviewing everything with Amber, who would be running the warehouse op from a mobile command post with Jesse. Trinity would run Eden's and Kiyomi's ops from here.

Footsteps came from overhead just as they finished up. The rest of the house was beginning to stir. Everyone except for Eden and Zack, who had spent the past few nights in a Birmingham rental near the yoga studio Tarasov's guys were planning to nab Eden from.

Seconds later, the sound of an uneven gait came from down the hall, the light tap of a cane becoming clearer, along with the patter of paws. Marcus emerged out of the shadowy hallway and into the sunlit room with Karas at his side.

"Morning," Trin said to him with a smile. He looked

much more like himself today, and the tension between him and Kiyomi seemed to have been resolved. For the most party, anyway. "Sleep okay?"

"Aye." He glanced at the empty table. "You two eat yet?"

"No, had some work to catch up on first, but we're done now," she said, closing her laptop and standing. "We'll help you get breakfast organized."

"I placed an order with Huffkins last night. Was just about to head out to pick it up, if you fancy joining Karas and me?"

"Love to." She could use the break, and she loved the village.

She followed him out to the side of the house where his old Land Rover was parked, slid in the front passenger seat while Karas jumped up nimbly into the back and Marcus got behind the wheel. Pale golden sunlight high-lighted everything, burning away the fine layer of mist in the hollows as they turned right out of the gate at the end of the long driveway and started up the hill toward town.

"It's so quiet here right now," she murmured as they reached the bottom of Sheep Street. Stow was a major tourist draw, and normally full of people this time of year.

"Aye. Give it a few hours and there won't be a parking space to be found anywhere."

They passed the Bell Inn on the left on the way up Sheep Street, and beyond it the road was lined on both sides with honey-stone cottages and shops decorated with flower boxes and baskets bursting with different color blooms. Climbing roses in shades of peach, pink and creamy yellow scrambled along the low stone walls and over doorways.

"I've missed it here," she said, feeling wistful. She had such amazing, complex memories of this place, and of her second family now gathered at Laidlaw Hall.

Marcus glanced at her. "You'll have to bring your young lad back with you next time you come across the pond, and stay for a proper visit."

The thought almost made her eyes sting. It was still such an incredible thought that she was going to be a mother soon. A completely different life was waiting for her, with the obstacle of the current mission standing in her way. She prayed her involvement wouldn't come back to haunt her in the form of the adoption being rejected.

"I'd love to do that." Once this was over, hopefully the rest of her trips would be for pleasure only.

He turned right up Digbeth Street, a narrow road that curved between more shops, none of them open yet. When it opened up into the town square at the top of the hill, he headed left past the stone market cross, and across the empty square to the row of stone buildings marking the south side of it.

Huffkins was near the end of the first row of shops. Behind it, the square tower of St. Edward's Church was visible above the gray slate rooflines, where generations of Marcus's ancestors had been buried. The sign on Huffkins' door read closed, but the lights were on inside and Trinity could see people behind the counter in the bakery section.

Marcus parked right outside the door and she went in with him. Their order was already waiting in a pile of neatly-stacked white boxes. Trinity's eyes widened when she saw how many there were. "You ordered all of this?"

His hard face broke into a grin. "Didn't want anyone going hungry on the big day."

Not a concern, based on the amount of boxes they carried out to the vehicle. "Did you get scones for Chloe?"

He snorted. "Of course."

Driving back down into the valley below was even more gorgeous than the trip into town had been. Stretching out in every direction for miles around, the rolling country-side was a patchwork of fields in every shade of green imaginable and bordered by dark green hedgerows, forest, and low, dry-stone walls. Flocks of sheep dotted the land-scape, their heads bent low as they grazed on the sweet summer grass.

She definitely wanted to come back here for a holiday with Brody and their son. Couldn't wait to start the next phase of her life without any further danger hanging over her or her family's heads.

Everyone was ready and waiting for them when they arrived back at the Hall. Chloe's eyes widened, a gasp coming from her when she saw the familiar boxes. "Are there scones?"

"Aye," Marcus said dryly, carrying his load into the breakfast room at the back of the house.

"With clotted cream, and jam?"

"It's the only proper way to eat them."

"Thanks." Grinning, she snatched the box he offered and scurried out of the room to hoard them all to herself.

"We should eat outside," Megan said, coming out of the kitchen with a big platter of freshly cut fruit. "It's such a gorgeous morning."

And probably the last one they would spend together in peace for a while.

Trinity followed the others out through the back doors to the flagstone patio beside the formal garden and dug into the offerings. This was so different from any previous op day. It was heaven to sit outside in the sun and enjoy some time with everyone while birdsong surrounded them.

Her phone rang when she was halfway through her maple éclair. Brody. "Hi. Was just thinking about you."

"Glad to hear that. I just got off a call."

She hurriedly swallowed the mouthful, her whole body tensing. "Caroline? Is she in labor?"

"She's having contractions every fifteen minutes or so. They're taking her to the hospital now to get checked out."

Shit, what was she going to do? She couldn't leave until the mission was over. But she'd so wanted to be there when their son was born... "Are you going?"

"No, it's still early. Might not be the real deal yet. I'm waiting to hear from them first."

She nodded, fighting off the wave of sadness and help-lessness. Her son might be about to be born, and she was trapped here across the ocean from him. "Yeah."

"Heads up," Heath said, standing in the middle of the patio to address the group. "Equipment check as soon as you've all finished chow. I'll be waiting on the south lawn."

Trinity bit back a frustrated sigh. "I have to go. Let me know what's going on?"

"You know I will. What uh... What time are you avail-able until?"

"Another hour, no more."

"All right. Don't worry. It'll all be okay."

She nodded, feeling torn. The others would have understood if she had flown home, but she had insisted on staying. She couldn't let them do this without helping. "Love you."

"Love you too."

Breakfast ended in a hurry, and after that it was a flurry of activity as the group broke into teams to do equipment, weapons, and comms checks. Firearm laws were strict in the UK, so none of them could get caught with one. Everyone but Briar would be using non-lethal rounds or tranq guns to keep the body count down and minimize the risk of collateral damage if any innocents got caught in the crossfire.

When everything was ready, the entire group assembled for one last briefing in the library, then everyone dispersed. Amber and Jesse left in their own vehicle that would serve as a mobile command center for the warehouse op. Kiyomi left with Marcus and Chloe. Briar drove with Georgia, Bautista and Heath.

Leaving Trinity all alone in the manor house.

Karas plodded over to her as she set up in an interior office for the duration of the mission. It had no windows, giving her complete privacy and quiet. She stroked the top of the dog's head, and Karas settled onto her side at Trinity's feet with a groan.

"You can stay, but no interrupting me," she told Karas, giving her another pat before opening her laptop and pulling up the programs she needed to access the video feeds Amber had hacked for their specific window.

The weight of responsibility settled heavy on her shoulders. As the eldest and most experienced of them, she felt like an honorary mother to her Valkyrie sisters. It was her job to look after them. She wished she was out there with them right now instead of here, but she knew she'd made the right call in sitting this one out.

It wasn't just her and Brody anymore. There was a

little guy about to come into the world, and he needed them to both stay safe—

She pushed out a breath, her heart aching. What if he was on his way right now? It would be another few days yet before she was able to fly home and see him. Being a mom was something she'd wanted for so long.

She shook herself, pushing it from her mind. She couldn't think about that now, or the baby. Her teammates were depending on her to help protect them and keep them informed.

Putting on her headset, she began monitoring the live feeds in Manchester near the yoga studio, and another in north London at Tarasov's place. Then she contacted Eden.

"All set up?" The yoga class started in fifteen minutes. Eden would take part, then walk the same route "home" that she'd taken when Tarasov's guys had scouted her before, with Zack nearby and ready to assist. Given her and Zack's skill sets, Tarasov's three guys stood no chance whatsoever.

"Roger."

They did another comms check, then Trinity activated the micro camera hidden on the zipper of Eden's yoga jacket. "Crystal clear," she confirmed as the inside of the rented flat appeared on her screen. Both she and Zack would be able to see everything happening in front of Eden during this part of the op.

"Perfect. I'm ready."

Her phone buzzed in her pocket. She muted her mic to check the screen. Brody.

She knew it was about Caroline, and her stomach knotted. "What's happened?" she said to him.

"False alarm. Braxton Hicks contractions. They're sending her home now."

She expelled a hard breath, shoulders slumping in relief. "Thank God." There was still time. She hadn't missed it.

But as soon as this mission was over, so was this life-style. No more ops. No more danger. She was ready to put their child first, above everyone and everything else.

"We're still okay."

She put on a smile. "Yes. Thanks for letting me know."

"Hoped it would ease your mind. You ready?"

As ready as she would ever be. "Yeah. Have to go silent now."

"Okay." An awkward pause followed, and it felt wrong on so many levels not to be able to tell him what was going on. But for the sake of his career, reputation and security clearance, he needed to have plausible deniability about all this. "Talk to you later?"

"For sure. Love you." Turning off her phone, she tucked it away and faced her open laptop, flipping the mental switch that put her into op mode. Eden and Zack were leaving the flat. The clock was officially running on this first phase of the op.

They'd done all they could to prepare. All she could do now was wait.

~

"Annnd, one last deep breath. Innnn…and…ouuuut."

Lying stretched out on her back on the yoga mat, Eden did as the instructor said, but for the past hour's class her mind had been on what she needed to do a few minutes from now. Heaver was out there right now, waiting for her to appear.

"Namaste," the instructor murmured, ending the hour-long class.

Energized after the gentle exercise and peaceful atmosphere, Eden rolled her mat and popped up to cross the hardwood floor before any of the other students had moved. The studio had a great vibe, especially since it was full of healthy, potted plants soaking up the natural light coming through all the tall windows.

She put on her socks and shoes, slid on her jacket and secretively activated the camera as she did up the zipper. Her mind was focused, her pulse calm. She was ready.

"Looks good, Eden," Trinity's voice said through her earpiece. "I'm muting my mic now, but Zack and I've both got you."

Having worked alone for most of her career, hearing those words was such a revelation. It was so nice to be working with a team again. Having backup made things so much easier and safer.

The timeline on this had moved quickly. Tarasov's goons had officially marked her as a target during her walk home from this same yoga studio the other night. Amber had intercepted their messages, as well as the confirmation call between Heaver and Tarasov last night, stating that they were planning to take her right after this class.

The whole thing was so messed up, and pissed her off. None of the captured women had been found yet. This was her chance to do her part to bring this ring down, and also hopefully expose whoever was behind the messages sent to Amber.

Show time.

Just before she hit the door she reached up and tapped the tiny earpiece hidden in her left ear to signal the others. "I'm in position," Zack answered quietly, his deep voice giving her another measure of calm.

It had been a while since she'd been operational, and damn it felt good to be back. Even better, she had Zack as a teammate on this one, and there was no one she trusted more. He wouldn't let anything happen to her.

Head up, senses on alert, she stepped out of the yoga studio into the warm summer sunshine flooding the sidewalk and took everything in. This street was busy with foot and vehicle traffic.

When she turned the corner at the end of the block in another couple minutes, things would get a lot quieter. It was somewhere along that stretch that the "kidnapping" was likely going to happen.

"I've got eyes on you, sweetness," Zack said, "just at the corner behind you. Heaver's halfway up the street on the other side, and the van's a couple blocks away."

She kept looking straight ahead and didn't respond as she started up the sidewalk, her fingers wrapped around the strap of the bag resting on her shoulder. It was decorated with metal trading pins, their points having been dosed with a custom-made sedative she'd mixed up before leaving Laidlaw Hall yesterday.

In addition to them, a thin, deadly blade also covered in sedative was hidden in a pocket she'd sewn into her jacket sleeve. If things got dicey all she had to do was break the skin with either weapon and her victim would be unconscious in a matter of seconds.

Turning slightly to let an elderly man with a walker pass her, she spotted Heaver across the street, dressed in jeans and a button-down shirt, leaning casually against the exterior of the florist part way up the block. A pair of dark shades covered his eyes, but she felt the moment his gaze locked on her, a telltale prickle at the back of her neck alerting her.

She lowered her gaze and kept walking up the sidewalk at a sedate pace, aware of him pushing away from the wall out of the corner of her eye and heading up the street with her.

Eden suppressed a smile, a tremor of excitement running through her. *That's right. Come and get me, sweetheart.*

They thought she was just another helpless victim. Another payment for their bank accounts.

These assholes were about to get the shock of their lives.

CHAPTER TWELVE

There she was.

Will spotted her the instant she came out of the yoga studio.

She was hard to miss. He'd captured some hot women before, but this bird was *lush* and he completely understood why the client had insisted upon her.

Clear, creamy brown skin, dark spiral curls that fell to her shoulders. Curvy, but fit, and those tight yoga leggings hugged her ass and long legs perfectly.

Target located, he messaged the two guys waiting in the van, and watched her walk toward him. She was on the other side of the street and hadn't noticed him. He'd make sure she didn't until the very last moment, and by then…it would be too late for her.

He pushed away from the wall he'd been leaning against and followed her. This order had been rushed, but the client had been insistent. Out of the list Will had provided Tarasov, the client had chosen this target personally, and paid nearly double the usual fee to make it happen. She was going to be the biggest payday yet.

There were too many people around here, however. He would have to follow her for a bit until they came to a less crowded spot. The guys would track his position and stay close until he gave the signal for them to approach just prior to his attack.

She was nearing the end of the street now. *Where you going, sweetheart?*

Her flat was to the right. If she headed home, taking her on the way there would be harder, especially at this time of day because of the number of people around. The area to the left was far quieter, lined with mostly attached terraced houses and a few small businesses.

Luck was running with him, because she turned left.

He sped up a bit, still holding his phone as he turned the corner. She was halfway up the block, but as expected this street was far less busy. There were several alleys up ahead that he could drag her into out of sight, places the CCTVs couldn't see into. Only the occasional vehicle passed by on the narrow, two-lane road.

But this was London. After this he was going to have to lay low for a while to stay off the radar.

Increasing the length of his strides, he started to gain on her. She glanced back over her shoulder and spotted him, but with his sunglasses on there was no way she could know he was staring at her. Facing forward, she quickened her pace and hitched the strap of her bag up higher on her shoulder.

Only a young guy walking a spaniel appeared on the sidewalk ahead of them. Will maintained his distance from the target until the guy passed him, then sped up again.

The woman glanced back again, and this time he could tell she was nervous of him. A flare of excitement hit. The thrill of the hunt. And the little alleyways were coming up soon.

He'd already typed out a command to the others on his phone. His thumb hit over the send button as he approached the woman. *Go.*

Less than twenty seconds later, he heard a vehicle turn the corner behind them. Glancing back, he saw the van.

He shoved his phone in his pocket as he faced forward again, his pulse accelerating under a burst of adrenaline. They'd already passed the first alley, but there was another one just a dozen meters or so farther up. And there wasn't another soul around who would see this. He'd scouted the area beforehand to make sure there were no cameras around.

As the van neared him, he broke into a run. The woman turned, but too late. He grabbed her from behind, clapped a hand over her mouth to cut off her scream and dragged her into the alley.

She fought him but he subdued her easily enough with an arm across her throat, applied with enough pressure to make breathing difficult, and his hand still across her mouth. She kicked at his knees and shins as she twisted but the flat, rubber soles of her trainers didn't hurt at all.

The van whipped into the alley, plunging them into shadow. As he dragged her toward it the passenger side door slid open, and the guy in the back reached for her. Together they quickly got her inside, and Will slammed the door shut behind him.

"Go," he snapped to the driver.

His colleague was struggling with the woman, his hand

over her mouth to muffle her screams. Will turned around to help subdue her and narrowly avoided a foot to the jaw. Then the van suddenly lurched to a sharp stop.

He stumbled back, slamming into the door. "What the hell?" he snarled at the driver.

"Arsehole's blocking me in," he responded.

Will looked back, and sure enough, a car was parked across the end of the alley. His heart lurched. Had they been seen? Was the driver calling 999?

"Ah, Christ," the guy struggling with the woman hissed. "We've been made."

"Shut up," Will barked, mind racing.

He faced their captive. The first thing they needed to do was subdue her and get her out of sight in case someone came to investigate. He had a sedative to use if necessary, though it usually wasn't once he got the cuffs and gag on.

But as he reached for her arms, Harry suddenly stilled. His face went slack, his eyes wide with surprise and confusion. He slumped to the side, his hand falling away from the woman's mouth.

Will went to grab a handful of her hair, but she blocked it with a move that told him she'd taken at least a self-defense plan. Then her expression shifted, going from terror to a smile of pure malice that made the hair on his nape stand up right before her hand shot out and something sharp jabbed into the side of his neck.

EDEN JAMMED THE end of the pin into Heaver's neck with a burst of pure satisfaction. He yelled and grabbed at her hand, his grip bruising, but it didn't matter. Her custom-blended concoction was already doing its job.

Within seconds Heaver blinked fast and started to topple sideways. Eden helped him out by planting the sole of her foot in his chest and sending him flying.

"Hey! What the hell are you doing?" the driver demanded, scrambling out of his seat and coming toward her.

She settled into a crouch and waited, coiled and ready. *Come and get it, asshole.*

His eyes widened when he saw his two buddies sprawled out in the back. A blade flashed as his hand came up. She dodged it as it swung toward her, striking the heel of her hand into his face.

His head snapped back, a sharp howl coming from him as he doubled over, cupping his nose. She swept his feet out from under him with her leg, and rolled out of the way just as the van door was ripped open. Zack started to lunge inside.

"No, I'm good," she told him, leaping lightly to her feet once more. The driver was lying crumpled on his side now, moaning and crying as he cursed at her. "This was almost too easy. Cocky bastards."

"You dose him?" Zack asked, voice taut.

"Nope. No need." And this way he'd be able to talk better.

Zack picked up her bag and held it open for her. Bastards should have dumped it rather than bringing it into the van, but whatever. These guys weren't nearly the pros they thought they were.

"I'm just the driver," the guy blurted. "I don't know anything, I swear!"

"Shut up." She capped the end of the used pins and put them in the bag, then grabbed the restraints and nylon rope

133

she'd brought and turned toward him.

He'd scrambled up onto one elbow but seemed afraid to move, glancing from her to Zack through streaming eyes as blood dripped over his lips and chin. "Listen to me, I don't know who you guys are, but just let me go and I won't say anything. It's them you want," he insisted, nodding at his two buddies lying unconscious on the floor. "They're the ones who know everything."

"Shut *up*." He recoiled when she grabbed his wrist, howled when she wrenched his beefy arm behind him and angled it upward, putting pressure on both the shoulder and elbow joints. One jerk, and she would pop them right out of their sockets.

It was tempting.

She curbed the impulse, jerked the flex cuff around that wrist and used his awkwardly-bent arm to steer him onto his stomach, keeping him in place with a knee in his back as she wrenched his other arm behind him.

"Who the fuck are you?" he snarled, his face wet with blood and tears.

Oh yeah, he'd talk, all right. "Your worst nightmare."

Seeing the driver no longer posed any kind of threat to her, Zack stopped hovering and climbed in the front and started searching for evidence they might find useful. "Got a cell phone and a radio here."

"Clone the phone and take the radio." Eden had no doubt that Amber could get all kinds of juicy things from them.

Working fast, she secured the driver's wrists behind him, bound his feet, then secured the others in the same way before tying them all together. In seconds she'd stripped them of their phones, wallets and weapons—

switchblades—and handed everything over to Zack to deal with.

"Found this too," he said, holding out a slim metal box containing loaded syringes, no doubt containing whatever sedative they'd intended to dose her with.

"Leave it for evidence." Straightening, she spotted the chain loop welded to the floor in the back, and paused. If she'd been like the other women they'd taken, they would have bound her and chained her to it, rendering her helpless.

A wave of rage hit. *Assholes.*

The driver let out a yelp as she seized his bound wrists, quickly tied a constrictor knot around the flex cuffs, then secured the rope to the chain loop in the floor and tightened it until there was no room for any of them to move more than a few inches.

She tapped her earpiece. "All three suspects neutralized," she told Trinity, holding the driver's fearful gaze.

"Good work."

"We're sending all the intel through the secure link now."

"Copy. You're clear to head to the drop point. Contact me when you're there, and we'll alert the cops."

"Roger." She tapped her earpiece to mute her mic. "We're good to go," she told Zack, who climbed out of the front and came around beside the open door.

The plan was for her to drive the van to the drop point, while he followed in the other vehicle to pick her up. "But stand guard for a minute first, will you? My friend here and I are gonna have a little chat."

The driver was already shaking his head, his expression frantic. "I told you, I don't know anything. I don't—"

135

She seized a handful of his hair and rammed the back of his head into the floor with a thud. "You either tell me everything I want to know, *mate*, or you'll die with your pals." The other men weren't dead and would start to come around in another ten to fifteen minutes or so, but he didn't know that.

"Jesus," he cried, writhing against his bonds and getting nowhere.

She leaned over him, putting a knee on his groin. He stilled instantly, gulping, his eyes wide with horror. "*Talk*," she snarled, increasing the pressure until he broke.

"Okay, okay!" he shouted, face slick with sweat.

Oh yeah, he was about to sing for her like a nightingale.

She hid a smile and twisted her hand in his hair, arching his neck back at a painful angle as he started to spill his guts. This first part of the op had gone exactly as planned. She hoped the others would go as smoothly.

~

Amber studied the multiple video feeds on Lady Ada from the back of the darkened cube van. Jesse was up front, watching the nearly empty parking lot he'd pulled into a few minutes ago. He was her backup and bodyguard, making sure she was safe so she could focus on her job.

Everyone was in place for the warehouse op. Briar in a fourth-floor window of the building across the street and down one. Georgia and Bautista standing by to breach the door, with Heath backing them up.

"Feeds look good," she told the team. "No changes since my last check in. Briar, can you confirm?"

"No changes here," Briar reported from behind her sniper rifle, aided by her high-powered binos. Unlike the others, she was using regular ammo. If she was forced to shoot, her target would die.

"Copy." All the recon they'd done for this had paid off beautifully.

By hacking into a few private security cameras in the immediate vicinity, she had a bird's eye view of the front and side of the warehouse, as well as the surroundings. CCTV footage would have been ideal, but hacking into that was trickier and more likely to raise red flags on the other end.

What they didn't have, was a camera inside the place. The team would have to do the breach before they would know exactly what was inside.

"On your mark, Briar," she said, and sat back to monitor everything. It was so much harder to sit on the sidelines than being part of the action.

"Go time?" Jesse asked, looking back at her.

She nodded, eyes on the screen just as Bautista and Georgia came into view near the side door of the warehouse.

A moment later, Briar's voice came over her earpiece. "Execute."

CHAPTER THIRTEEN

I t had been a damn long time since he'd been able to put his skill set to use. Even longer since his enemies had shuddered with fear at the name "El Santo."

Dressed all in black with a balaclava hiding his face, Miguel Bautista placed the breaching charge on the side door of the darkened warehouse and retreated out of sight around the corner to wait. There were two armed security personnel inside, and an unknown number of others.

It felt good to be back in action, and even better to be on an op to rescue women, with a team that included his wife. This was a far cry from their comparatively sedate life back in Miami, and they were both enjoying the rush of conducting an op again.

All their intel indicated one or more women were currently being held somewhere in the building for the next hour or two. His team's task was to neutralize whatever threat lay inside, and rescue any prisoners.

"You're clear," Briar said in his earpiece, providing overwatch from across the street while Heath kept an eye out for them from ground level. As a former PJ, Heath had the best medical skills on the team. He would guard their rear and assist in treating the hostages and any wounded after the building was secure.

Miguel withdrew his weapon and stood poised there, his body tensed and ready to go. Once he and Georgia entered the building, they would have mere seconds to distinguish foe from friendlies.

No sooner had the thought formed than Georgia's hand landed on his right shoulder. She might not be able to put her incredible sniper skills to use on this op, but she had an entire arsenal of other badass tricks she could pull out of her sleeve as needed.

She squeezed him, signaling she was ready to go.

He hit the trigger on the charge. The metal lock on the door disintegrated under the force of the explosion.

Go.

Bursting from around the corner, he drove the sole of his boot into the edge of the warped door, smashing it inward. The moment it gave way he ducked back around the corner to wait.

Seconds later, two men burst through the open doorway, carrying rifles. As Miguel raised his pistol to engage them from behind, the faint sizzle of bullets ripped through the air and both the men dropped almost simultaneously in a spray of blood.

"Two tangos down," Briar reported coolly. "Entry's clear."

Without missing a beat, he emerged from cover and plunged inside the gaping doorway, weapon up as he checked the left side and scanned to the right in the dimly-lit interior of the warehouse. As he stood there, Georgia swept past him to scan from the right side and meet him in the middle.

Shouts came from the back somewhere out of sight. Both of them pivoted at the same moment to face the new threat. Four more guys appeared from the hidden hallway, scrambling for their weapons left on metal tables. One of them upended a table and dove behind it for cover, disappearing from view.

He and Georgia charged forward, weapons up. Two guys grabbed pistols sitting on the other table and whirled to face them, ready to fire. Miguel squeezed off two shots at the first tango and kept going as the guy dropped to his knees, clutching his chest. Non-lethal rounds still hurt like a bitch and could cause fractures or internal damage.

The other tango dove behind the flipped table with his buddy.

"I'll go right," Georgia said.

Miguel automatically shifted left as they both slowed, circling the sides of the table hiding the two tangos. "Give it up," he growled to the cowardly shits hiding there. "Toss your weapons on the floor and put your hands up." The other tango was still down, groaning in pain.

Miguel flicked a glance to the entrance to the hallway at the back left corner of the warehouse, where one of the four guys had gone earlier, then focused on the upended table.

"Fuck you," one of them yelled back.

"Last chance," he said, steadily moving forward with Georgia, primed and ready to react to the merest hint of movement. If they didn't surrender, he was going to make it hurt.

Too stupid to realize who they were up against, neither

one took the out he'd offered. He took another step to the left, aware of Georgia mirroring his movements on his right, his gaze pinned to the left edge of the table. If the bastards decided to shoot their way out, he would have only a split second to react.

A flicker of movement came from the left edge. He froze, automatically adjusting his aim. The instant the black pistol appeared he stepped left and fired at the man crouched there.

A cry echoed along with the gunshot. The enemy's pistol clattered to the concrete floor, followed by shuffling and a string of low, guttural curses.

The idiot's friend suddenly popped up from behind the table, pistol raised, a livid expression on his face. "You motherfu—"

His face contorted and he stumbled back as Miguel and Georgia both hit him center mass almost simultaneously. He blinked at them in shock, his arms falling. His weapon hit the floor, both his hands going to his chest as he fell to his knees.

Miguel surged forward and kicked the table aside with a noisy clatter. All three men were down now, clutching their chests, their wide eyes full of terror as he stalked toward them while Georgia stood guard.

"Where are the women?" he growled out while Georgia quickly bent to tranq them with Eden's sedative, then took their weapons and frisked them. She came up with phones and blades, tucking them away in the pockets of her black tactical pants.

"Where?" he snapped when they just kept staring at him, their eyes going hazy from the drug. There was at least one more tango to contend with somewhere to the left down the hallway. But there could be more.

"In the back," one of them gasped out. "Oh, Jesus, you shot us. You fuckin' shot us," he moaned, trying and failing to move away.

"How many more of you are there?" he demanded, unmoved by their suffering. They deserved to suffer. They deserved to *die* for what they'd done, and were lucky his team couldn't afford to rack up a high body count on this mission. Otherwise these assholes would all be facing their maker right now.

One guy let out a sob and started wheezing. "You... broke my ribs," he gasped out.

"How many?" Miguel snapped, his voice cutting through the room like the crack of a whip.

"T-two," the first one wheezed, collapsing onto the floor.

Georgia had already secured their hands behind them and straightened. "Heath?" she said, glancing toward the other end of the warehouse where they'd entered.

"Clear back here," the former PJ answered, dragging the second of Briar's kills inside and pushing the warped door shut to mostly cover the opening. "We need to hurry." He jogged toward them, taking in the captured men with a single look. None of them posed a threat anymore.

Miguel turned to his wife. She was calm and composed as she visually swept the room, her blue eyes cool. Seeing her in operator mode again was unbelievably hot. And incredible as it still seemed to him, she was *all his*. "Let's go," she said.

He took point as they moved down the hallway. It was

dark except for the light filtering down it from the main room they'd just left.

Their boots were all but silent on the concrete floor as they moved, scanning for any hint of a threat ahead. Two doors stood at the end of the hallway, one on either side.

He used hand signals to indicate that he would enter the one on the left. Pausing briefly with his back to the wall beside it while Georgia stood back to assist, he drew a breath and reached for the knob. Surprisingly, it turned.

Throwing it open, he whirled and swept the room from the doorway, his eyes adjusting slowly to the faint amount of light coming through the edges of the blind on the window. The room was empty except for a massive wooden desk in the far corner.

His gut tingled, telling him there was someone hidden behind it.

He crept toward it, weapon aimed. When he got halfway across the room, he caught the faint sound of movement from behind the desk. He dove to the right, rolling as shots exploded in the silence. Bullets slammed into the wall behind him, raining down a shower of drywall.

Rolling to one knee, he aimed to the right side of the desk and fired when a shadow moved there. A faint grunt sounded, then a shuffling noise. He rose to a crouch and eased forward, finger on the trigger.

The shadow moved again. He stopped, waiting.

His prey sprang from cover and tried to dart past him in a desperate attempt to escape out the door.

Miguel fired, hitting him in the back before he'd cleared the desk. The man cried out and dropped to his knees, cursing as he put a hand to his back.

Quickly disarming him, Miguel drugged and bound the asshole, then rejoined Georgia, now standing guard in the doorway. "Any movement in there?" he murmured, nodding at the closed door across the hall.

"I heard a woman crying inside."

If the bastards in the other room had been telling the truth, there was only one more man left. But criminals rarely told the truth, and could never be trusted.

This door was locked. He loaded a fresh magazine of rubber-tipped ammo before approaching the final door, and glanced at Georgia. At her nod, he reared back and drove the sole of his boot into the lock.

Once. Twice. Three times, until it finally broke and the door groaned open.

Shots exploded through it immediately, ripping across the hall and slamming into the wall behind them. Georgia dropped to one knee and returned fire.

Everything went eerily silent.

Was the shooter down? Or just fucking with them?

He surged inside with Georgia right behind him.

In the dimness he made out the two women bound and gagged in the far corner, and a man lying crumpled on the floor, holding his belly. He looked up and raised a pistol.

Georgia fired, hitting him in the chest. He flopped back and went still. Miguel stalked forward to drug and sedate him, holstering his weapon.

He barely caught the flash of movement in his peripheral vision before someone burst out from behind the opened door. He was half-turned toward the threat when an arm suddenly locked around his throat.

Instinct took over.

Grabbing the arm, he reached his other hand down to

draw the blade strapped to his waist and pivoted, slicing across the man's inner thigh. A howl of agony rent the air and the arm barred across his throat let go.

Teeth bared, Miguel whirled and slashed again, laying open the man's chest. Not deep enough to kill, but enough to hurt like a bitch and make him bleed like a stuck pig. They were keeping this one alive for interrogation.

The man yelped and tried to stumble back, but there was nowhere to go except straight into the wall. Miguel drove his elbow into the side of the bastard's face and swept his leg out to buckle the guy's knees.

The man went down hard, bleeding and cursing. Miguel seized him, pinning him facedown on the nubby carpet as he secured the asshole's hands behind him without sedation, then tied a blindfold across his eyes.

When he looked up from his crouch, Georgia had already freed the women's hands and feet and was removing the second one's gag. "Are either of you hurt?" she asked in a low, calm voice.

"M-my leg," one of them gasped out in a strong Manchester accent. "I c-can't walk."

"It's okay. We're going to get you out of here." Georgia looked up at him.

"Take them to Heath," he told her, sheathing his blade as he stood, towering over the whimpering lump at his feet. "I'll handle this one."

ONLY ONE OF the three tangos on the floor was still conscious when Georgia appeared, but he was fading fast.

Dismissing him, Heath pushed to his feet and shifted his full attention to the women coming toward him, rushing over to help the one Georgia was half-carrying. The second one appeared unhurt, following under her own power. They were both wearing the clothes they had been kidnapped in.

"I've got her," he told Georgia, bending slightly to scoop the first woman up in his arms. "Where are you hurt?" he asked as he carried her across the warehouse, while Georgia and the other woman followed.

"My knee," she choked out. Both of them were crying.

"Okay, let's take a look," he said, setting her down in a chair halfway across the floor. He could feel the seconds ticking past. They needed to bug out of here fast.

Briar was still keeping watch from across the street, and Trinity had eyes on a whole bunch of views of the exterior. So far neither of them had reported any additional threats coming their way. He had time to assess and treat before leaving.

The seated woman had on a thigh-length dress. She was trembling from shock as he took her wrist to check her pulse. He went to one knee beside her and reached for an ACE bandage from his vest. Georgia was talking to the other woman about twenty feet away.

"Are you Holly?" She was pale and her pulse was fast, but she was breathing fine, her pupils were okay, and she didn't show any signs of being critically dehydrated.

"Yes," she said in a shocked tone. "How d-did you…"

He didn't answer, still assessing her. There were no obvious wounds anywhere, only some minor bruising and scratches. Probably because the assholes who'd kidnapped her didn't want to damage the merchandise before handing her off to the buyer.

"Your left knee?" he asked, examining it with gentle,

146

gloved hands. It was a little swollen on the medial aspect, with some bruising on the kneecap.

"Y-yes." She wrapped her arms around herself, shivering. "Who are you guys?"

"We're here to get you out," he told her, and began wrapping her knee in a figure-eight pattern.

"They were going..." She swallowed, fought for composure. "Going to sell us," she whispered.

A hot stab of anger punched through him. "We know. But they won't hurt you or anyone else ever again," he vowed, tucking the edges of the bandage in, then taking out a Mylar blanket and draping it around her to conserve warmth. "There. You sit tight for just a bit longer, and we'll have you out of here." He glanced up just as Bautista appeared out of the hallway, dragging a bleeding man behind him.

Heath turned Holly's chair to face away so she wouldn't have to see her captor, gave her a reassuring smile through his balaclava and squeezed her shoulder gently. "Be right back."

Bautista dumped his blindfolded cargo on the floor and folded his arms as he glanced at the women. "How are they?"

"Scared out of their minds, but otherwise okay." He nodded at the bleeding guy. "What's his story?"

"He fucked around and found out."

Heath felt zero sympathy for the asshole, glad he was hurting after what he'd done to these and other women.

"Just patch him up enough to stop him from bleeding out until at least after the cops get here."

Amber would call the cops as soon as the team had cleared the area with the freed hostages. "Roger." The restraints made it easier to work on him, but the slice across the inner thigh was deep enough that muscle showed. Bautista didn't fuck around.

With anyone else, Heath might have thought it was pure chance that had made the knife miss the femoral artery, but given Bautista's expertise with a blade, he knew better. A few more ounces of pressure, and it would have been a bloodbath. Although this bastard didn't realize it, he was only still alive because Bautista had allowed it.

"How much longer?" Briar asked.

"Two minutes," he replied, working as fast as he could to staunch the bleeding.

As soon as he'd finished applying the pressure bandages, he pushed to his feet. "We're coming out, two females in tow."

"Copy that," she replied.

Bautista bent to lever the wounded guy across his massive shoulders and stood to carry him back to the other prisoners, ignoring the uttered curses and threats while Heath went back for Holly. Georgia took point, the other woman behind her. Heath followed her, and Bautista brought up the rear.

They paused inside the busted side door, waiting for confirmation that it was safe to exit. At Briar's reply, Georgia stepped outside, weapon in a double-handed grip as she began to lead the way across the asphalt courtyard at the center of the group of buildings.

Heath was part way across it when the faint sound of an engine caught his attention, immediately followed by the screech of tires.

Automatically, he set the woman he was carrying down and drew his pistol, looking around.

"On your left," Briar said in a hard voice.

He turned. A car was screaming toward them. Georgia whirled around. The woman she'd been escorting stood frozen in terror in the glare of the headlights.

With a mental curse, Heath sprinted toward her. The car sped up. He raised his weapon and fired as Georgia did the same, but the non-lethal rounds didn't hit the driver. The car kept coming.

Heath lowered his weapon and ran, charging for the woman. She took a startled step to the side and tried to run.

The car raced right at her.

Suddenly there was a loud thud, and a large bullet hole appeared in the windshield.

Briar.

The car veered, the driver slumped over the wheel. The woman stopped and darted the other way, but too late.

Heath dropped his weapon and dove at her, knocking her out of the way. But the forward momentum threw him directly in the path of the vehicle.

Pain exploded like a lightning bolt when it hit him.

The impact threw him upward, launching into the air. It spun him twice, then slammed him hard into the ground.

For an instant he stared up at the sky, his brain kicking in. *Shit, no. Chloe…*

Then blackness swallowed him.

CHAPTER FOURTEEN

"Twenty seconds."

Chloe didn't respond to Trinity's announcement in her earpiece, too busy connecting the wires to the device she'd just planted beneath the car's fuel tank. Man, what a rush. She'd forgotten how good this felt. And while bringing down a building would have been a lot more fun, they couldn't afford that much damage.

This was better than nothing. And she got a big kick out of knowing she was about to destroy Tarasov's favorite toy.

Her time window was rapidly closing, however. Tarasov's security patrols weren't the primary concern. They were scattered and didn't appear to be on any kind of set schedule here at the garage.

The problem was, the patch Amber had coded for them to upload to the security cameras in this building was about to end. Chloe needed to be out of here by the time that happened, or someone might see her and her team would lose the element of surprise necessary to pull this off.

With a practiced hand, she finished connecting the detonator under the Audi R8 and climbed to her feet. "Done," she whispered, giving the car a longing, regretful look. Such a pretty car. Was such a total waste to destroy it, except that it was sure to piss Tarasov off.

If Kiyomi let him live.

Chloe secretly hoped she wouldn't.

"You're still clear, but we're cutting it close now," Trinity answered. "Move."

Picking up the pace, Chloe hurried to the workbench lining the back wall of the luxury garage and boosted herself onto it. Standing, she reached up for the sill of the partially-open window and jumped, catching the edge of the sill and levering her body up to push it open.

A quick check outside assured her that no one was back here. She slid one leg through, then the other, balancing momentarily on the sill before jumping to the ground.

She landed in a crouch on the pavement below and paused to ensure the window was mostly closed, as it had been when she'd arrived, then darted around the side of the building and disappeared into the gathering shadows. Picking her way through the maze of easements and lanes to reach her ready position for the next phase of the op, she crouched in a tiny back alley between two brick, terraced houses to wait.

"I'm good to go," she murmured, alerting the others. From her vantage point she could see Tarasov's place on the opposite side of the block through the end of the alley, about sixty meters away.

"Copy that," Trinity answered, monitoring everything back at Laidlaw Hall. "Stand by."

Kiyomi spoke a few moments later. "We're in position." She and Marcus were currently tucked away out of sight in a blind spot near the back of Tarasov's house that the cameras couldn't pick up. As soon as Trinity gave the word, Chloe would blow the charge and get this party started.

Waiting was never easy for her. On an op she was able to focus better, but she was still restless, and this time she had another distraction, wondering how things were going for Heath's team. Eden should be in the middle of or have completed her op by now too.

Not wanting to distract Trinity at such a critical time by asking for an update, she took the custom detonator button from her pocket, then pulled out the radio she'd brought and switched to the frequency that allowed her to hear Amber's communication with Heath's team.

But nothing could have prepared for what she heard on the other end.

"Briar, give me status," Amber demanded, her tone curt.

Chloe tensed. Something was wrong.

"A car just went at them," Briar said. "I put a round through the windshield and took out the driver, but—"

"Are the hostages hurt?"

"It's Heath," Briar answered. "He's down."

The blood drained from Chloe's face. She shoved the radio into her pocket and yanked out her phone, frantically texting Amber.

"Chloe," Trinity said in her ear before she could get the message off. "On my mark."

"Not now," she whispered to herself, her gut a giant block of ice. Heath was down. How bad was he hurt?

"Five. Four. Three."

No. No, no, no, she couldn't do this. What was happening with Heath?

"Two. One. *Go.*"

Clamping her jaw shut, she shoved the phone into her pocket and hit the button. The concussion of the blast a block over reverberated in her ears.

Heath. Please be okay...

She tucked the detonator stick away and drew her pistol, torn, and sick with worry. The others didn't know what was happening. And it was too late to stop this now. She was desperate to know what was happening with Heath. Everything in her screamed to drop everything and go to him.

You can't leave the others. They're counting on you.

Kiyomi and Marcus were about to enter Tarasov's private lair, not knowing exactly what they would be up against inside. They needed backup, and while Marcus had served in the most elite unit in the British military, his physical limitations meant Chloe couldn't leave them to face this on their own.

The front and side doors of Tarasov's place flew open. Three men raced out, running across to the burning garage.

Her mind filled with images of Heath. Lying crushed beneath the vehicle. Or lying broken and bleeding on the ground. Maybe dying.

Oh God, I can't do this.

"Now," Trinity commanded. A heartbeat later, Marcus and Kiyomi appeared around the side of the house, weapons up as they raced for the open doorway.

"Chloe, go," Trinity ordered.

Heath…

But she had no choice. She had to stay.

"Goddamn it." Her choked whisper clogged in her throat as she shoved up and bolted from cover, terror for the man she loved filling her with every step.

LUKA PAUSED WITH the china coffee cup partway to his mouth, his attention on his phone screen. He'd been checking it every few minutes for the past half an hour, with no luck. And now worry pricked at the back of his neck.

Will was late checking in about the pick-up. He should have sent word by now.

Setting his phone down, Luka continued drinking his coffee, only half his attention on the newspaper in front of him. He had too much on his mind. Today was a massively important one for his business. There were a lot of moving parts to keep track of, too many things to monitor at once, and it made him feel scattered.

The timing was critical. Breaking protocol, he had two women at the warehouse right now, being guarded while his men waited for the buyers to show.

Luka wanted them all gone from the warehouse before Will's new target was brought in. Cleaner that way. Less chance of any fuck-ups, and he couldn't risk two buyers coming into contact. Guaranteeing his clients' privacy was paramount.

He jumped in his seat when a loud boom suddenly shook the air, making the house rattle and spilling his coffee into the saucer. Heart thumping, he whirled to face his bodyguard, standing across the room. "What the fuck was that?" he demanded in Russian.

"I don't know." Face grim, Ivan turned and rushed out of the room.

Luka jumped up and followed on Ivan's heels, heading for his office in the basement.

One of his other men came running down the hall toward them. "What happened?" Luka demanded.

"There's been an explosion."

He drew his brows together in a menacing frown. "No shit. Where?"

"The garage. It's on fire."

What the fuck? All his cars were in there. Over a million pounds' worth of vehicles.

"I've sent three men to try to contain it."

Fury burned hot in his gut. No way this was some freak coincidence. Someone had targeted him. Taunting him. Was there another attack coming? "Stay here and guard the doors," he said to the man.

"People will have called 999. We don't have much time. We need to get you out of here."

Luka let out a stream of curses. "Stall them." When the cops came, he needed to be out of sight.

Leaving the man to do his bidding, Luka and Ivan ran down the stairs to the basement and shoved open the door to the office. One of the computer screens mounted on the wall showed the exterior security camera feeds, including coverage of the garage.

Sure as hell, orange flames were pouring out of the shattered windows of his state-of-the-art garage. All his vehicles would be lost in a blaze like that.

He leaned forward to curl his tattooed hands around

the edge of the desk, the muscles in his arms and shoulders knotting. "Find out who did this," he growled, and Ivan immediately left.

Whoever it was, would pay. In blood. *No* one fucked with him. Not even his former Bratva brothers, who had learned that the hard way.

His mind raced as he toggled back and forth through the various camera feeds, checking all views. Finding nothing else of concern, he reversed the video of the garage coverage.

Again, there was nothing. Not a single suspicious thing in the past twelve hours to indicate that anyone had been casing the building, let alone attempting to break into the garage. He needed to go back farther. But something told him he still wouldn't find anything.

How? How had the person responsible pulled this off? Unless...

Unless it was an inside job. Unless one of his own wasn't as loyal as he thought. Maybe hungry enough for more money, or perhaps out of jealousy, and had fed security information to one of his enemies.

He straightened, checking all the other cameras one last time. He had plenty of enemies. Including his surviving Bratva brothers, who would love to boast of killing him. Whoever was behind this was a professional. No one else could have pulled this off without his security noticing something.

Shouts echoed from the hallway overhead. He stiffened, pulse tripping when the sharp crack of gunshots rang out above. His gaze snapped to the middle screen. Two black-clad figures appeared there, rushing past the camera before he could see any details about them.

The enemy was here. And they were coming for him.

Abandoning the office, he rushed out into the hall, headed for the safe room at the end. It was hidden behind a false wall, and accessible only with a code and a biometric scanner that only his and Ivan's palm and fingerprints had been entered into. He would be safe in there, and the cops would never find him.

More shots echoed out overhead as he ran. He heard Ivan's voice, shouting something behind him. The clatter of running feet on the tile floor.

Coming closer.

He reached the fake wall and pushed on the hidden panel to expose the security pad. He punched in the code and pressed his palm flat to the scanner, his heart thudding hard against his ribs and a film of sweat coating his back. "Come on, come on," he growled under his breath, waiting for the scanner to confirm his prints.

Finally, the little light at the bottom switched from red to green and the concealed door popped open. He swung it wide, was just about to step inside as the interior light flickered on.

Then he heard it. A faint whisper of movement behind him.

He froze and turned his head slightly, catching the outline of the shadow thrown against the wall.

Darting a hand inside to grab the weapon attached to the wall, he whipped around to confront the threat. Too late.

Something slammed into his back. He jerked and cried out, instinctively reaching for the wound. But there was no slickness against his fingers. Only a tight, burning circle where the round had hit him.

He leaned toward the open doorway but the attacker slammed into him, knocking him off his feet. He grunted as they flew backward into the safe room, the impact with the floor knocking the pistol from his hand. It spun across the tile floor and out the door before he could grab for it.

He rolled, knocking the person aside, and jumped to his feet as the door automatically closed, locking them inside. Shock ripped through him when he saw a woman standing on the other side of the room. She was dressed all in black, her face concealed by a balaclava.

She stood not fifteen feet away, her body so still it sent a wave of unease through him.

One gloved hand reached up and removed the balaclava, revealing stunning Asian features and deadly black eyes. "Julia sent me."

~

Eden parked the van in an empty lot outside an abandoned building near the police station and paused only long enough to glance into the back to check the cargo. All three men were bound and unconscious. She'd sedated the driver the instant she'd finished her quick interrogation, which she'd recorded on her phone and sent to both Trinity and Amber.

The resulting confession—in which she had remained off camera—and the rest of the evidence her team would turn over pretty much guaranteed his and the others' conviction. She hoped they rotted behind bars for the rest of their lives.

"Sayonara, assholes."

There was no time to wipe down the van, but any DNA

she or Zack had left behind would be minimal because of their gloves. Besides, the men should start to come around within the next few minutes. By the time the cops got here, they should be mostly awake and she would be long gone.

Exiting the vehicle, she used her burner phone to take a picture of it to show the plate and location, then sent it to Trinity with a message. *It's done.*

Trin would take it from there, sending the evidence and the edited video from the kidnapping attempt to local police to deal with these pathetic excuses for human beings.

She jogged past the end of the chain link fence and around the corner where Zack was waiting in a rental vehicle. She pulled open the door and slid inside with a smile, but it faded when she saw the look on his face. "What's wrong?" she asked, hand frozen on the door handle.

"Heath's down. Car hit him," he said grimly, firing up the engine.

"Shit. What about the others?"

"No word yet," he said, quickly turning onto the road and heading south. "But we need to get there A-fucking-sap to back them up."

CHAPTER FIFTEEN

Georgia jumped out of the car the moment Miguel pulled up to the curb down a side street a block from the police station, grim-faced and adrenaline still pumping through her from what had just happened a few minutes before.

Heath was being rushed to the hospital right now in the back of the van Amber and Jesse had been using as a mobile CP. Amber and Briar were both in the back with him while Jesse drove, but given his injuries, there wasn't much they could do to help him. Heath needed emergency care if he was going to survive.

She ripped open the rear passenger door and reached for the woman seated there. "Come on." Grabbing her hand, Georgia pulled her out and steadied her before reaching in for Holly.

Holly slid across the seat and allowed Georgia to help her out, balancing her weight on her one leg, the buggered knee meant she couldn't walk without help. Georgia could put her across her shoulders, but that would draw unwanted attention, and Holly had been through more than enough already.

She draped Holly's arm across her shoulders, grabbed her around the waist. "Come on," she said to the other woman, and started along the sidewalk.

There was no one back here, and that was a good thing. Georgia had ditched the balaclava to avoid suspicion if anyone saw her, but being caught on CCTV between here and the police station was a given. She intended to only get as close as absolutely necessary.

Holly hissed in a breath and made muffled sounds of pain as Georgia hurried her along. "I know, I'm sorry," Georgia said. "But we have to make this quick."

"What about your friend?" the other woman asked, hurrying alongside them. "Is he going to be okay?"

"I don't know." None of them would know anything until the medical team assessed him at the hospital. "Come on. Keep going."

Holly hobbled along with her around the corner. Cars zipped back and forth on the next street, and there were people on the sidewalks.

Georgia stopped, instinct telling her she'd gone as far as she could. "You'll have to take her," she said to the other woman. Georgia removed Holly's arm from across her shoulders and placed it across the other woman's instead. "I can't go any closer."

"Wait, where are you going?" Holly blurted, voice tight with fear.

"I'll wait here until you enter the police station. Just tell them the truth about everything that happened—except that one of our guys was hurt." The cops would start figuring out things soon enough. The team didn't need them showing up at the hospital already linking Heath to the op.

She gave a terse nod at the other side of the street. "Go."

The two women hesitated, looked at each other, then started off. At the corner they stopped. Holly turned back to call to her. "Wait, what's your name?"

Georgia shook her head and jerked her chin at the police station. The less they knew about her and the others, the better. The team was going to have enough problems trying to cover up this shit show as it was.

She waited until the women had struggled up the concrete steps and entered the station before whirling and running back to the car. Miguel had pulled up behind a building just out of sight. He threw open the door for her and she jumped in. "They're in?" he asked.

"Yes." She strapped on her seatbelt, anger burning deep in her gut. They'd been so close to pulling off a perfect op. Had been moments from getting out of there unscathed. Losing Heath was a blow to the entire team, and Chloe...

Jesus, Chloe was going to fucking explode when she found out.

～

Kiyomi dropped the balaclava and straightened to face Tarasov.

This wasn't how she and the rest of the team had planned to do this, but with Marcus and Chloe taking on the handful of security personnel upstairs, she'd seen the bodyguard appear at the top of the stairs and gone after him, knowing he would be protecting Tarasov.

And not a second too soon, because Tarasov had been about to enter this room. If she hadn't made her move when she had, she would have lost her only shot.

Now the two of them were trapped in here together. At least no one else could get in the way. And in the meantime, Marcus and Chloe could more than handle whatever happened upstairs.

Tarasov's eyes flared in shock as he stared at her.

"…yomi… are you?" Marcus's worried, disjointed voice came through her earpiece. By now he would be clearing the second floor with Chloe. This room must have seriously thick walls to interfere with the signal.

She shifted her weight to the balls of her feet, ready for anything.

More static hissed in her ear. Urgent words from Marcus, then Trinity. The noise was too distracting. Irritating. Like the hair-raising scrape of fingernails on a blackboard.

A quick tap turned off the earpiece. As silence engulfed her, her focus narrowed to the enemy waiting across the small room.

Seeing him up close was harder than she'd expected. Reminding her of the night she'd found Julia. Seeing what the animals had done to her.

Ruthlessly, she blocked the rush of emotion, shoving the memories and feelings into a vault at the back of her mind. She had to stay sharp. Couldn't let emotion cloud her mind for even an instant.

She'd already taken down two men to get to him. Much

as she craved being able to avenge Julia by killing Tarasov here and now, she had promised Marcus she wouldn't. Besides, a predator like Tarasov would suffer far more by going to prison. There he would finally taste karmic justice and experience what it was like to be preyed upon.

He was crouched on the balls of his feet as he stared at her, tattooed hands up in a fighting stance that told her he was used to using his fists.

She sized him up, letting her hatred for him wash over her. He and his Bratva brethren were all thugs, trained to fight dirty and take what they wanted.

But with his weapon lying outside this locked room and no one to save him, it was down to hand-to-hand. While he had the advantage in size and strength, she was fast, and trained in skills he could only imagine.

Confusion flared in his dark eyes for a moment. "Who the hell are you?" he bit out, his accent holding a slight British edge.

"You're about to find out," she answered, her blood pumping, muscles warm and limber. She feinted toward him. He dodged right, eyeing her warily, scanning her for a weapon.

She feinted again. He moved to the other side, anger stamped into his features. She had a blade strapped to her calf, but she wasn't pulling it unless it was absolutely necessary. In this confined space, a knife could be turned on her in the heat of a fight.

Realizing that she was taunting him, his face reddened, the muscles beneath his trimmed beard bunching. "You got a death wish, bitch?"

His expression said it all. He arrogantly assumed he

had the upper hand because he was a man, knew some Krav Maga and a few other street fighting tricks.

Well, she knew all that too. And a lot more besides.

Letting action speak for her, she dropped down and kicked his feet out from under him. He hit the floor hard on his ass but leapt to his feet in a practiced motion, fury contorting his features.

Do it, she silently taunted him.

With a bellow of rage he came at her.

She ducked the tight punch he threw at her face, used his momentum against him and caught him upside the head with a quick elbow as he pivoted. He staggered sideways, his shoulder crashing into the wall while she danced back and readied herself for another attack.

He pivoted to face her again, baring his teeth in a feral snarl.

He didn't realize it, but his ego posed the greatest danger to him. Soon enough he would lose his cool because he wasn't gaining the upper hand against her and make a mistake.

The moment he did, she would seize the advantage and stab him with the loaded syringe waiting in her thigh pocket. Eden had loaded a dose strong enough to knock him out within five seconds, and keep him out for fifteen to twenty minutes.

Kiyomi held his hateful stare, ready for whatever he dished out. *Yeah, come on. Come at me and see what happens.*

She tensed when someone pounded on the other side of the door. "Luka!" the muffled male voice shouted, barely audible through the soundproofing.

Tarasov lunged forward to throw a hook at her jaw, his

other fist going in for a jab at her ribs. She ducked, blocked the jab with her forearm and danced out of range.

Before she could reset, he reached to the side and hit a switch on the wall. The lights went out, plunging them into blackness.

Now it was real.

She couldn't see him, but she could hear him. Could hear his quickened breathing and sense his movement as he shifted to her right. She reached a hand down, going for her thigh pocket.

The door suddenly clicked open, the narrow strip of light revealing Tarasov still across the room from her, and a man entering the room.

If he got in it would be two against one, and even with her blade, in this confined space, she would be in trouble.

Kiyomi ran at the door and slammed her weight into it, crushing the man in the opening as he tried to enter. He howled, jerked back and disappeared from view. She reached out with her foot to kick the door shut and started to turn to face Tarasov, but he slammed into her from behind.

He drove her into the wall with his big body, his coffee-scented breath hot on her cheek. "I won't kill you yet, *malyshka*," he purred in her ear. "But by the time I'm done with you, you'll wish I had."

There wasn't enough room for her to slam the back of her head into his face. Kiyomi set her jaw and started to curl her fingers into a claw, ready to plunge it between his legs to grab and twist his balls.

But the door opened again before she could move. A ribbon of fear twisted through her as Tarasov's hold tightened.

Something was wrong. Marcus and Chloe should have been down here by now and dealt with this other guy.

But they weren't. So she had to fight them both on her own.

Tarasov turned his body slightly, moving his head away. With a low snarl she threw her head back and twisted sharply to the side.

The back of her skull hit his jaw with an audible crack of teeth. He grunted, his hold easing for just a moment. Kiyomi dropped to the ground and spun her body in a hook kick, her foot sending the door flying closed.

The man outside bellowed in frustration, catching it just in time to prevent it from slamming shut.

She jumped up, drove her foot into Tarasov's side as he came at her, and pivoted to ram her hands against the edge of the door. This time she caught the intruder's forearm in it. He screamed, reflexively shoved the door open enough to withdraw his arm.

The instant he did she drove it closed with a click and hit the light switch, just as shouts came from farther down the hall.

Marcus—

Tarasov hit her from behind, tackling her to the floor. She hit the unforgiving tile hard, the impact of his weight bruising her ribs and pelvis and driving the breath from her lungs. Spots danced in front of her eyes as she struggled to adjust to the sudden brightness.

"Got you now, bitch," he snarled, seizing a handful of her hair and wrenching her head back.

Her gaze shot to the wicked blade in his other hand. A military-issue knife poised in front of her throat, turning her blood to ice.

. . .

WHY THE HELL wasn't she answering?

"Kiyomi, come in," Trinity demanded for the third time.

No answer. Just an awful, hollow silence that told her something had gone terribly wrong for her friend. On top of that, Heath was hurt bad. She had dispatched other team members to assist his team, but it might be too little, too late.

You can't do anything else right now. Focus on Kiyomi.

Where was she?

She shut off the static in her head, put aside all the other things happening at the same time, and concentrated on the task before her. Kiyomi was downstairs somewhere. A hidden room maybe.

She quickly scanned all the feeds currently showing on her laptop screen. One of the burning garage a block away from Tarasov's place, a tall plume of black smoke billowing into the air. Various calls to 999 had gone out just seconds after the explosion, and others after the gunshots had begun.

First responders would be there in minutes. Trinity needed Kiyomi and the others out of there before crews arrived. And then she would have to tell Chloe about Heath—

She shook the thought away and checked the cameras showing the exterior of Tarasov's house. One gave her a view of two armed men who looked like the type to work for him running toward the side door.

As for what was happening downstairs, the situation was worse. She was running blind now. No video feeds to tap into. No way to see what was happening, where Kiyomi was, or what she was up against.

Dammit…

She keyed the radio again. "Marcus, where are you?"

"Moving to the stairs," he answered, breathing hard. "Kiyomi followed the bodyguard. She's down there alone."

"Two more tangos are heading your way, through the west door. I can't reach Kiyomi. I think she's in—"

"I'll find her," he said grimly, his clipped tone telling Trinity all she needed to know. He was worried as hell.

"Hurry," she urged him. "Fire crews are en route, and the cops won't be far behind them. I'm sending backup to you, but Kiyomi's down there alone with Tarasov and maybe one other tango. It sounded like they're hand-to-hand, but the audio cut out and now she's not responding."

"On it," he said, and there were sounds of a scuffle near him. A pained grunt came next, then a sharp cry and a gunshot.

Trinity held her breath, waiting, every muscle pulled taut.

"I'm going after her," Marcus said.

She exhaled at the sound of his voice, willing him to go faster. "Roger that."

It was a race now. She prayed Marcus got to Kiyomi in time.

CHAPTER SIXTEEN

M arcus finished securing the final man's hands behind him and stiffly pushed to his feet, urgency beating at him as he faced Chloe. "I'm going after Kiyomi."

She nodded, but he could tell she was far from okay. Her expression was pinched, and she was uncharacteristically quiet. Little wonder, as she'd just found out Heath had been injured, and couldn't go to him. "Go," she said.

He nodded and took off, leaving her to guard the prisoners and watch the door. His hip burned like hellfire as he ran for the stairs, and he cursed the hobbling gait that slowed him down. Kiyomi was downstairs engaging Tarasov alone. He had to get to her.

Precious time had been eaten up dealing with Tarasov's men. There had been more than they'd expected. He hoped the hell no more were coming, because Chloe would have to face them alone. He wasn't leaving Kiyomi, and every second counted.

His pulse raced, shards of pain shooting through his

hip and down his leg with every step. Pushing past it, he shoved aside his fear for Kiyomi and fell back on his decades of training. He was no good to her incapacitated or dead. And before he could help her, he had to deal with any other threats standing between them.

He paused at the edge of the wall next to the staircase, waited a beat, then ducked around the corner to check for targets.

A shadow moved down below. He broke from cover and started down the stairs, watching below him intently, finger on the trigger.

There was no sound to indicate how many men he might be facing, or where Kiyomi was, or whether she was still all right.

A flicker of movement caught his attention as he neared the bottom of the stairs. He instinctively dropped to one knee and took aim, waiting.

Hands appeared, holding a weapon, and two shots exploded in the quiet, thudding into the wall above him and shattering the plaster.

The shooter's hands vanished from view. Marcus moved to the other side of the staircase, giving him a better angle, and crept down two steps.

The weapon appeared again. Marcus fired, and the shooter backed off.

He was too exposed here, and needed to move. Staying here on the stairs waiting for the shooter to make a mistake left Marcus vulnerable, and wasted time Kiyomi didn't have.

Decision made, he acted. This time he saw the shadow before the shooter's hands appeared. He shifted left to get a better angle, then paused, waiting. The instant the weapon appeared around the corner he fired, hitting an arm.

A bitter curse followed.

He kept moving, his hip screaming at him to stop, on the verge of giving out. But he couldn't stop. He had to neutralize this threat, no matter what. He pushed past the burn, focused on taking this man down so he could get to Kiyomi.

More movement alerted him a split second before the shooter tried again. Marcus pivoted, caught sight of the shooter and aimed center mass. Two quick non-lethal rounds to the chest dropped the man.

But now he was out of ammo, and more vulnerable than ever.

Marcus rushed at him. The man rolled to his back and swung his pistol upward, the shifted position revealing his face.

The bodyguard.

There was no time to hesitate. Bracing his weight on his good leg, Marcus kicked out with the other. The top of his boot connected with the man's wrist, snapping it and knocking the weapon to the floor as fire ripped through his hip.

The kick had saved him from being shot, but cost him dearly. His weaker leg buckled, sending him crashing to one knee as the disarmed man scrambled away to the right.

Dizzy under the onslaught of pain, Marcus sucked in a breath, sweat breaking out over his body as he struggled to his feet. Both pistols lay on the floor out of reach down the hall to the left. The bodyguard was halfway down the hall in the opposite direction, racing to what looked like a dead end.

Gritting his teeth, bracing for more pain, Marcus shoved upward. The room spun for a moment, but his focus remained locked on the man at the other end of the hall. The guy was pressing something in the wall. A panel popped open, revealing a keypad and screen.

Safe room.

His heart pumped hard and fast. Was Kiyomi in there? Was she trapped inside with Tarasov?

He drove himself forward, every choppy, running step a separate agony. His bad leg threatened to buckle every time his foot hit the floor.

Kiyomi. He would endure any amount of pain to get to her.

The bodyguard was still frantically trying to get through the security measures. With a mingled roar of pain and fury, Marcus launched himself at his target. They hit the false door with a bone-jarring thud and dropped to the floor, rolling away into the wall.

Marcus came up on top, balancing his weight on the knee of his good leg, then grabbed the bastard by the throat with one hand and drove his fist into the man's face. He barely felt the impact on his knuckles, the pain in his leg eclipsing everything else.

The bodyguard let out an enraged snarl and twisted, throwing up a palm-heel strike and tried to buck him off. Marcus dodged the blow but his leg buckled again as he tried to maintain his balance. Alerted to his weak spot, the bastard delivered a sharp punch into the side of Marcus's damaged hip.

The breath exploded from his lungs. Agony engulfed him, all the muscles protecting the joint seizing.

He clenched his teeth and drew his fist back to deliver

another blow, temporarily blinded by the pain. This time bone crunched under the impact of his fist. The bodyguard's head snapped back, his skull ramming into the unforgiving floor, momentarily stunning him.

That single pause was all Marcus needed.

Sucking air into his nose and trembling, Marcus pinned the man to the floor with all his remaining strength and locked a forearm across the front of his throat. "Where is she?" he growled, his voice low, guttural with a mix of rage and pain. "The woman. Is she in there?"

"Fuck you," the bodyguard snarled back, struggling to break Marcus's grip.

Marcus shoved his forearm harder against the man's throat and landed another punch to the side of his face. "Give me the code," he snapped, out of patience. Kiyomi was on the other side of that fucking door, and he would get to her even if he had to break it down with his body. "The code, goddammit!"

The man groaned, flopped as Marcus seized him by the front of the shirt and dragged his upper body from the floor. His head lolled, blood streaming from his nose and lips.

Jaw set, Marcus squeezed his eyes shut and bit back a scream as he forced himself to his feet, dragging the man with him. The guy stumbled, threatening to unbalance Marcus.

He wound up shoving the asshole against the false door, holding his face turned toward the panel inches away. Marcus could see now that the screen was a biometric scanner. He prayed the bodyguard's prints were in the system.

He grabbed the bastard's right hand, hanging limply at

his side, and wrenched it up to the keypad. "Enter the fucking code," he snarled, giving his prisoner another shove into the hidden door, all his weight on his good leg.

Fear stirred low in his gut when the bodyguard resisted, the frantic need to get to Kiyomi beating at him. He couldn't maintain the position for much longer. His muscles were already trembling with the strain of holding the both of them up and the pain was making him dizzy.

"Now, or I snap your sodding neck!" he shouted.

The limp hand started to move, the battered, bloody fingers stretching toward the metallic buttons. Heart in his throat, Marcus could only hold him there and wait, dying a little with each passing second.

The bodyguard entered the first number. Then the second.

Sweat slicked Marcus's skin, his injured leg shaking. Weakening more and more with every heartbeat. *Come on, come on, dammit!*

He heard something behind him.

Snapping his head around, he stared at the bottom of the staircase as someone ran down them. Ice slid through his veins.

He was trapped. Had no weapon, and his strength reserves were draining fast.

But he couldn't release the bodyguard. Kiyomi's life depended on getting through this door.

Marcus tightened his grip on the man and braced himself for whatever was about to come at him.

~

"Hold on." Megan shifted her grip on the wheel as they approached the last turn. Barely letting her foot off the gas, she turned hard.

The car's back end swung around the corner, tires squealing on the asphalt, but she didn't dare slow down. Marcus and Kiyomi were in deep shit, and Trinity had dispatched her and Ty to stave off disaster.

The road ahead was full of cars. She didn't hesitate, merely eased out of the controlled skid and pressed harder on the accelerator, shooting past the other vehicles as she wove in and out of slower traffic. Beside her, Ty didn't say a word, one forearm braced against the door.

Up ahead, a few pedestrians were using a crosswalk. Megan zipped back into the correct lane and laid on the horn without slowing. The people's heads jerked around, and they quickly scrambled out of the way as she barreled toward them.

At the intersection she made a hard left, swerving to avoid a BMW parked at the curb. She sped for the next corner, laid on the horn again as she made a right turn, narrowly avoiding a collision with a delivery truck. Tires screeched around her, angry horns blaring as she shot past the restriction and kept going.

Tarasov's place was only another two blocks away. They were almost there.

She navigated her way through the maze of narrow lanes behind the house, finally coming to a rocking stop a few dozen yards from the back of it.

A column of black smoke billowed high in the sky above the garage. Sirens were screaming in the distance, more first responders on their way. They had to get Kiyomi and the others out of the house *now*.

Ty threw open his door and started racing for the side entrance. Megan jumped out and ran after him, drawing her weapon. It was loaded with non-lethal ammo, but if killing was the only way to protect Marcus and Kiyomi, then she would use other means. She would face whatever consequences came as a result.

Chloe met them at the door, face grim. "They're both still down there. This floor's secure now."

"We'll get 'em."

"How's Heath?" she demanded as Megan and Ty started to rush past, expressions set. "Trinity wouldn't say."

Megan couldn't lie to her. "He's being taken to the hospital. You need to get there fast. We got this."

Tears shimmered in Chloe's brown eyes as she swore and ran for the door.

"Let's go," Megan said to Ty, racing past the unconscious prisoners lying on the floor, with him right behind her. She kept her weapon up, even though Chloe had assured her the floor was clear. She wasn't taking any chances.

They paused at the top of the stairs for a moment and looked at each other. Someone was fighting down there.

Megan turned and rushed down the steps, trusting Ty to guard her back and keep an eye on the upstairs doorway, just in case Tarasov had any more reinforcements on the way.

Meeting no resistance, she reached the bottom and ducked her head around the corner to peek at what lay down the hall, weapon outstretched. Her heart lurched.

Marcus stared back at her, face strained and streaked with sweat as he struggled to hold a large, heavily muscled man upright. "Ty, Marcus is here!" she shouted, holstering her weapon and running for him.

She grabbed the shoulders of the man he was holding, using her weight to prop him up.

"The palm scanner," Marcus panted, his face etched with an agony that was magnified in his eyes. "Kiyomi. Tarasov."

Then she understood. Kiyomi was on the other side of a false door, locked in with Tarasov. They had to get through it at any cost.

The man they were holding suddenly bucked hard, lashing out with an elbow. Megan jerked her head out of the way just in time to avoid a blow to the face, but Marcus stumbled sideways, cursing as he fell to one knee.

His hip.

Enraged, Megan clamped her teeth together and rammed her elbow into the back of the prisoner's neck. His bleeding face hit the hidden door with a satisfying thud and he yelled, his body slumping.

She grabbed him under the arms, strained to shove him upright, and then Ty was there, grabbing the bastard and hauling him off the floor in one quick move.

Megan took a half step back, waiting for her chance to help. The guy struggled but was no match for Ty, fresh and primed for a fight. Ty subdued him within seconds, yanking his hands behind him, wrenching the shoulders at just the right angle to make the man freeze and gulp.

"Don't you fucking move," Ty warned, his voice low and deadly.

"I need one of his hands," Megan blurted, shoving close to grab one. She muscled it upward while the man resisted, cursing and snarling at her in Russian, his face turning from red to purple as he strained.

Marcus was struggling to get to his feet. Ty grabbed the prisoner's wrist, and together they slammed his right hand against the screen.

But, of course, the asshole had squeezed his fingers into a tight fist, preventing them from getting a palm reading.

Megan dug her fingers into the inside of his wrist, pressing as hard as she could to hit the median nerve while prying his fingers away from his palm. Christ, the bastard was strong.

"Just knock him out," she snapped at Ty. *Or cut his damn hand off.* They didn't have time for this shit.

Without missing a beat, Ty pulled the guy back a foot or two from the door, then slammed him into it with a loud thud. Then again. Until the guy went limp, his head lolling, arms falling to his sides.

Megan lunged forward, seized a meaty wrist and yanked the hand up to press its palm flat against the screen, her gaze locked on the red light beneath it, willing it to turn green. They all waited, precious seconds ticking past while Kiyomi fought for her life on the other side of the door.

CHAPTER SEVENTEEN

idden deep in the shadows of a room in the vacant building across the street, Ivy watched the scene unfolding around her through her high-powered binos. The fire at the garage was big enough that they'd had to call in a second fire crew to battle it, probably in the hopes of keeping it from spreading to the adjoining buildings.

The diversion had been clever, but also brought additional risk with all the first responders now in the area. As for Tarasov…

She shifted the binos to peer across the street at his house. Chloe had left not long ago. Ivy had glimpsed her running out the side door, blond ponytail bouncing. Wherever she was off to, she was in a hurry, leaving Megan and her man inside with Kiyomi and another guy.

The rest of them hadn't come out yet. And neither had any of Tarasov's men.

Staying here any longer was risky, but she wanted to see what happened. Wanted to know whether Kiyomi had survived, but it was getting more dangerous by the minute with all the police starting to arrive at the garage. She would do a drive by instead to see if she could find out anything more, the shadowy shelter of her vehicle hiding her in plain sight.

Tucking her binos away, she zipped up her jacket, tugged the ball cap low over her wig and made her way down the empty hall to the second staircase. She paused at the top, making sure no one else was around before descending quickly, running down the four flights of stairs to the ground floor.

At the exit door she stopped again, drawing her weapon and pausing a moment. When she didn't hear or sense anything amiss, she opened the door and stepped out into the alley.

Empty.

Walking at a brisk pace, she hurried away from the chaos at Tarasov's, back toward the car she'd left parked at the curb three blocks over. But just as she neared the end of the alley, she felt it.

Eyes on her. Someone watching her from behind.

She whirled, weapon up as she scanned for the threat she knew was there. An instant later a shadow appeared from around the corner at the end of the alley. She fired two quick shots, center mass.

The figure grunted and dropped, the clatter of a weapon hitting the ground following an instant later. She didn't wait to see if the shooter was dead.

Tucking her pistol out of sight, she turned and ran, slowing only when she reached the main road and stepped onto the sidewalk with the other pedestrians. Head down, she remained hyper vigilant as she made her way back to her car. Having to leave now sucked, but the police presence and that shooter left her no choice.

There was no way to do what she'd come here to do now. Her real mission would have to wait just a little while longer.

∾

Kiyomi remained frozen, all her attention focused on the wicked edge of the blade poised inches from her neck. Twisting or pulling away would slit her throat. But she wasn't letting this bastard kill her.

In a lightning quick move, she thrust both hands up to lock around Tarasov's wrist and shoved the knife away, then rammed her head back as hard as she could. He grunted when the back of her skull slammed into his jaw, the instant of surprise giving her enough slack in his arm to shove the knife a few more inches away from her neck.

She twisted to the side, using all her strength to buck him off, and twisted his arm away from her. He came up on his knees, one hand still locked in her hair, and slowly forced the knife closer.

Their arms shook under the strain as they each fought for supremacy. But he was stronger, and if she didn't do something fast, that knife was going to plunge into her.

A guttural snarl of rage came from between her clenched teeth as she twisted hard, a sharp, quick movement that caught him off guard. She managed to throw his upper body off her for just a moment. Seizing her chance, she struck, ramming the heel of her hand into his chin.

His head snapped back and he toppled sideways. She

scrambled from underneath him and shot to her feet, adrenaline coursing through her in a wild riptide.

Staring at her, he slowly got up, flipping the knife over with a flick of his wrist. The way he gripped it with his fist, blade sticking outward from the bottom of it, told her he knew what he was doing.

And that the next few minutes would be a fight for her life.

Holding his stare, she slid the switchblade from her calf with her left hand and freed the blade with a snick that was overly loud in the quiet room, the only other sound their heavy breathing. She raised the weapon in a defensive posture, leaving her right hand free to grab the syringe from her thigh pocket when the opportunity came.

She couldn't risk pulling it out now. Couldn't let him see it until the very last moment.

Tarasov's gaze flicked to the weapon in her hand, and his lips twisted in a sneer. "Come on," he taunted, a gleam in his eyes, as if the idea of her fighting back excited him.

She'd met so many men like him. A predatory animal who enjoyed preying on anyone weaker than him.

She circled him warily in the enclosed space, mindful of the walls around her, how limited her range was. There was nowhere to go. And from the look on his face, only one of them was leaving this room alive.

He lunged at her. She pivoted, ducking at the last moment to avoid the edge of the blade as his hand swung out, and struck back.

A loud hiss filled the room as he whirled to face her, a red ribbon appearing across the outside of his shoulder. His expression turned cold. Deadly. And in spite of herself, fear curdled in the pit of her stomach.

He came at her again, and didn't stop with one step. He slashed inward with the knife, took another step toward her and swung his leg out to sweep her feet from under her. She jumped just in time to avoid being toppled over, twisting in mid air to keep from having her guts spilled on the floor by the lethal point of his KA-BAR.

Her back hit the wall. Her heart thudded.

His arm whipped out in a diagonal slice, aiming for her torso. She whirled left, sucked in a breath when a hot pain kissed across the side of her ribs. Beneath the burn she felt the warm wetness seeping over her skin.

Trapped.

In desperation she leaned back against the wall and jumped up, using the leverage to drive both feet at him as hard as she could.

She caught him in the chest and sent him reeling back with a grunt, allowing her some breathing room and space to get away from the wall. Tarasov crouched slightly and circled her again, feinting with his blade.

A jab to the right. Then toward her neck.

She ducked and wove, moving fast, weight balanced on the balls of her feet and her knife at the ready. She had to get in close to stab him with the needle.

He lunged forward. She danced back, pivoting to give herself room as she swung her knife at him. He ducked back, then twisted and drove the point of his blade toward her. She reared her head to the side, narrowly avoiding the deadly end as it sunk into the wall with a blood-curdling *thunk*.

Before he could yank it out, she landed a sharp punch to his kidney and stabbed the knife into his side. He howled like a wounded animal and wrenched away to the side, knocking her loose. She tucked into a somersault, rolled and leapt to her feet, whirling just as he came at her again.

But he was too close. Without the leverage to keep him at arm's length, without room to move, she was on the defensive. The only thing she could do to protect herself against the next attack was to draw her arms in tight to her body, her locked forearms and clenched hands protecting her face, neck and belly as best they could.

The first blow glanced off her forearm. Fire seared the path of the blade.

She braced her weight, the pain galvanizing her, and drove her right foot straight out, smashing his kneecap. He went down on his other knee, allowing her to spring up.

The wound in her arm burned. Blood dripped down, slicking her palm, making the hilt of her blade slippery.

She faced him, breathing hard. She wanted to kill him. Wanted to slash her knife deep across his throat to sever his jugulars and carotids. She thought of Julia. Of what her friend had suffered in her final hours because of this monster.

But dying was too easy for a piece of shit like Tarasov. She wasn't letting him off that easy.

Twisting, she lashed out with a sharp sidekick, hitting him in the chest as he turned. He stumbled back into the wall.

Now.

She straightened, reached for the syringe in her pocket. He sprang, diving at her, blade outstretched, aiming right for her belly.

She pivoted at the last second, whirling away. But not fast enough.

His blade caught the inside of her upper left arm as she wrenched to the side. It caught her flesh and sliced deep. Her left hand instantly went numb, the knife falling from her nerveless fingers. A spray of blood arced across the wall next to her.

Cold swept through her belly. She was wounded bad, her left arm now useless and hanging at her side.

Tarasov climbed to his feet, an evil smirk on his face. "Gonna carve you up, bitch," he snarled, triumph glowing in his eyes as he stalked toward her, blade up and ready to strike.

If she didn't take him down here and now, she was going to die a horrible death. Marcus's face appeared in her mind.

She couldn't die here like this. She had too much to live for. Couldn't let Marcus suffer any more pain.

Bracing herself, fighting to ignore the blood pumping from her wound, she waited, every heartbeat an agonizing eternity. When Tarasov lunged toward her, she pulled the syringe from her pocket with her right hand and flew at him.

The needle plunged deep into the side of his neck as his blade whipped past her face, missing her by inches.

He jolted in shock, his eyes widening as they locked with hers, their faces close together. She jerked the needle out just as he drew his blade back for another strike, but suddenly the hidden door burst open.

A body hurtled through it, slamming into Tarasov in a flying tackle. Kiyomi fell back as they hit the floor with a thud. She scrambled up, grabbing her wounded arm, pressing hard to control the bleeding. And then she saw who it was.

"Marcus," she rasped out, a strange mix of fear and relief hitting her. Then Ty and Megan swept in.

Marcus didn't answer, too busy pounding his fist into Tarasov's face. Twice, three times until the other man toppled over, his whole body going slack.

Panting, Marcus looked over at her. And when he saw the blood pouring from under her clamped fingers, he cursed, fear tightening his features. She took a stumbling step toward him as he struggled to his knees, then one foot.

Ty was reaching for her, but Marcus cut him off to snag her right wrist and tug her toward him, clamping his hand around the wound in her left upper arm. "Tourniquet," he snapped to the others. Tarasov was out cold on the floor, his wounded shoulder bleeding onto the floor.

"Here," Ty said, quickly undoing his belt and handing it over.

How much blood had she lost? Her knees were unsteady, her breathing choppy as Marcus quickly wrapped the belt around her arm above the wound and tightened it mercilessly. She cried out, automatically trying to pull away, but Ty was there, holding her fast.

"Get her out of here," Marcus ordered, struggling to stand, jaw tight and his eyes full of torment as he stared at her.

His hip. He couldn't get up.

Her throat tightened, the pain and fear finally hitting her. "Marcus—"

"Go," he snapped, pushing her at Ty. "They'll be here any minute."

The cops? Or more of Tarasov's men?

Before she could ask, Ty scooped her up and ran out of the room. "Keep pressure on it," he told her.

Kiyomi pressed down on the knot in the tourniquet Marcus had tied, the world already beginning to fade away around her. But she wanted Marcus, not Ty. She glanced over Ty's shoulder as he raced down the hall, looking back at Marcus.

Her last sight of him was of Megan helping him to his feet and looping his arm across her shoulders to help him from the bloodstained room.

CHAPTER EIGHTEEN

Marcus's insides were a tangle of fear as he fought his way up the last of the stairs in Tarasov's house, using Megan as a human crutch. Ty and Kiyomi were nowhere in sight. It killed him not to be carrying her out of here himself, but with an arterial bleed there was no time to lose, and Ty was faster.

"She'll be okay," Megan said as she helped steady him with the last hop up the final stair. "Ty's got her."

"Just get me to her," he grated out. He trusted Ty, but he needed to be next to her. Needed to be the one taking care of her and protecting her.

They moved down the upper hallway as fast as he could go, every step sending a searing jolt of agony through his hip joint and down his thigh. The men he and Chloe had sedated earlier were still unconscious on the floor where they'd left them.

They were the police's problem now, as was Tarasov. Right now, he and the others had to get the hell out of there before they were discovered.

He hobbled out the door into the warm evening air, his skin slick with sweat, the constant pain making him nauseated. The fire Chloe had started was still burning, but the smoke had changed from a tall column into a flat cloud above the building, so the crews must have it well in hand. Sirens echoed through the streets, signaling the imminent arrival of more police.

He blocked it all out and hurried along the side of the house, his sole focus on saving Kiyomi. He'd get to her if he had to drag himself every inch of the way.

A thin trail of blood droplets glistened on the ground, marking Kiyomi's passage. Marcus swallowed hard. Was the makeshift tourniquet holding? Had it slowed the bleeding enough?

First responders were so close, but they couldn't risk taking her over to the fire crews already on scene. They had to get her to the hospital themselves without being detected by the cops, or the entire mission and everyone involved would be compromised.

"Just around this corner," Megan said, panting as she adjusted her grip around his ribs. He was big and heavy but she didn't complain, just helped muscle him along as fast as he could go.

The instant they rounded the corner of the house he spotted Ty, his back to them as he bent inside the backseat of the car. He glanced over his shoulder at them briefly, and Marcus caught a glimpse of Kiyomi lying stretched across the seat, limp and still.

His chest constricted. "How is she?"

"We gotta get her to Emergency, fast," Ty answered without looking at him.

"Cops are already on scene," Megan said, releasing

Marcus as they reached the car. Ty shifted his body to allow Marcus past him into the back. "Hold this dressing down tight," he warned.

Marcus dragged himself onto the seat, lifted Kiyomi's head into his lap and took hold of her injured arm, clamping both hands around the bandage. It was already turning red in the middle in spite of the tourniquet.

Her eyes opened, focused on him in the twilight. But she was pale. Too goddamn pale, and listless. "I'm okay," she mumbled.

No, she wasn't. Not by a bloody long shot. "Aye. I've got you."

Satisfied Marcus had a good hold on her, Ty let go and stepped back. He and Megan jumped into the front seats and the engine roared to life.

Marcus swallowed past the lump in his throat as the car shot forward. "We'll have you to the hospital in no time," he told her, his voice rough. She seemed so fragile at that moment. Had lost too much blood already.

"It's not as bad as last time," she said with a wry smile, but for the life of him he couldn't smile back. She stared up at him for a long moment, her dark eyes glazed. "You okay?"

No. He was furious and terrified, the fear twisting in his chest unbearable.

Three times now he had almost lost her. Three fucking times.

He was done. Would never let her put herself at risk again, no matter what consequences came because of it.

He tightened his grip on her arm until his fingers went numb. He wouldn't let up. He would never let go. Because he loved her more than life itself. "I'm fine. Just rest now, love."

Her eyes closed and she turned her face toward him, pressing it into him as though seeking comfort. He couldn't let up on the pressure of his hands for an instant. Not even to stroke her face or hair. The only thing he could give her for comfort was his presence, his solid grip, and his voice.

He talked to her while Ty raced them through the darkened streets, navigating the maze that was north London. Kept his voice low and calm, hiding the panic and dread clawing at him.

He told her he loved her. That she was going to be all right. Told her how brave she was, how much he admired that courage, and that she had given Julia justice tonight.

"Tarasov is spending his last moments as a free man right now. Because of you."

He'd been furious when she had gone after him alone, but he understood why she'd done it. If she'd waited for him or Chloe, Tarasov would have locked himself in that safe room and been out of reach. With all the evidence the team had compiled against him, he would stay locked up for the rest of his life.

She nodded but didn't say anything, pressing closer to him in a way that made his heart squeeze so hard it hurt.

"We're eight to twelve minutes out," Megan said to him, phone to her ear. "Trin says Heath's already there."

"How is he?" Marcus braced his body to keep Kiyomi still as Ty made another hard turn, wincing as more pain jolted his hip.

"Don't know. They're doing an assessment right now and not letting anybody in."

"What do I tell the hospital staff?" They were going to ask questions. Questions he couldn't answer, and the police were going to be involved if they weren't already.

"As little as possible."

No shit.

"Trin's coordinating with Amber now on how they're going to handle everything."

Marcus stared down at his wife, her suffering twisting his heart. "Not long now, love. Almost there." And after this, never again.

~

Chloe jumped out of the cab she'd flagged down fifteen minutes before and ran up to the A&E doors, only to pull up short when Briar and Georgia suddenly appeared out of the shadows to block her path.

"Out of my way," she warned, stepping to the side. She didn't want to fight them, but if they didn't move right the hell now, she wouldn't hold back. Nobody was stopping her from getting to Heath. Not even them.

Briar stepped in front of her and held up a palm. "Stop. You go in there all ballistic like this, you'll get yourself arrested and not only not get to see Heath, but compromise the rest of us too."

She opened her mouth to argue but Georgia cut her off.

"You can't see him anyway, they've got him some-where in the back running a bunch of tests right now." The other sniper stood shoulder to shoulder with Briar, barring Chloe's way. They were both wearing street clothes. Chloe was still in her tactical outfit, having raced straight here from Tarasov's.

She sucked in a deep breath and drew herself upright, knowing they were right, but hating it all the same. Every instinct she had was screaming at her that Heath was inside that building, and that he needed her. "How is he?" Obviously it was bad. "I mean, how bad?" She glanced between them anxiously. "No bullshit."

"He was unconscious when we brought him in," Briar said, her dark eyes full of empathy. "Head injury, and maybe internal ones too."

The blood drained from her face, leaving her dizzy. "But he's not... He's not going to die, right?"

Briar hesitated an instant too long before answering. "We don't know anything yet, but he's in good hands and they're doing everything they can."

Not the answer she'd been hoping for.

"Shit." She spun around, dragged her hands over her face and stood facing the parking lot, battling tears. The cars and lights all blurred, everything funneling out under the frantic thud of her pulse in her ears.

After a moment Briar came up and wound an arm around her shoulders. "We're here for you, okay? Not going anywhere."

Chloe nodded, lips clamped together, her throat tight and burning with unshed tears. "What happened?" she finally managed when she could speak past the restriction.

"He was protecting one of the female hostages. One of Tarasov's men was behind the wheel of the car. I hit him, but he must have slumped forward instead of back, because the car suddenly veered at them and sped up. Heath dove at the hostage to knock her out of the way, and took the brunt of the impact."

Chloe closed her eyes, pulling in a shuddering breath.

194

"That others may live," she whispered. Didn't matter that Heath had been out of the Air Force for a while now, he was still a PJ to the core. The Pararescue motto was fundamentally part of who he was.

And also a big part of the reason she'd fallen in love with him.

Unable to stay still, she spun away and began pacing up and down the sidewalk, battling the fear and panic clawing at her insides. This shouldn't be happening. Heath hadn't liked the idea of the op from the outset, but he'd taken part because of her.

He'd spent his adult life putting himself in harm's way to rescue and protect others. Now it was his life hanging in the balance.

"Chlo," Briar said softly.

She shook her head and walked faster. Up and down the sidewalk, desperate to burn off some of the frantic energy building inside her. She wanted to see Heath. To hold his hand and talk to him, to be there for him. But Briar was right about one thing. She needed to calm the hell down first.

"What about Kiyomi and Marcus?" Georgia asked, pulling her from her distressed thoughts.

She drew in a shaky breath. "She found Tarasov. Marcus went after her. Then Megan and Ty got there to back them up, and I left. I couldn't stay. Not when Heath was—" She choked up and had to stop, wiping at her eyes. This should never have happened to him. This was her fault, for getting him involved.

"Hey." Briar walked up to take her hand, gripping it tight. "I know you're scared. But you don't have to go through this alone."

Before she could answer, a car raced up and stopped in front of them at the curb. The front passenger door opened and Amber hopped out, revealing Jesse behind the wheel.

Amber looked at the two of them in concern as she shut the door and Jesse drove off. "How is he?"

"We don't know," Briar said, rubbing Chloe's upper arm. "What about the others?"

She sighed. "Kiyomi's hurt bad, and Marcus can't walk. Ty and Megan are bringing her here now, should arrive any minute."

"How bad is Kiyomi?" Briar asked sharply.

"Tarasov sliced her up and hit her brachial artery."

Fuck.

"But she got him," Amber said with grim satisfaction.

Thank god for that. "Dead?" Chloe asked.

"No, but sedated and contained along with the rest of his crew. The cops are on scene there now, and Trin's already been in contact with Rycroft. Under the circumstances, we're gonna need some help with cleaning all this up."

Yeah, no doubt.

The sound of a racing engine made them all glance to the left. A sedan roared up and Megan jumped out of the front passenger side. "Gimme a hand," she blurted, opening the back door. Marcus was inside, Kiyomi's head in his lap, his hands clamped around her upper arm.

Chloe rushed forward but Briar beat her to the car, bending with Megan to help lift Kiyomi out of the back. She was limp and pale, the bandage and makeshift tourniquet saturated with blood, and more of it dripped in a thin ribbon as they moved her.

"Hold that bandage tight," Marcus commanded.

196

"We've got her." Megan took over applying pressure, one arm around Kiyomi's shoulders while Briar scooped up her legs and raced for the entrance.

Marcus set his feet on the ground and struggled to stand, both his hands bloody as he shoved up against the doorframe for leverage. His face was drawn, lines of pain that were more than physical etched around his eyes and mouth.

His silent suffering tore at Chloe. She went to him, looped an arm around his waist and helped steady him. He laid his arm across her shoulders without protest, the breath hissing out of him as he tried to take a step. Georgia moved in to bolster him on the other side.

"Get me inside with her," he grated out, and Chloe's heart twisted. She knew exactly how he felt, and it sucked.

She and Georgia half-carried him to the automatic doors as fast as they could. They walked into a flurry of activity in the A&E department. Staff had already swooped in to whisk Kiyomi into the back.

A nurse came out from behind the admissions desk, her expression concerned as she eyed Marcus. "Sir, I'm going to need you to—"

"I'm not here for me," he said curtly. "I'm here for her." He nodded at the door they'd just taken Kiyomi through. "She's my wife." His voice cracked a bit on the last word.

Georgia looked up at him, frowning. "You should get looked at too."

"No," he said, his tone final. "I'm fine." His body was rigid, tension pouring off him in palpable waves, magnifying Chloe's.

"You can't go back there," the nurse told him, running

a clinical gaze over the length of his body. "And I would strongly advise you be seen by a doctor."

"I'm fine. I just want to know what's happening with my wife."

"She'll be well taken care of. After you fill in some paperwork, you'll have to stay out here, or in the waiting room down the hall," the nurse said just as Briar and Megan came back out through the door.

"They kicked us out, but they're on it. Kiyomi's in good hands," Megan said, hurrying over to take Georgia's place on Marcus's left side and looking up at him. "There's nothing more we can do right now. Come on, let's go wait with the others."

Marcus's jaw was clenched, but he didn't argue, took the forms and allowed Chloe and Megan to escort him down the hall. Bautista was standing beside a door partway down, looking like a sentinel. He opened the door for them without a word and stepped back to maintain his post. Eden and Zack rose as they entered.

Chloe helped Megan get Marcus into a chair. They lowered him slowly, his hiss of pain slicing through the room. "Marcus," Megan said in a low voice. "At least let them do an x-ray."

"No. It's just soft tissue damage. Nothing to be done," he grated out, sweat beading his brow as he gingerly stretched his bad leg out in front of him.

He didn't want to risk missing something about Kiyomi.

"Here, Chloe." Eden came over to slide am arm around her waist and usher her to an empty seat.

Chloe dropped into it and put her head in her hands, closing her eyes. It was killing her not to know what was going on with Heath. Was he still unconscious? Were they dealing with a simple concussion, or was it a brain injury? Was there a risk of a coma? Worse?

Too many thoughts raced through her mind, and the waiting was hell. She was conscious of Eden's hand gliding up and down her back, the touch gentle, but not in the least soothing because Chloe was in total turmoil and the only thing that could calm her was finding out that Heath was going to be okay.

She thought of him lying on a gurney right now, unconscious. Or awake and in pain, confused, wondering where he was and what was going on. Maybe he was asking for her. Not understanding why she wasn't at his side. Because he would have been at hers.

More tears stung her eyes, Kiyomi's situation and the fallout from the op landing like another hammer blow on top of her already chaotic mindset. Too much had gone wrong. Everything felt out of control.

She didn't know how much time passed. Quiet murmurs flowed around her. She tapped her foot on the worn carpet, struggling to calm her racing thoughts, to slow her thudding heart. Every minute that passed without answers was torture.

The waiting room door finally opened. She looked up, bit back a groan of disappointment when Amber walked in instead of a doctor. "Got you both some civvies to change into," she said, handing clothes to her and Marcus.

Changing was the last thing she felt like doing, but their tactical clothes would only bring more questions if the cops came, so she did it anyway, standing and stripping down to her underwear right then and there, not giving a shit who saw her.

"We can't stay here," Megan said. "Especially not all together."

"No," Amber agreed. "Everyone but Chloe and Marcus need to go. A few of us will stay close and act as lookouts. The police will probably be here soon, because by now the staff will have called them. You'll have to stick to the cover story we came up with."

Chloe nodded dully. "What about Trin?"

"She's working with Rycroft. I need to head back to HQ to meet with them, but I'll stay if you want me here."

Chloe appreciated the offer, but shook her head. "You go. I'll be okay." Marcus was here. She wouldn't be alone.

Amber and her sister shared a questioning look, then Megan nodded at her. "All right. But I won't be far. Text me if you need me. You too, Marcus."

He and Chloe both nodded, and the others all filed out of the room.

In the sudden silence that followed, a flood of despair swamped her. "Oh, dammit," she breathed, bending over and rocking, arms wrapped around her waist. She felt like she was about to split apart.

"Here," Marcus said. He reached out a hand, surprising her.

She was well aware that she wasn't everyone's cup of tea, so to speak, and that she definitely wasn't Marcus's. Her high-energy, impulsive personality was the polar opposite of his quiet steadfastness, and she knew it had rubbed him the wrong way more than once. Yet now, with the two of them here suffering in silent, mutual solidarity, he was offering her his support.

She got up, sat in the chair next to him and put her hand in his, a bittersweet pang hitting her at the way his fingers closed around it and held fast. At the moment she was thankful he wasn't a talker. She couldn't have handled inane conversation right now. And his solid presence, the reassuring grip of his hand letting her know she wasn't alone, were comforting.

Neither of them spoke as the clock kept ticking, each lost in their own thoughts. When the door opened again, she sat up straight as a doctor walked in. He glanced at them, then down at his clipboard. "Is someone here for Heath Barrett?"

"Yes." Chloe shot to her feet, her heart trapped in her throat. "How is he?"

"In surgery."

Her heart constricted. "What—"

"He had internal bleeding that needed to be addressed immediately."

"What kind of internal damage?" Her voice sounded strained. Strangled.

"His spleen, and possibly his liver. His kidneys were bruised by the impact, and he sustained a head injury as well. But he regained consciousness before going to the operating room. He was alert and responsive."

She exhaled in relief, then frowned. Head injuries were dangerous and tricky. "That's good, right?"

He gave her an understanding smile. "That's very good. It will be a few hours before you're able to see him, so if you wanted to perhaps leave—"

"I'm staying. I'll wait as long as it takes to see him."

The doctor nodded, then focused on Marcus. "I understand your wife was brought in with stab wounds earlier?"

"Aye."

"She's currently in surgery as well, and we've called in

a neurosurgeon to try and save the damaged nerve in her arm. It could be a long wait until she's in recovery too."

Marcus let out a slow breath, all but slumping back against the wall. "I'll wait as well."

When the doctor left, Chloe immediately texted the others to update them, relief and hope making her throat thicken. She dropped back into the chair beside Marcus with a hard sigh and rubbed a hand over her face. "Holy hell."

He grunted in agreement and gave her back a reassuring pat before folding his hands across his middle.

The quiet started to grate on her within a few minutes, the urge to get up and move making her squirmy. "I never understood what it was like until now," she said softly.

Marcus glanced over at her. "What what was like?"

"How it felt to be on the other side of this. What it's like for one of you guys. Being involved with one of us, and having to deal with the risks and then the aftermath if anything went wrong." Her and the other Valkyries, she meant.

She continued, taking care to put her thoughts into words. "When I was alone and it was just me risking my own neck, it was different. I didn't care as much if anything happened to me, as long as the job got done and the target was neutralized. I never stopped to think about how it must have felt for Heath once we got together, and never understood how awful this helplessness feels. But now that it's him in that operating room...I get it. The cost is too high."

Marcus was silent for a moment. "Aye. Way too high."

She swallowed, thinking of everything she would tell

Heath when she saw him. "I think Kiyomi will get it now too."

"I just want to protect her," he said in a low, tired voice. "I want to keep her safe."

Yes. It was so clear to her now, and it hadn't been before. All this time, that's what Heath had wanted to do for her as well. That's why he'd come here with her. And it was why he was lying on that operating table right now.

Her eyes ached with unshed tears. She fought them, channeled the sorrow and regret into choosing the words she would say to him the first chance she had.

Hours more passed before a nurse popped in and smiled at her. "Your husband is up in his room now, if you want to see him."

She exploded out of the chair, was already partway to the door before she realized she was leaving Marcus here all by himself. She stopped and faced him. "Will you be okay if I...?"

One side of his mouth tipped up in the hint of a smile. But his exhaustion was clear. He was emotionally and physically spent. Her heart went out to him. "Aye. Go, be with him."

She rushed from the room, followed the nurse up to the correct floor and down the hall to a semi-private room. The woman pulled the curtain partition partially aside and nodded at her.

Chloe stepped around it, and her heart clenched at the sight of Heath lying in the bed, his face all bruised and swollen, head bandaged up and various tubes and leads attached to him. She grasped his hand, curled her fingers around it.

His lashes stirred. He opened those beautiful, piercing

blue eyes to look at her, and the weak, lopsided grin he gave her broke the wall that had been holding all her emotions in check.

The tears she'd managed to fight back until now suddenly flooded her eyes, scalding hot as they ran down her cheeks. She bent over him, trying to stifle a sob as she gripped his hand tight and touched her cheek to his.

"I love you," she choked out. "I love you so much, and I'm sorry. So sorry, I didn't understand what it was like for you before."

"Don't cry, firecracker," he said, his voice hoarse. Tired.

It only made her cry harder. "I'm sorry, and I'll never, ever put either of us at risk ever again."

He made a low sound that sounded like something between a grunt and a chuckle.

She raised her head, frowning down at him as she shook her head. "I won't. I swear."

His blue eyes searched hers, the tenderness there almost unbearable. "Even if you did, I'd still love you anyway."

It broke her heart and healed it at the same time. This man was one of a kind. She would never take him or his love for granted ever again.

Gently taking his battered face in her hands, she kissed him, infusing it with every ounce of love in her heart.

CHAPTER NINETEEN

"Heath *and* Kiyomi?" Alex said, staring at Trinity in disbelief as they stood in the middle of his hotel room. She'd called him two hours ago for help and he'd told her to meet him here in London.

He'd had a bad feeling about this from the start. The added concern of the radio silence from her and the others since he'd arrived in London the other day made his suspicion worse. Now he knew what had been going on behind the scenes.

Three almost simultaneous ops, and two had wound up going sideways.

She nodded, pale and somber. "Yes, they're both in surgery right now. Kiyomi's going to be okay once they get the bleeding under control. But Heath... Pretty sure he's going to have a long road ahead of him due to the internal damage."

He bit down hard on his back teeth for a moment to hold in the words he was a hair's breadth from shouting at her. He'd warned them. Fucking told them point blank to be careful about what they did, because his ability to run interference for them was severely limited now.

"And the body count?" There would absolutely be dead bodies to deal with after an operation of this scale. Especially when Valkyries were involved.

His blood pressure went up another ten points when she told him. He inhaled slowly. Let the breath out even more slowly until he could get a chokehold on his temper. "I told you my hands were tied."

"Yes." The word was soft. Contrite. But it was the guilt in her eyes that dispelled the brunt of his anger.

Guilt because two of her teammates had been WIA tonight. Yet for Trinity he understood that it was also more than that.

She was beating herself up over what had happened, wondering if she could have done anything differently to prevent this, or somehow made the difference in everyone getting out unscathed if she had been engaged in person tonight instead of running things behind the scenes.

She looked so upset he couldn't take it. *Aww, fuck.* "Come here," he muttered, grabbing her and pulling her in for a hug.

"I'm sorry," she whispered.

"I know." He held her tight, incredulous at how he could be so mad at her and the others and yet still love them all to death at the same time. "I'll handle it." Somehow.

When they pulled apart she wiped at her cheeks and her eyes were damp. "What do you want me to do?"

He sighed and put his hands on his hips. "I want you to go back to Laidlaw Hall so you're not involved anymore than you already are, and let me deal with this." He'd start with his contacts at MI5, but MI6 would probably get involved as well. He still had some pull there, and Marcus did as well.

Trinity wrung her hands, the action so out of character his eyebrows rose. "What about the adoption?" she whispered. "What if someone finds out I was involved and they take my baby away—"

"That's not going to happen."

She blinked fast, more tears glistening in her eyes. "But what if it does?"

He laid a hand on her shoulder, a fierce protectiveness forming as he held her gaze. "I'm not going to let that happen. I promise." The US government had sanctioned the Valkyrie program that had taken away Trinity's choice and ability to have a baby. She was meant to be a mother and wanted it more than anything. Alex would do whatever it took to safeguard this adoption.

She closed her eyes and bowed her head, releasing a shuddering breath. "Thank you."

"Trin." He waited until she looked up at him, exasperated and scrambling to figure out how he was going to tackle this. "Call Brody and talk to him on the way back to the Hall. You'll feel better. Now go, and leave this to me."

"Are you sure?"

He raised an eyebrow at her, and she gave him a little smile that put a bit of sparkle back in her eyes. "Thank you, Alex," she whispered, throwing her arms around him.

He grunted and patted her back. "Yeah. Now get going. I'll give the others hell later."

She let go and stepped back, her lips curving. "I'm glad you decided to jump on a flight to London, just in case."

"Yeah. Me too." This was going to be a nightmare to clean up, and would mean calling in every favor he was owed here in the UK. But Trinity and the others, securing their futures, made it worth every bit of the shit storm he was about to endure.

~

"Who *are* you, and why the hell did you go silent all of a sudden?" Amber muttered, looking at the intel on her laptop.

She leaned back in her chair and rubbed a hand over her face. She'd been at this for hours already. Her eyelids felt like they had sandpaper under them. It was almost one in the morning. She hadn't slept in more than twenty-six hours, and right now she was feeling every single one of them.

Hushed footsteps fell on the carpet. She looked back as Trinity walked into the room, looking as tired as she felt. "Hey. How'd it go?" She had been meeting with Rycroft.

"It went." Trinity dropped into the chair next to her with a weary sigh. "He was actually already in London when I first called him."

Amber's eyebrows shot up. "For real? Why does that not surprise me as much as it should."

"I know. He'd banked on us going operational, so my call wasn't totally unexpected, but obviously we've put him in a bind and he's not happy with us. I gave him all our intel and all the details of what happened. He's working with MI5 right now to try to keep everything under wraps. Pretty sure no one but Tarasov and his crew saw us, but there's no way the story won't get out, so they're going to spin a story about us in the media. Making up a fake name and saying we're a homegrown vigilante group or something, while hiding our identities."

Rycroft was the best for a reason. "What about Tarasov?"

"In custody at MI5, along with the others. Including Heaver and his crew. You're going to need to scrub any evidence of us from all the video feeds before you send them."

"Been working at it since I got back." Amber studied her. "You okay?"

She nodded, staring at the computer screen, her shoulders rigid. "I hate that I wasn't out there with the rest of you. I should have been there. I might have been able to mitigate the risk more. Reduced the damage."

"Doubtful, given how it all played out. And besides, we needed one of us to run the other two ops."

Trinity sighed again and finally looked at her. "How are Kiyomi and Heath?"

"Both out of surgery. Kiyomi could be looking at some permanent nerve damage in her forearm and hand. They'll release her in the morning. Heath's going to be in there for at least a few days longer, for tests and observations." They'd stopped the internal bleeding, but he also had a concussion, broken ribs and bruised kidneys that needed to be monitored. He faced a lengthy healing process.

"And what about Chloe and Marcus?"

"Both still at the hospital. Don't worry, Megan's keeping an eye on them and sending me updates."

"Good. Chloe's come a long way since she and Heath got together, but this has got to be really hard on her."

"I'm just glad he's going to be okay. And Kiyomi too."

"Same." Trinity focused back on Lady Ada. "How much more video do you have to edit yet?"

"Not too much left. What did Rycroft say when you told him everything?"

"Like I said, he wasn't happy, but I think secretly he was pleasantly surprised that the body count was as low as it was. He was on the phone to Briar when I left him in London. I think he senses she was the one who took out Tarasov's guys at the warehouse. Including the driver."

"If she hadn't, there would have been more casualties."

Trinity nodded. "True. And there's something else I wanted to tell you."

Amber watched her curiously. Trinity's posture and tone were relaxed enough, but her words set Amber on edge. "What?"

"Rycroft called me on my way here to tell me the final body count doesn't match our numbers."

That wasn't possible. She and Trinity had made sure they knew *exactly* how many men their team had brought down, how many dead, and how many had been left alive.

"The police found a body in an alley near Tarasov's place. Identified as a Russian national known to have ties to him. Two small caliber rounds to the chest at close range."

The unease that had been gathering in her gut all night suddenly intensified, sending a prickle of alarm up her spine. "Where and what time," she demanded, reaching for the keyboard.

Trinity gave her the location where the body was found. The timeframe was near the end of the op at Tarasov's place, when Kiyomi had been fighting him in the safe room in the basement, and the others trying to get to her.

Amber pulled up the feed from the one camera she'd accessed near the spot, and reversed it to the right time frame. Together they watched the footage, looking for any sign of movement in the immediate vicinity.

Amber was stunned to see a figure appear at the end of the alley. Dressed in dark clothing. How the hell had she missed this before?

"Can you enhance it enough to see the face?" Trinity asked.

Amber paused the feed on the best frame and did what she could, but the image remained blurry. Yet there was no mistaking the gender of the person involved. "Definitely female."

"Yep." Trinity's voice was taut. "Who the hell is she?"

"I don't know. Dammit, she must have been watching us the entire time from that building." And there was only one explanation Amber could come up with.

Trin gave her an uneasy look. "Have you heard anything more from our source yet?"

She'd just read Amber's mind. "No." They went back to staring at the shadowy image on screen.

Was this their mystery source? Holy shit, if so, there was no telling what kind of intel she had on them now. "Call Rycroft. But tell him to only talk to his most trusted source at MI6 about this, not MI5. We can't risk a leak." Whoever this woman was, they had to find her, because if she'd seen them today, she could do untold damage to the team.

"On it." Trinity got up and left the room, phone to her ear.

Amber kept studying the video feed, then went back to another one showing the front of the building the woman had come out of. She zoomed in on every window visible, looking for any hint of a shadow that might indicate where the woman had been hiding.

Nothing. And it didn't bode well when combined with having nothing but radio silence from their source for days now.

When she'd done all she could think of to begin the hunt, she let Lady Ada work on the problem while Amber edited the rest of the video feeds to ensure no team members appeared on them. After sending everything to Rycroft along with any other pertinent intel, she turned her attention back to the mystery female in the alley.

There was nothing new. No additional angle for her to examine.

She needed something more. Some other bit of intel or some clue to find out who their source was, and whether the person was connected to the woman on the video. Amber's gut said they were.

Going on a hunch, she opened the chain of encrypted messages between them and typed out a new one. *Put the intel you sent to good use. Ring destroyed. Tell me who you are.*

The program automatically coded the message, then Amber hit send. Who knew if she'd get a reply, but at least there was a chance.

Hushed footsteps on the carpet behind her made her look up. Jesse was there, and his presence eased some of the anxiety grinding in her belly.

He looped his arms around her from behind and bent down to kiss the side of her neck, sending distracting little tingles all over the place. "Trin said there was an uninvited guest at the party at Tarasov's."

"Yes. And the way things look right now, she's going to remain a mystery."

He straightened and spun her chair around so that she faced him. Six-feet-plus of lethal, protective male encased in muscle, staring down at her with dark, sensual eyes. "It's almost three in the morning, and it's been a long day. Come to bed, *belleza*."

Automatically, she shook her head. She was tired, but needed to keep monitoring the situation, just in case. "I need to keep looking." The clue she needed had to be out there. Somewhere.

"Not tonight." He scooped her up and lifted her from the chair, pulling her snug against his chest.

Amber stiffened and opened her mouth to argue as he strode for the door, then stopped herself. He was right. There was nothing more she could do right now. And when he held her like this, took care of her like this...

She slid her arms around his neck and curled into him, reminding herself how lucky she was to be his. Laying her head on his solid shoulder, she closed her eyes and let him carry her up to their room.

～

A new message.

"Well, well. What've we got here?" Ivy murmured, absently scratching Mr. Whiskers behind the ears with one hand as she opened the message. It had been a while since she and Amber had been in contact.

Put the intel you sent to good use. Ring destroyed. Tell me who you are.

Yeah, she wasn't telling her that. By now the cops, and probably Amber too, would know about the body in the alley. Would have scoured any security and CCTV video feeds in the area, looking for the shooter.

Her.

That had been an unfortunate but unavoidable complication in the op. Yet she was pleased by the outcome.

They'd passed the test.

Tarasov was in custody. The captive women were free. And the kidnapping ring was destroyed.

Now there was one more, equally important test they had left to pass. One that could prove deadly for them *and* her.

It was finally time to put the second phase of her plan into action.

She set the cat down on the rug and straightened, thinking up the appropriate wording for this final coded message she would send. It had to be something unique. Something clever that only a Valkyrie would recognize.

When she finally had the right words and method in mind, she composed it using various cheater programs in her arsenal, then stopped to check it. Satisfied that it did everything she wanted it to, she sent the message to Amber in the same way she had before, and leaned back with a tight, satisfied smile, anticipation stirring her blood.

This was it. Everything she had wanted was on the line now.

Within a few hours she would know what course of action to take for the final part of this mission.

CHAPTER TWENTY

Bleary-eyed after dragging her ass out of bed when the birds had woken her with the sunrise, Amber let out a jaw-cracking yawn and sat at the breakfast room table to check what Lady Ada had uncovered in the past few hours. Her to-do list was long and complicated, including retrieving the big chunk of money she'd paid from her investments from the Architect op to Tarasov to secure Eden's kidnapping before authorities investigated.

Before she got to that, she had more important things to tackle first.

Trinity popped her head in. "Marcus and Kiyomi are home."

Amber jumped up and followed her out the front door to wait on the top step. Karas raced after them, her whole back end wagging in doggy glee.

Ty was driving the car, Megan in the front passenger seat. It pulled up to the bottom of the stairs. Amber and Trinity rushed forward as the back doors opened. "Welcome home," Amber said, sweeping her gaze over the rear passengers.

Kiyomi was pale, her left arm bandaged up and cradled to her chest with a sling. She gave them a tired smile. "Good to be back."

Marcus's face was strained, lines of exhaustion bracketing his mouth and eyes. "There's a pair of crutches in the hall closet."

"I'll get them." Trinity hurried back inside.

"Let's get you up to bed," Amber said to Kiyomi, bending to curl an arm around her friend's waist, careful not to knock her bandaged arm as she helped her from the car. "How you feeling?"

"Just tired."

And sore as hell, no doubt. "I'll bet. We'll get you upstairs and tucked under the covers." She guided Kiyomi up the steps as Trinity came back down with the crutches for Marcus.

"Any news?" Kiyomi asked as they stepped into the house, Karas dancing from them to Marcus and back.

"Some. Rycroft is in London working his magic right now."

She nodded and started up the staircase to the second floor. "Megan said there was another player involved yesterday."

"Yes. Haven't been able to ID her yet, unfortunately."

"Is it our source?"

"Don't know yet. But I'm betting the two are connected."

Crutches thumped on the floor behind them as they climbed the stairs. Amber took Kiyomi straight to her and Marcus's room, pulled back the covers and set her friend on the edge of the bed. "Need anything? Tea? Toast maybe?"

Kiyomi shook her head, shifting gingerly. "Just sleep."

Amber moved aside as Marcus came in, Karas next to him, wagging her tail. He was hurting bad, his movements stiff and slow, and his jaw locked tight. "We'll leave you guys in peace so you can get some rest. Text me or Trin if you need anything."

Karas jumped up on the bed and settled herself in the middle of it, watching Marcus expectantly. "Thanks," he said to Amber. He winced as he gingerly lowered himself onto the mattress and set the crutches aside.

Amber backed out of the room and shut the door. When she got downstairs, Trinity was in the breakfast room with Megan, Ty and Jesse. Eden and Zack hadn't come down from their room yet. "They're going to try to sleep for a while. What's the update on Kiyomi's prognosis?" she asked Megan.

"The surgeon managed to patch the nerve together. She's got partial movement in her hand, but the whole thing's numb right now. We won't know more until the swelling goes down," she answered, pouring herself a cup of coffee from the carafe on the table. "Heath's in rough shape though. He'll be in for another few days at least."

"Chloe's going to stay with him, I'm assuming?"

"Yes. Now fill us in on what you found last night."

Amber told them everything over breakfast. Trinity got called away by Rycroft partway through, asking her and Briar to come back down to London.

After they ate, Megan and Ty went up to bed. Amber went straight back to her work, opening Lady Ada to take a look.

Her pulse kicked when she saw the new message alert waiting for her, and glanced up momentarily when Jesse walked into the room.

"Morning," he murmured in a deep voice, coming over to kiss the top of her head. "Get any sleep?"

"Some." She opened the message, barely aware of her husband putting a plate of pastries together for himself five feet away.

Like all the others had been, the message was encrypted. And once her program cracked it, there was yet another hurdle to overcome. It was written in a complex code.

Maybe there was something wrong with her, but she enjoyed it when someone challenged her like this. It was her kink.

She took several cracks at it, attacking the problem from various angles. She had to admit, whoever the mystery source was behind all of this, they were damn good. So good it made nerves bubble in the pit of her stomach.

She muttered to herself under her breath and kept trying. A thrill raced through her when she began to uncover several letters in the message. Bit by bit she kept at it, slowly unscrambling the coded characters and using the same process to reveal the letters they symbolized.

Finally, the full message was revealed. She read through it several times. It gave no hint about the sender's identity or any other clues that Amber could see. But the final line seemed cryptic enough to warrant a closer look.

My last point is the most important of all.

"Last point," she muttered, the only sound in the room Jesse eating his breakfast a few chairs away. Last point. It had to mean something, because the sentence before it was too benign and random.

Her eyes went to the period at the end of the sentence. What if...

Following her hunch, she pasted the final few words and period into a different program and enlarged it. Bigger. Bigger still. Until the black pixel dots began to reveal some kind of image embedded inside it.

Her breath caught. "Jess."

Jesse dropped his pastry and hurried over to peer at the screen. "What've you got?"

"Look at this." She showed him the cryptic line, then toggled to the screen where she'd blown up the period. Magnifying it even more, she stopped, staring at it in stunned disbelief. Holy shit. What did it mean?

Reading over her shoulder, Jesse let out a low whistle and straightened. "You better go wake Kiyomi up."

～

Kiyomi woke to a wet nose snuffling at her cheek. She opened her heavy eyelids and groaned, exhaustion and pain weighing her whole body down. "Karas, why?"

Marcus snapped his fingers and the dog immediately jumped off the bed to sit at attention next to it, staring up at him. Ears perked, tail wagging, an adoring look in her eyes.

"Down," Marcus ordered. Karas's ears flopped. She stared at him with a pleading expression. "Down," he said, more firmly this time, and she sank down onto all fours on the floor with a dejected sigh.

Kiyomi grimaced as she gingerly turned onto her back

to look at him. The blinds were drawn over the windows on the far wall but it was bright enough in the room to see his face.

He lay on his side, facing her, and reached out to stroke a finger down the side of her face. "Did you sleep?"

"A little. You?"

He nodded, studying her, then lifted his arm to glance at his watch. "Time for your next dose." He sat up, ignoring her protests, and it hurt her to see the way he winced as he reached for the bottle of pills and the water glass next to the bed.

She pushed herself up with her good arm and leaned against the headboard to take them from him. Being sliced open sucked. The wounds on her ribs and forearm burned, but the deep one on her upper arm was the worst by far. "Now you," she told him, handing back the water glass.

"I'm fine."

"No, you're not." And there was no reason for him not to take the pain relief now that they were safe at home.

His jaw flexed. "I don't like the way they muddle my brain." He took the glass from her, set it on the bedside table beside him, and turned back toward her.

She could tell he was still angry about what had happened. They needed to talk this out. "I had to go after him when I did," she said quietly. "If I'd gotten there even a few seconds later, I'd have missed any chance to get to him."

Marcus averted his gaze and started petting Karas's head, since she had propped her chin on the side of the bed at his hip. "I almost didn't get inside in time."

Sliding her free hand across the bed, she reached for his, curling her fingers around it. Needing the contact. She couldn't stand it when he was angry with her, especially now. "But you did, and I'd already injected him anyway. I'm okay."

Something raw and vulnerable flashed in his eyes. "You're far from okay."

"All right, I'm banged up, but alive. And I'm *going* to be okay." Eventually. She hoped.

She wiggled her swollen fingers, winced as the motion pulled on her incision. She had stitches along her ribs too. Hopefully Tarasov was suffering more than her.

Her phone buzzed. She grabbed it from the bed beside her and read the message. "It's Amber. She's found something, and says she needs me to look at it ASAP."

"Tell her to come up."

"No, I'm sick of lying in bed. I want to move around a bit." She swung her legs over the side of the bed, paused a second to steady herself when the room spun a bit. She'd lost a lot of blood yesterday. Her body was still trying to stabilize itself.

A grunt sounded behind her. She glanced back to find Marcus struggling to his feet, reaching for his crutches. "No, you stay. I'll—" She stopped at the hard look he gave her. She hadn't meant to wound his pride. She just hated to see him hurting, and it was worse knowing it was because of her.

They found Amber and Jesse in the breakfast room. The couple looked up from Lady Ada, and the identical expressions on their faces set Kiyomi on edge. "What is it?"

"Come see this." Amber pushed the laptop toward her. Jesse rushed around to pull out chairs for them.

Kiyomi sat and read the message on display. "Is this it?" It made no sense.

"No. Check this out." Amber brought up another screen and zeroed in on the period at the end of the sentence.

When she enlarged it enough for the image to material-ize, Kiyomi inhaled sharply. "A microdot."

"Yeah, but not just any microdot." Amber kept magni-fying it.

The pixelated blob began to reveal its secrets. And the final image was stunning.

A crow with spread wings holding a sword in its talons. And beneath it, a scroll bearing the word *Valkyrija*.

The Valkyrie symbol. A badge of honor earned only by those who had graduated from the secret, elite program. Each of them had it either tattooed or branded on their left hips.

A series of numbers was tucked inside the upper and lower halves of the circle it formed. The whole thing was encased by a wreath made of what appeared to be ivy. Interspersed with the letters of Kiyomi's name.

A sharp pain lanced through her. She swallowed, refusing to believe what she was seeing. It was a trick. A fucking cruel trick. This couldn't be real. Someone was fucking with her.

"What?" Amber demanded, staring at her. "What does it mean?"

She could feel the weight of Marcus's and Jesse's stares too. She shoved her emotions aside and focused on the problem at hand. "They're coordinates. Plus a date and time." She indicated the coordinates with a tap of her forefinger.

Amber immediately reached past her and typed the numbers into a program. "Bourton-on-the-Water." She looked at Kiyomi. "That's only four miles from here."

Kiyomi nodded, something tight and hard settling in her chest. "And the meeting time is ten-hundred tomorrow."

"You're not going," Marcus said in a low voice. "It's a trap."

She shook her head. "Maybe. But I have to be there. We need to see if anyone shows."

"Why do I feel like you're not telling us something?" Amber said.

Because I don't know if I'm right. And because it seemed impossible. "I don't know anything yet. Except that I have to be there."

"You're not going anywhere alone," Marcus growled, bristling beside her.

"No," she agreed, putting a hand on his arm to reassure him. "But I am going."

CHAPTER TWENTY-ONE

Having lived freely in the Cotswolds for the past eight months, Kiyomi had explored the area and been to Bourton-on-the-Water many times. Visiting this place was like stepping into an English postcard.

The picturesque village was nestled along the banks of the Windrush River, and made of pretty golden-stoned cottages and shops. Five low-arched stone footbridges spanning the shallow water had earned it the nickname of Venice of the Cotswolds, and as it was the height of summer, it was already packed with tourists at nine-thirty in the morning.

Yet as pretty as it was, Kiyomi barely noticed the scenery or ambiance.

Tucked up a narrow pedestrian lane off the walkway by the river with Marcus, she surveyed the stream of people walking past, heading east up the near side of the channeled river, pausing along the row of shops and bakeries in the center of town.

She had tried to convince him to stay home and rest his leg, but of course, he'd shot that down hard. He wasn't letting her out of his sight until the person behind the messages had been caught, and the threat was over.

The rest of the team was here as well, including Trinity and Briar, having returned from London late last night. All of them wore various disguises while they watched for any sign of the person who had sent the message yesterday.

There was no sense of overt danger at the moment, only a sense of building anticipation and frustration. With this many people around, the chances that their mystery contact would try and take a shot at any of them were minimal. Still, Kiyomi couldn't shake the sense of unease.

They still weren't certain whether they were looking for a man or a woman, since the culprit might not be the same person from the video. Or whether the person would actually show.

Maybe this was just another ruse to see if they reacted to the message. Looking for a weakness. Maybe to follow them from here, and attack them when their guards were lowered.

Marcus shifted on his crutches, standing on her left side to protect her from anyone bumping into her sore arm. Sticking out of the end of the sling, her fingers were still swollen, numb, and difficult to move. She hoped things would improve drastically once the swelling dissipated. If they didn't, she wasn't going to be able to use her left hand for much of anything.

"See anyone?" he asked quietly.

She shook her head and kept watching. "You?"

"No. Only quarter to, though. They might show yet."

How was she supposed to recognize the person?

Whoever had sent that message was either manipulating them once again, or had something far more nefarious in mind. It was unsettling as hell to know their source could identify each of them visually, while Kiyomi and her team had no idea who they were looking for, or how many others were involved.

It put them at a distinct disadvantage. There could be an entire team here right now, scoping them out in plain sight, looking for an opportunity to strike. And the message had expressly named *her* as the one to be here.

Ten o'clock came and went. She scanned each face that passed by them, kept checking behind them every so often.

Quarter past. Still nothing. She covertly tapped her earpiece to activate her mic. "Anything?" she murmured.

"Nothing here," Trinity answered, and the other couples replied with the same answer.

Impatience seized her. She felt restless and twitchy, instinct telling her to move. Heading out into the open for a bit should be okay as long as they stayed near other people along the walkway.

"Let's take a little walk," she said to Marcus.

They turned onto the walkway hugging the south side of the river and headed east, walking slowly in deference to Marcus, and the growing throng around them. A line had formed out the door of the most popular bakery in town, the mouthwatering scents of coffee and cinnamon carrying on the air.

Kiyomi visually checked every single person they passed, watching for any hint of interest or recognition in their faces. It felt so strange to be on high alert, looking for a potential enemy amongst these people, all of them oblivious to the potential threat that could be hidden out of view —or in plain sight.

She and Marcus walked to the last footbridge and stopped. Standing on the bridge itself was too much exposure, but they had now walked the entire length of the main waterfront area and Marcus should rest. If someone was here watching for them, there was no way he or she could have missed them.

She studied the people on the opposite bank, some sitting on the grass, and others perusing the shops and cafés on the north side of the river. There was no one staring at them. No one quickly looked or turned away when she made visual contact. Yet a faint tingle prickled the back of her neck, as though someone had eyes on her right now.

Watching her, though she couldn't see them.

"Let's go," she murmured, not wanting to stay in such a visible spot any longer.

Had the person she'd sensed been on the far side of the road across the river? There were so many little walkways running into the main road. Someone could be hidden out of view in any one of them.

They retraced their steps back to the west side of the busy area and turned up a different walkway, stopping in the shadows of the stone building there. "I thought I felt something earlier," she said to Marcus.

He looked at her sharply. "Where?"

"By the last footbridge. Didn't see anyone suspicious though, and then it disappeared."

She scanned the buildings and cottages on the opposite side of the road beyond the river. Was someone watching through binos or a scope from a window in one of the buildings?

There was no telltale glint of light, no twitch of a curtain or blind. If someone had been watching her, they had chosen their hiding place well.

She checked in with the others again. It was quarter-to-eleven already. Forty-five minutes past the meeting time specified. "Anything?"

"Negative," Briar answered, and everyone else reported the same.

Dammit!

Kiyomi bit back an irritated sigh. "I'm calling it. It's a bust. Head out whenever you want. We'll see you back at the house." She switched off her earpiece and glanced at Marcus. "Maybe whoever it was spotted some of the others and got spooked." Though she doubted it. The others were all experts at blending in, and the sender must know she wouldn't show up alone here.

"Maybe," he murmured, though he didn't look convinced.

They stuck with the stream of tourists on their way back to the large parking lot on the north end of a walkway leading from the village. Large tour buses were offloading their passengers for the day amongst all the cars crowding the lot. Kiyomi rounded the hood of the rental car Zack had picked up for her last night and opened the driver's side door.

The tingling started up at the back of her neck again.

She froze, her head lifting. Her gaze shot to one of the tour buses, and the group of passengers milling around its door. A woman with strawberry blond hair stood there in black capris and a T-shirt.

The face was unfamiliar, but their eyes met. Recognition flared in the woman's stare.

And in that fleeing instant, something inside Kiyomi jolted. Shock and denial flooded her, sucking her back in time.

The damp, mildew scent of the moldering brick surrounded her as she picked her way through the fog up the alley. She had been searching for her friend for weeks now, but the latest tip had been days ago and the trail had gone cold. Until tonight.

Please don't let me be too late, she prayed, pistol in hand as she neared the shadowy end of the alley. Only minutes ago she'd seen some of Stanislav's thugs leave this place, speeding away in vehicles. And she hoped she was wrong about why they had come here. And who they had left in this desolate place.

There was no sound other than her hushed footsteps. No light here, and no one behind her. Holding her breath, she switched on the tac light on the top of her weapon. The thin beam of light lit up the end of the alley, outlining the body lying there.

A woman.

No...

Kiyomi ran toward the woman, heart in her throat. She couldn't be too late.

Dropping to her knees beside the figure sprawled on her stomach, Kiyomi set the weapon down so that the light bounced off the nearest brick wall and gingerly turned the woman over.

Her heart clenched, a cry of denial locking in her throat. "Julia," she croaked, horror swamping her.

Her friend's face had been beaten almost to the point

of being unrecognizable. Her nose had been flattened. Her lips were split open, dark, congealed blood telling Kiyomi it had been done hours ago. One swollen eyelid twitched, and slowly opened a slit, revealing a bloody eye with a hazel iris. The recognition in it as it looked up at her made the backs of Kiyomi's eyes sting.

They'd bound her arms behind her. Kiyomi pulled out a knife and quickly freed Julia's hands. Her friend moaned in pain.

Her fingers had been broken. Methodically.

Julia's breathing was shallow and uneven. Raspy from the blood in her lungs.

Kiyomi had no medical supplies with her. And even if she had, Julia was beyond all that. She was dying. Needed immediate, emergency surgery.

"Hold on," Kiyomi commanded, pulling out her phone to call for an ambulance. She cradled the side of Julia's face with her free hand, maintaining eye contact with that one, slitted eye as she spoke to the emergency operator and gave them Julia's location.

Julia's arm twitched. One mangled, bloody hand lifted slightly. Brushing Kiyomi's before falling. "H...help."

The plea was barely loud enough to be a whisper. Barely audible in the awful, hushed gloom of the alley.

"I will," Kiyomi vowed. "Help is coming. You have to hold on. For both of us." She leaned over her friend, rage and agony howling inside her. "I'm sorry," she said in an anguished whisper. "So sorry." She'd been so close to finding Julia these past few days. So close to being able to free her and spare her this painful, hideous end.

Julia didn't answer, struggling to breathe, the sound

wet and gurgling and awful. But that one eye stayed locked on Kiyomi, as if it was the only thing keeping her alive.

She stayed as long as she could. Until the wail of the ambulance siren was so close that she barely had time to get away before it arrived. No one could find her. No one could know of the connection between her and Julia. It was too dangerous.

Kiyomi held her friend's face and forced a smile. "You're going to be okay," she lied. "Help is here. And I swear I'll find who did this and make them pay. I swear it."

The eye focused on her for one last moment, then closed. And Kiyomi's time was up.

Pain clawing at her, she shoved to her feet, stole one last helpless glance at her dying friend, then turned and ran back up the alley and disappeared into the murky darkness just as the ambulance turned into the alley.

Pulling in a sharp breath, Kiyomi returned to the present. The woman suddenly broke eye contact and disappeared into the moving crowd.

Kiyomi broke away from the car, heart thudding. She ignored Marcus's worried call behind her and headed straight for the group of people filing out of the lot into the narrow walkway.

But when she reached the edge of it and scanned the crowd, the red-headed woman was gone. Or perhaps she'd been wearing a wig and removed it.

Damn, and the team was all off comms now. Kiyomi pulled out her phone and shot off a desperate text, pushing her way through the crowd, searching for the woman.

Female. Early to mid-thirties. Black capris and gray T-

shirt. Heading south on walkway from parking lot. Possibly red wig in possession.

She shoved her phone into her pocket and moved faster, studying every single woman she came across. All too soon she reached the end of the walkway.

She followed the crowd out onto the street and paused to look around, turning every which way. There were too many people around to easily pick out the woman now.

She spotted Eden moving toward her, Zack a few paces behind. Eden shook her head as she got close. "Do you see her?" She stopped next to Kiyomi to look around.

"No." *Dammit.* She couldn't have disappeared into thin air.

The rapid thud of crutches made her glance over her shoulder. Marcus was rushing toward her, a deep scowl on his face. "What the hell?" he demanded. "What's going on?"

She shook her head and kept looking around, frustrated. "I thought…"

He caught the side of her face and turned it toward him, worry lurking in his eyes. "You look like you saw a ghost."

"I…thought I did," she murmured, wondering if she'd misread this completely. Or if she'd imagined something that wasn't really there. Maybe she'd seen similarities simply because she wanted to so badly.

Whoever that woman was, she was long gone now. "Hurry," she told him and the others. "I need Amber and Lady Ada."

She was silent on the speeding drive back to the manor, her mind in turmoil, and thankfully Marcus didn't press

232

her. Amber was waiting for her the moment she stepped through the door. "What's going on?"

"I need you to dig into Julia Green's death," she said, aware of all the others gathered around them.

Amber nodded and rushed to get Lady Ada. Kiyomi stayed with her, the thump of Marcus's crutches close behind them.

Kiyomi stood tensely while Amber worked her magic.

It couldn't be her, she argued with herself. *You know it's impossible. You saw the death certificate. Verified for yourself that she died.*

Yet there was no quashing the hope beating inside her. Pressing against the inside of her ribs until it felt like they would split.

Marcus wrapped an arm around her and held her firmly to him. She leaned into his strength, her heart thudding as she waited, watching the information Amber pulled up on the screen.

After a few minutes, Amber spoke. "She was pronounced dead at this hospital in Moscow on the night you found her. October eleventh."

Kiyomi stared at the screen, disappointment hitting her hard. "You're sure?"

"Positive. These records list her as an unknown prostitute, cause of death internal bleeding from being beaten. And here are the police reports confirming it." She looked up at Kiyomi questioningly.

Shit.

Deflated, Kiyomi released a hard breath and ran a hand over her face. It was stupid of her to allow herself to hope. Stupid to even think it could be possible that Julia had somehow survived. She'd seen for herself the extent of Julia's injuries. Had known she was dying even as she'd knelt beside her.

Still… She couldn't let this go in case there was even a sliver of a chance that she was right. That maybe this had all been an elaborate test of sorts, to feel them out.

She had to know for certain whether she was right or not. And there was only one way to do that.

"I need to verify something. For my peace of mind. Just because the source didn't come forward today doesn't mean she wasn't there."

"She?" Amber said, raising her eyebrows. "Fine. What do you want me to do?"

"Send one last message, using another microdot—and use cherry blossoms around the circumference instead of ivy."

"Okay," Amber said slowly, glancing from her to Marcus. "And the message to go with it?"

"Say 'you're safe; it's okay to come in now.' And then…" She let out a breath, bracing for the reaction she was about to get. "Give the coordinates to somewhere in Stow. Somewhere public, along with tomorrow's date and a morning meeting time."

"Why? And that's way too damn close to us," Marcus said.

"No, that's why it's perfect. I want to try again."

Marcus and Amber both frowned. "Kiyomi, what the hell's going on? What aren't you telling us?" Marcus asked.

"I thought it might be Julia." She shook her head, realizing it sounded stupid and desperate even as they both stared at her in shock. "But it doesn't matter. This is our last hope of finding out who's behind this."

One way or another, by noon tomorrow, it would be over and she would have her answer.

CHAPTER TWENTY-TWO

B ack in her London flat with Mr. Whiskers curled up and purring like an engine on her lap, Ivy toyed with the beaded bracelet around her wrist and she stared at the message on screen she had just received from Amber.

You're safe. It's okay to come in now.

It's a trap, her brain said immediately.

Afraid to believe the message was real, let alone true, she searched for some other clue embedded in the unscrambled message and honed in on the final period. She isolated it and began enlarging it, her pulse picking up when it revealed an image.

The Valkyrie symbol, with a wreath of cherry blossoms encircling it, and the letters J U L I A embedded in them.

Kiyomi. Only Kiyomi could know to use the cherry blossom symbol with her.

Seeing her old friend this morning in Bourton had been like a knife in the heart. Walking away when Kiyomi had been that close had been one of the hardest things Ivy had ever had to do. She hadn't been certain, but it seemed her old friend had recognized her somehow.

It could be a trap.

Yes. The risk was real.

The meeting date beneath the symbol was for tomorrow. Kiyomi suspected it was her, and wanted to see her again tomorrow. To embrace her? Or kill her?

A sheen of tears blurred her eyes for a moment before she blinked them away and entered the coordinate numbers into a GPS program. A map popped up, showing the Cotswold village of Stow-on-the-Wold. Then the program began shrinking the area. Smaller and smaller, isolating an exact location.

The satellite image paused on the middle of town. Along with an address. When she entered that, she got a name.

Huffkins.

She looked it up, then sat back, staring at the image of the cute little stone façade of the tearoom, trying to make sense of it. It was located smack in the heart of the village, a public place that would be crawling with tourists by the time the meeting took place. Making it unlikely that Kiyomi or anyone with her would try to kill her in plain view of any bystanders.

Mr. Whiskers yowled and she jerked her hands off him, realizing she'd unconsciously been squeezing him half to death. He leaped off her lap, landed lightly on the rug and paused to give her an indignant look before retreating to the safety of another room while she focused on the screen again.

You're safe. It's okay to come in now.

She had never wanted to believe anything so badly in

her life. But the fear was real, raw and icy. If she was wrong about Kiyomi's intentions, she could be killed tomorrow.

It went around and around in her mind all day, torturing her. After forcing herself to eat something for dinner that night, she lay awake in bed once the darkness finally came, staring at the dim lights coming in her bedroom window.

She had lived so long in suspicion and fear, motivated by hatred and revenge. Yet at every turn since this had begun, Kiyomi and the others had proven themselves to her without realizing it.

She was still afraid to trust them. Afraid this would turn out to be just another manipulative lie. Another disaster she would pay for, this time with her life. Could Kiyomi and the others really be waiting to embrace her after everything that had happened?

It was too tantalizing to ignore. Going to the meeting tomorrow was a huge risk. Kiyomi would be ready for anything, and she likely had at least some of the others there as backup.

Don't go. It's a trap, that bitter, fearful voice in her mind whispered.

"But it could also be my salvation," she told it, her voice strong in the silence.

Her chance to be free. To have a life of her own. To form friendships and maybe even find people who might care about her.

Her heart pounded. She had to do this. Had to know for sure, and she was so damn tired of her lonely, superficial existence. She wanted her freedom, and a future. A life of her own, as the others had won for themselves.

Also, they hadn't turned around and hunted her down after Kiyomi had spotted her this morning. That was a big indicator that she was probably safe to go see them.

Her mind was made up. She was going.

~

At nine-fifty the next morning Ivy parked her rental car along Old Forge Lane and cautiously walked toward Stow-on-the-Wold's famous market square. It was already busy, the car park full, people wandering around taking photos and popping in and out of the shops ringing the square. A tour bus was offloading passengers at the visitor's center in the middle of it.

Ivy joined the crowd milling around the bus and used it as cover to take a good look around. She had come without a disguise today and put on a black and white sundress. Kiyomi should be able to pick her out again if Ivy didn't spot her first, even though her new face looked nothing like Julia's.

No telltale tingle at the back of her neck. Just a bubbling anticipation in the pit of her stomach, and a painful bubble of hope in her chest.

Huffkins was a short walk away, across from her and to the right. She headed for it, hyper aware of everything that was happening around her, watching the people and faces she saw.

There was a line outside the door at Huffkins. She paused a few dozen yards away and looked around. Beside her, the bus drove past. She glanced back to where she'd been and did a double take as her eyes stopped on the lone figure standing away from the knot of tourists in the shadow of the visitor's center.

Female. Slender. Right height. Left arm in a sling.

The woman stepped forward, emerging into the sunlight, her gaze locked with Ivy's.

Ivy caught her breath, her pulse accelerating. *Kiyomi.*

She couldn't move. Could barely breathe as Kiyomi came toward her with a slow, cautious gait, her beautiful, familiar face a blank mask, giving nothing away. There had to be other Valkyries here too, but Ivy didn't care, couldn't tear her eyes away from her old friend.

Kiyomi stopped about thirty feet away, assessing her with that dark, fathomless gaze. "Are you alone?"

Ivy nodded, not trusting her voice. The uncertainty was killing her.

Kiyomi lifted her chin, staring right at her. "Who are you?"

"Ivy," she managed to get past the constriction in her throat. "I'm Ivy now. But I used to be…" Nope. Her throat closed up before she could get out another word.

The look in Kiyomi's eyes softened slightly. "Julia."

"Yes," she whispered, and to her horror, tears blurred her eyes.

Kiyomi didn't move, her expression still guarded. "What did I give you when we graduated together?"

She held up her wrist. "This."

Kiyomi zeroed in on it, and the blank mask dropped, avid interest taking its place. "What's on the bead?"

"A cherry blossom." She blinked, the tears spilling over.

Kiyomi started toward her again, and stopped within

reach. She searched Ivy's eyes a long, breathless moment before reaching for her wrist and examining the bracelet.

A shaky smile trembled on Kiyomi's lips, and when she met Ivy's gaze again, her eyes were wet too. "It really is you," she whispered.

Ivy nodded and pressed her lips together to hold in a sob. She hated the weakness, hated it even more that she was falling apart in plain view of anyone here who cared to watch, but this was too much.

Still smiling, Kiyomi released her wrist and reached up to wipe away the tears on Ivy's face. "It's so good to see you."

That did it.

She crumpled. Just fell to pieces right there in the middle of the square.

Kiyomi's arm came around her, holding on tight. Ivy clung to her fiercely, part of her still terrified that this was all a dream. That someone would tear them apart at any moment and she would lose her only friend yet again.

She didn't know how long they stood like that while she desperately tried to get a grip on herself. It took everything she had to lock her emotions back in the box she kept them in and pull back, wiping her face in embarrassment.

Kiyomi's smile was genuine. Soft. "Looks like we've got a lot of catching up to do, huh?"

"Yes." Her voice was rusty.

"Feel like meeting the rest of your sisters?"

Oh, God, were they here? She glanced around, horrified that she'd dropped her guard so badly.

"They're not here. But they're close. Come on." She hooked an arm around her and led her back across the square. "Where are you parked?"

Ivy took her to the rental car, glanced up as an old Land Rover pulled up close by, and tensed.

"Don't worry, it's just my husband, Marcus." She flashed a grin and turned toward the vehicle. "You'll love him."

Marcus undid the window and lifted a hand. Ivy echoed the gesture, feeling awkward. He must have had eyes on them the entire time, and Ivy hadn't had a clue. She was slipping.

"Are you okay to drive?" Kiyomi asked. "You can follow us. It's not far, only a few minutes away."

"Where?"

"My home."

Feeling like she was having an out-of-body experience, Ivy got in her car and followed the old Rover up the lane, then onto Digbeth Street. They wound down it to where it intersected with Sheep Street and became Park Street, both sides lined with pretty, golden-stone cottages.

From the top of the hill, the lush, rolling green countryside spread out in all directions. She barely saw it, too caught up in her head.

Marcus drove a few miles east, then turned north up a quiet road. Another couple of miles later, he turned west and slowed at a driveway marked with a large wrought iron gate flanked with tall Cotswold stone pillars.

Ivy stared through it, looking past the gatehouse at the large, imposing manor house that stood at the top of the long gravel driveway.

Holy shit. Kiyomi lived *here*?

The gates opened and Marcus pulled through. Ivy followed, palms damp on the steering wheel and her pulse thudding hard in her ears when the Rover suddenly stopped, barring her way.

Someone stepped out of a door in the gatehouse and walked toward the gate. Ivy's heart skipped a beat when she recognized Megan, and a tall man behind her. He was armed, a pistol in the hand resting at his side.

Ivy unlocked her doors, lowered her window and turned off the ignition. Taking a deep breath, she raised both hands in the air so they could see them, palms out.

Megan and the man approached her door cautiously, watching her every move. "Need you to step out of the car," Megan said.

Ivy nodded and kept her hands where they were, the intense vulnerability of the moment scraping over her like razor blades. The man opened her door. She stepped out and faced them, hands up as Megan approached.

"Gotta pat you down, just in case."

Ivy didn't move as Megan frisked her, couldn't help staring at the other woman. She'd searched for the surviving Valkyries for so long, it seemed surreal to finally meet another one. The man was searching the car for weapons.

Megan grasped the bottom of Ivy's shirt in one hand and tugged down the left side of her waistband with the other. As soon as she saw the Valkyrie mark on Ivy's hip, she looked up at her with a little smile. "Are you really Julia?"

"Not anymore. I'm Ivy."

Megan nodded. "Okay then. Come on. The others are waiting for you."

Ivy got back in her car and followed Marcus and Kiyomi up the long, sloping driveway while Megan and the man followed on foot. Ivy relaxed slightly, focused on the manor house. Her heart beat faster and faster as they approached the front of it, until it raced in a dizzying rush of hope and joy.

Kiyomi stepped out of the Rover with Marcus as the front door opened and a medium sized brown-and-white dog charged out to greet them. Kiyomi's teeth flashed as she smiled. "You ready?"

"Think so." She was so damn nervous.

So many terrible things had led them to this moment. So much pain and fear and hatred that had stolen everything from her but mere existence.

Kiyomi reached out a hand to her, fingers closing tight around Ivy's. "All this time I thought you were dead. I found you lying in that alley and I knew there was no way you were going to make it..." She trailed off, shaking her head.

Ivy smiled through her tears, her heart about to explode. "I'm too stubborn for that."

They both laughed. Kiyomi squeezed her again and officially introduced her to Marcus. "Come inside and meet the others."

Inside, other familiar faces were there to greet her. Amber, who grinned and pulled her into a bear hug. "Hey, hacker sister."

Ivy almost teared up again, but there wasn't time to get all emotional because she had a lot more sisters to meet.

The fabled Trinity. Briar. Georgia. Eden, and their significant others, including Megan's husband, Ty.

"Where's Chloe?" Ivy asked, looking around for her.

The happy smiles dimmed. "She's with Heath," Kiyomi answered, her arm around her husband's waist. It was so strange to know her friend had married, but it thrilled Ivy to see her settled and happy, and to know that she had been able to love and be loved in return. "He's still in the hospital, but at least he's going to make it."

Trinity took her by the hand. "Come into the library for snacks and tell us everything."

Seated on a tufted velvet sofa, Ivy regaled her story to the captive audience gathered around her, ending with being taken captive in Moscow. "Tarasov and his men dumped me in that alley thinking they were leaving me to die. But I beat the odds. The paramedics managed to keep me alive on the way to the hospital, and apparently they took me straight into surgery."

She let out a breath, pushing aside the terrible memories. "It took several transfusions, three more surgeries and two weeks in the ICU before I regained consciousness."

"But there was an official death certificate," Amber said.

She nodded. "I forged it right after I escaped the ICU. Then I went to ground in a place I found outside of Kiev. It took months for me to recover enough to come out of hiding. I siphoned some money from Tarasov and found a plastic surgeon to repair the damage." Gesturing to her face, she smirked. "Had him take off a few years while he was at it. After I recovered, I stayed off grid and started working on my plan."

"To kill Tarasov," Amber said.

"Yes, but something else just as important." She looked around the circle of faces before her. "I didn't know until now whether it was safe to resurface. I knew Zoya and Hannah had sold me out to Tarasov and his crew, but I didn't know if it went farther than that, or whether some or all of you were involved too. So I started tracking all of you to find out. Not that you made it easy," she added with a wry grin that made everyone smile.

"So you *were* testing us," Kiyomi said. "You sent us the intel on Tarasov and the kidnapping ring to see whether we would go after him. And ever since, you've been watching us, trying to decide whether you could trust us enough to come out of hiding."

"Yes." She clasped her hands in her lap, looking from Kiyomi to all the others. "I'm sorry I put you all at such risk." She focused back on Kiyomi, nodded at her sling. "And for the damage I've caused. Truly."

"Taking out Tarasov was my pleasure," Kiyomi said. "He'll never be a free man again."

"Be surprised if he lived more than a few weeks in the clink," Jesse said, his arm around Amber's shoulders. "Convicts hate rich, arrogant assholes like him."

Ivy sighed and rubbed her palms on the skirt of her dress, shaking her head. She wasn't sure she deserved their understanding or forgiveness, especially since Kiyomi and Heath had been injured so badly because of her. "I was so envious of what you all did after banding together to kill The Architect. That you all made it out alive and were able to make new lives for yourselves."

"Rycroft's going to want to meet you," Trinity said.

Ivy hedged. "I'm not sure I…" She was so close to having the chance she'd been dreaming of. Gambling it by talking to Rycroft about everything seemed too big a risk.

"His bark is way worse than his bite. And we should know. We've put that man in a lot of awkward positions, and he's come through for us every time." Kiyomi smiled at her. "You can trust him."

Briar nodded. "You really can. And us, though I under-stand why it'll take you time to get there."

The tension in her belly eased. "It feels so surreal to think that I might have the chance at a future now."

"Welcome back," Kiyomi told her with a grin.

Ivy returned it, wanting to pinch herself. Against all odds, she was finally, truly alive again.

Because she was free.

CHAPTER TWENTY-THREE

I ncredibly, they had gained another sister through this whole ordeal.

It still seemed unbelievable as Trinity lounged in the library that evening with the other Valkyries. She had fulfilled her obligation with assisting Rycroft with the cleanup efforts, and was due to fly out the following afternoon. She was anxious to get home to start the next phase of her life.

Ivy was understandably still a bit guarded, and seemed most comfortable with Kiyomi. The two of them were cozied up on a loveseat in the corner, laughing about something.

Hearing that happy, carefree sound and looking at the women around her, Trinity's heart swelled. The threat that had been hanging over them all this time was gone, and Tarasov's network dismantled.

Five of the missing women had been located and rescued across the world, thanks to intel Amber had sent to Scotland Yard and MI5. Sadly, two had been killed before their whereabouts were known. But at least their kidnappers were all being brought to justice.

Eden walked into the room with an eager look on her face. "Hey, guys, Chloe and Heath are here."

Everyone except Ivy jumped up and followed her to the door. Kiyomi paused on the way to alert the guys, all gathered in Marcus's study for brandy and cigars, then opened the front door.

Chloe was partway up the steps with Heath, holding his hand. "Hey. Heard there was a party going on, and we didn't want to miss it," she said cheerfully.

Poor Heath didn't look nearly as chipper. He was bent forward at the waist, jaw set and his lips compressed into a thin line as he struggled up the steps toward them. Trinity and Eden grabbed their bags for them and carried everything up to their room on the second floor.

Upstairs, Heath lowered himself gingerly to the bed, face white, a pained groan coming from between his clenched teeth. After a moment he opened his eyes and blinked when he saw the crowd of people standing in the bedroom doorway. "Hey," he said with a wan smile. "Glad to be home."

Chloe helped him lie down flat, and within minutes people had brought up food and drinks for them both. After tucking him in and covering his face with kisses, Chloe shut off the light and stepped out into the hallway. "Poor guy. He needs to sleep. The doctors weren't thrilled about discharging him this early but he insisted, and it was a rough trip from the hospital." Facing them, she raised her eyebrows expectantly. "Heard we have a new family member I need to meet?"

Trinity and Kiyomi looked at each other. *Awkward.*

Chloe could be unpredictable at the best of times, and Ivy had ultimately been responsible for putting Heath in harm's way.

"Oh, come on, I'm not gonna shoot her or anything," Chloe said in annoyance.

"All right, but don't spook her," Trinity warned, taking her by the arm and leading her downstairs. "She's still trying to adjust to all of this, and all of us. I don't want you scaring her away."

Chloe snorted. "Please, I'm like, the *least* intimidating one of all of us."

She probably believed that, too.

Trinity led her to the library. Ivy looked up, saw Chloe and stiffened, her expression shuttering like a switch had been flipped.

Yep. Awkward.

Trinity put on a reassuring smile and squeezed Chloe's arm in warning. "Chloe, this is Ivy." She could feel the others behind them, almost holding their breaths.

Chloe didn't move, staring at the newcomer for a few tense seconds. "Hey," she said finally, expression unreadable.

"Hi." Ivy shifted slightly, her only outward betrayal of nervousness. "I don't know what to say to you except that I'm glad Heath is going to be okay. And I'm *really* sorry about what happened to him. I didn't mean for any of you to get hurt."

Chloe nodded. "I'm sorry too." She pulled free of Trinity's grip, grabbed a handful of chips from a bowl on the table on the way by, and went to sit in a chair beside Ivy. "So, fill me in on everything I missed," she said eagerly, shoving a handful into her mouth.

Crisis averted. A collective sigh came from the group.

With the tension broken everyone filed back into the room, including the guys. A few minutes later Trinity's phone vibrated in her pocket. Rycroft. "Hey."

"Hi. What's all that racket going on in the background?"

"We're having a reunion party, just like we told you in the first place."

He huffed out a laugh. "Well, open the damn gate, will you? I want to meet this new Valkyrie."

She blinked. "Wait, you're here?"

"Drove out from London the second I heard about her. And I'm taking Briar to Heathrow with me tonight anyway. So, you gonna let me in, or what?"

She got up and started for the door. "Is it safe to?" she teased, hitting a button on the keypad by the door to open the front gate.

"See you in a minute."

Trinity waited at the door while he parked and walked up the stairs. "How's the clean up going?"

"As well as can be expected," he said with a bland look, then glanced past her down the hall. "So, what's she like?"

"She's like all of us were before we came out to the world," she answered, leading the way to the library.

A cheer went up when Rycroft stepped into the room. He grinned, shook hands with the guys and Chloe, then hugged the rest of them.

Finally, he stopped in front of Ivy, hands on hips, that penetrating silver gaze pinned on her. "So. Another one for me to worry about."

Ivy rose and shook hands with him. "No, you don't need to worry about me now."

He raised an eyebrow. "Heard that one before." He glanced around at the rest of them. "Didn't believe it then, and still don't believe it now."

"Oh, come on, you know you love us," Chloe insisted, reaching for a leftover cream bun from Huffkins. Lucky for her, her metabolism was as hyperactive as her brain.

Rycroft grunted, giving Trinity, Briar and Amber a hard look. "I distinctly remember you saying I wouldn't have a mess to clean up this time."

Chloe brushed his reprimand away with a careless wave. "Not as much as last time," she said, as if what had happened was no big deal.

He stared at her. "You blew up a building. In *London*."

She rolled her eyes. "A single vehicle in a *garage*. Not even close to the entire building. I made sure. Because I'm a *pro*. I know what I'm doing."

"But thanks for looking out for us," Eden interjected, coming up to curl an arm around his waist and giving him a fond smile.

The legendary NSA agent's eyes narrowed at her for a moment, then he visibly melted and shook his head. "You guys drive me crazy, but for some damn reason I can't stay mad at you."

After that the party got into full swing. The whole room rang with conversation and laughter, and once again Trinity was struck by the joy and comfort of it. Everyone in this house shared a bond like no other—but now she just wanted to get home.

Over on a couch talking to Marcus and Ty, Rycroft suddenly pulled out his phone and answered it, standing.

He covered his other ear with his hand and strode for the doorway as he spoke. Then he stopped abruptly and faced her, holding out the phone. "It's for you."

Brody. He was the only person it could be.

Trinity set down her wineglass and took the phone, stepping out into the hallway where it was quieter. "Hello?"

"Hey, gorgeous. How's it going?"

"Going so great. Wish you were here to see it and meet Ivy."

"Yeah? You might change your mind about that when I tell you why I called."

She stilled, everything funneling out but the sound of his voice as he spoke.

The chatter and laughter in the next room faded into the background. The walls and hallway seemed to blur around her.

Heart thudding after she ended the call, she walked back to the library with a lump in her throat and tears pricking her eyes.

Conversation ceased immediately, all eyes turning to her. "What's wrong?" Kiyomi said, frowning in concern as she stood.

Trinity shook her head, a smile trembling on her lips. "That was Brody. Apparently we're having a baby."

A collective gasp echoed around the room. "*Now?*" Briar demanded, rushing over, eyes wide.

"The birth mom's in labor. They said it's going to still be a long while, but…" She looked at Rycroft. "Got room in the car for one more on the trip to Heathrow?"

An instant later she was surrounded by Valkyries, all hugging her and talking excitedly. Chloe put her hand on top of Trinity's, and one by one they all stacked hands in the center of the semicircle they'd formed.

"Wait." Kiyomi waved Ivy over. "Come on, get over here. Hand in."

Ivy complied, a little smile tugging at the corners of her lips as she placed her hand on the top of the pile.

Chloe grinned and threw her head back, shouting to the ceiling. "Bitchilantes ride or die!"

A collective shout went up, but Amber let out a shrill whistle. "No time to celebrate this momentous occasion right now—we gotta get this mama packed and on her way to the airport."

In moments she was being ushered up the stairs in a happy swarm to help her get ready to leave.

"I'll get her suitcase," Eden said, hurrying to the closet. "The rest of you start grabbing her stuff."

"Man, this is one lucky kid you're about to have," Briar said, giving Trinity a squeeze. More than anyone else, she knew exactly what becoming a mother meant to Trinity. "I'm so happy for you guys."

"Yeah, and just remember, if anyone messes with him, he's got a whole crew of aunties ready to step in and kick ass," Chloe added from the en suite.

Trinity had never felt so loved. She and Brody might be about to start their own family, but nothing would ever replace this one in her heart.

～

Ivy's euphoria dimmed when Alex Rycroft stepped back through the doorway. Tall. Broad-shouldered. Mostly gray hair but still powerfully built, his commanding presence instantly changing the atmosphere in the room.

She stiffened, her pulse picking up. If he'd come to single her out, it couldn't be good news for her.

He sat on the chair Chloe had been in minutes before, leaning back to pin her with his intense silver stare. "I'm going to be leaving in a few minutes, so we need to do this now. And I'm going to be checking every single thing you tell me, so if you lie, I'll know, and then you and I are gonna have a serious problem."

If she hadn't spent her entire adult life as the weapon the government had transformed her into, he would have intimidated the shit out of her. As it was, he wasn't the sort of man she wanted to be on the wrong side of, especially when she was trying to get her life back.

She dipped her chin in acknowledgment of his statement, wishing at least one of the others were down here with her.

"Good. First, were you working with anyone on this?"

"No."

"Did you kill Tarasov's man in the alley?"

Lying was second nature, and a denial was right there on the tip of her tongue. But she was tired of lying. Tired of hiding.

She believed him when he said he would check everything she told him, and didn't doubt that he would find out the truth anyway. More than that, Kiyomi and the others said she could trust him. "He came after me, not the other way around."

"Did you kill him?" he repeated.

"Yes. In self-defense. I was on my way out of the area when it happened."

He nodded, his expression thawing slightly, and she got the sense that she had just passed a critical test. As if he'd already known all of it before he'd asked. "So you were there while Kiyomi's part of the op was happening."

"For a while." It didn't surprise her that he was considered a legend in his field. Even with all her training and experience, she couldn't read him or figure out what was going on in his head.

"You can fill in the details later when you and I meet with my MI5 contacts—and yeah, that's happening. If you're wanting to go straight and get your life back like the others, then you're going to have to play by the rules now."

She didn't like it, was naturally suspicious of others and especially people who worked for the government, but she understood. Besides, Rycroft was semi-retired and trying to get out. There was no reason for him to try to screw her. "Okay."

"It's going to take me a while to dig up your records, if they still exist, so it'll be way easier if you just tell me what I need to know. Are you still a US citizen?"

"My citizenship as Julia was never revoked, but technically she's dead and I never got around to getting a US passport for my new identity."

"I'll handle it." He folded his arms across his wide chest. "How did this whole thing unfold from your end?"

That was a loaded question. One that could potentially get her into a lot of trouble.

"Bear in mind, it's not possible to shock me at this point. Not after dealing with the rest of you for this long. So whatever you need to say, just say it."

Dredging up everything about her past was the last

thing she wanted to do. It had to happen, though, so doing it here and now would allow her to get everything out into the open and hopefully allow her the fresh start she was dying for. "How much do you know about my past?"

"Not nearly enough. So enlighten me."

She ran through it quickly in as straight forward a manner as possible, starting with just before the disaster with Zoya and Hannah, and ending with the Tarasov op. When she finished, Rycroft sat in silence for a few moments, silver eyes assessing her.

"That everything?"

"Yes." The details she'd left out didn't matter and could be filled in later. He had everything he needed about her now.

He inclined his head, the hint of a smile tugging at his lips. "All right. Thank you, Ivy." He rose and held out his hand. They shook. He didn't let go, his grip firm as his gaze bored into hers. "I'm warning you now, don't run. I can't help you if you do."

"I won't." Not when Tarasov was in custody and she'd finally been reunited with Kiyomi. "I'm done running."

"Good." He released her. "I'll be in touch within the next day or so. Gotta get two Valkyries home to their families first." He turned and strode out.

Ivy watched him go, a poignant smile spreading across her face. Weird as it seemed, she felt like she might have just found an ally in Alex Rycroft.

CHAPTER TWENTY-FOUR

H ow long was this going to go on for?
Trinity popped out of the chair again and began pacing the length of the waiting room, unable to bear it.

"You're gonna put a hole in the carpet," Brody mumbled from the chair he was slumped in, ball cap pulled low over his eyes.

"It's like time's moving backward," she muttered, rolling her head around to ease the tight muscles in her neck and shoulders. It had been two days since she'd slept. She was tired and restless and edgy as hell, and the waiting was killing her.

Everything since leaving Laidlaw Hall with Briar and Rycroft was a blur. As soon as she'd been let off the plane, she'd hoisted her carry-on luggage and run through the airport, cleared customs and jumped straight into a taxi to come here. The labor was now well into hour nineteen, and Trinity was scared something was wrong.

"Come sit down. Better yet, come curl up here next to me and get some sleep."

"Can't. Need to move." The waiting and not knowing was torture. So many things could go wrong.

Not to mention the legal issues, and the potential consequences for her involvement in the Tarasov op were still up in the air. Rycroft had promised to make sure it didn't affect the adoption, but he could only do so much.

Brody sighed, stood up and grabbed her around the waist, hauling her back to the chair while ignoring her protests. "Just shh for a minute," he told her, pulling her into his lap and holding her securely.

She remained stiff for a few moments, then gradually melted. He had to be anxious too, and here he was trying to soothe her.

"That's better." He stroked her hair, kissed her forehead. "It's you and me, Trin, no matter what happens. We're our own family. And everything's going to be okay."

She cuddled close, drinking up his love and comfort. "I'm glad you finally gave in and married me," she teased. They both knew it was the other way around.

He snorted. "Brat."

The door opened. She jumped up like she'd been launched off Brody's lap by a catapult, heart tripping as she stared at the nurse. "What's happened?"

The nurse smiled. "Congratulations, Mom and Dad."

Trinity clapped a hand over her mouth, a high-pitched sound coming out. Brody was beside her in an instant, hooking his arm around her shoulders. "He's here?"

She beamed at them. "Yes. Are you ready to meet him?"

Trinity followed her into the hall, clutching Brody's hand. This was happening. After all these years, all the sadness and heartbreak, she was about to be a mother and hold her child for the first time.

"Oh my God, oh my God," she whispered, barely able to hold it together.

Brody squeezed her hand, his excitement palpable.

A door down the hallway opened and a doctor stepped out holding a precious, blanket-wrapped bundle in her arms. "Mr. and Mrs. Colebrook, I'd like you to meet your son."

Tears flooded Trinity's eyes. She might have run the last few yards, she wasn't sure, but her outstretched arms were already reaching out for the baby when she stopped in front of the doctor.

A moment later her newborn son was carefully transferred to her arms.

Trinity stared down at his pink, scrunched face, struck by how tiny he was and blinking furiously to see him through the rush of tears. "Oh my God, Brody…"

He chuckled and stepped up close behind her, reaching out one big hand to touch their son's forehead. "He's a good looking kid."

He was perfect. The most beautiful thing she'd ever seen.

A torrent of love poured through her, along with a fierce wave of protectiveness. "Hi, Rory." They'd picked the name out months ago, and it suited him perfectly. She pushed back the edge of his little knit hat. "Oh, wow, look at all this dark hair!"

"He's gorgeous, healthy, and has quite a set of lungs on

him. He'll definitely let you know when he wants something," the doctor said.

"Oh my God, I love him so much already." She tore her attention from him for a moment, remembering it wasn't just them involved in this process, and spoke to the doctor. "How's the birth mom doing?"

"Great. The delivery was tough, but she'll be fine, and will feel a whole lot better after a well-earned sleep." Her eyes sparkled at them. "I'll leave you three to get acquainted."

Trinity was already back to staring at their son, completely absorbed, then realized how selfish she was being and turned toward her husband. "Here, you need to introduce yourself properly."

Brody took him, naturally holding him in the crook of one muscular arm, Rory's fragile little body tucked to his broad chest. "Hey, little man. I'm your daddy."

The awe and love shining on her husband's face as he smiled down at their tiny son almost burst Trinity's heart. This was everything she'd ever secretly dreamed of and been afraid to hope for.

It seemed that sometimes dreams really could come true.

$\sim$

Ten days later

Marcus paused just inside the door of his study, and listened.

Quiet. Blessed, wonderful quiet.

Karas nudged his hand with her nose, impatient to leave. "Right," he said, mentally gearing up before exiting his private sanctum, ready to be social and play host once again.

Hard to believe a week and a half had passed since the day of the ops. He was back to being able to use his cane now, the pain in his hip bearable again, but he wouldn't be going on a hike anytime soon.

Trinity had made it home in time for the birth of her son. The baby boy was healthy, the adoption finalization had all gone smoothly, and Trinity and Brody were both over the moon to be parents.

Most of the others had left the day after Ivy's sudden arrival, with the exception of Chloe and Heath, since he hadn't been in any kind of shape to travel yet. Ivy and her cat were staying with them for a while longer yet, until she figured out where to go and what to do with her newly found freedom. Kiyomi had been there herself not too long ago, so she was helping guide Ivy through the process.

While he was looking forward to having his quiet life, house, and wife all to himself again, he didn't begrudge her more time with Ivy. It warmed his heart to see Kiyomi so happy. He knew she'd been lonely without her fellow Valkyries around, even if she wouldn't admit it and had never said it to him.

He opened the study door just as Chloe came down the stairs with Ivy and Kiyomi helping her carry the luggage. His wife no longer wore her sling, but still couldn't use her left hand much. The doctors and physical therapists on her rehab team were all hopeful that she would be able to regain most, if not all function in the coming months. He was diligent about making her do her exercises and getting her to rest.

Heath was a few stairs behind them, slowly making his

way to the foyer. He no longer looked like he would keel over and die at any moment. His face had better color, and he was moving with far less pain. He still had a long way to go in terms of recovery, however.

Marcus hoped Chloe made a concerted effort to curb the impulsive part of her nature and took it really easy on him in the months ahead.

Though that was likely a tall order where she was concerned.

Chloe looked up at him and set her suitcase down on the stone floor. "I know, I know, you're devastated to see me leaving and missing me already. But don't worry, I'll come back to stay with you and Kiyomi again someday."

One side of his mouth lifted. The cheek on this one. "I'm glad to hear it. Because I want to invite you both and all the others back here for Christmas this year."

Chloe and the others all stopped and stared at him in surprise. "For real?" Chloe asked, eyebrows hiked up.

"Aye." He glanced at his wife, and her face broke into the most gorgeous smile. It was like watching the sun break through the clouds on a cold, stormy day, bathing him in instant warmth. "I'd like us all to celebrate the holiday together when we can make the dates work." That would be the best Christmas gift he could ever give his wife. And it was more than enough reason to give up his peaceful existence here for a few days more.

Chloe narrowed her eyes, pretending to consider the offer. "Will you make Yorkshires?"

He grinned. "More Yorkshires than you can eat."

A wicked smile spread across her lips. "Ooh, I'll take that as a personal challenge." On impulse she flung her arms around his neck and hugged him. "We'll be here. And I knew you'd warm up to me eventually."

He patted her back, shooting a grin at Kiyomi. "You wore me down." He couldn't forget that Chloe had stuck around to watch their backs on the op after she'd heard about Heath. For someone who struggled with impulse control, that would have been even harder for her. He respected her discipline and integrity a lot.

Heath finally made it to the bottom of the stairs and paused to catch his breath. Marcus shook his hand. "You take care of yourself." He shot Chloe a hard look. "Go easy on him."

"Of course I will," she replied in a tone that said he was ridiculous, hooking an arm around Heath's neck and gave him a smacking kiss on the cheek. "He's my everything. Oh, and by the way," she added to Marcus, "business has been sloooow. So if you hear of anyone needing something blown up, send 'em my way."

Heath groaned and shook his head, mouthing the words *please no* to him.

Marcus smothered a smile and opened the door for them. Heath paused on the way out and gave him a rueful look. "Wanna make a bet now that next time you see me, I'll have more gray hair than you? Might even be a silver fox just like Rycroft," he added, making him and Kiyomi chuckle.

After they'd left, Chloe waving a hand out the driver's side window and a trail of dust coming from under the speeding car's tires, Marcus shut the door. Ivy was nowhere to be seen, but Kiyomi was leaning against the newel post at the bottom of the stairs, head cocked as she watched him.

"What?" he asked.

She straightened and walked toward him with that sexy, sensual stride that made him wish they had no more houseguests so they had absolute privacy and could be as loud and sexually creative as they wanted. "I can't believe you invited them here for Christmas."

She wound her good arm around the back of his neck, her scent teasing him, her breasts pressed to his chest and the look in her dark eyes making it hard to concentrate on what she was saying. He caught her by the hips. "I thought you'd be happy."

"Oh, I am. But I'm always happy when I'm with you." She lifted on tiptoe to settle her lips against his.

Marcus sank a hand into her hair and kissed her slow and tender, then deeper, the need she always ignited in him bursting into flame. She was a bundle of contradictions, and sometimes he thought he would never be able to peel all her layers back in this lifetime. But one thing was certain.

Whatever else lay in store for them in the future, there were bound to be more surprises along the way.

EPILOGUE

L aidlaw Hall was a beautiful place, but never more so than when it was all done up for the holidays, with a real tree decorated in every reception room, and other adornments scattered throughout. Outside it was chilly and damp, but inside all was warm, cozy and full of life, voices floating down the hall from where she stood alone, admiring the huge, decorated tree in the library.

Wood fires crackled in the grates and heat radiated from the huge Aga cooker in the kitchen. Strands of white and multicolored lights made everything twinkle and glisten, glowing against the oppressive darkness outside, revealed by the windows.

To Ivy, it was nothing short of magical.

She couldn't remember having a real Christmas. She'd been abandoned when she was a toddler, then put into an orphanage before being taken into the Valkyrie Program. For her, Christmas was something other people got to celebrate with friends and family, and something she saw in movies.

Ivy had accepted their invitation to stay with them for a few months. She and Mr. Whiskers had moved into the gatehouse where Megan and Ty had once lived.

"I think it's almost that time." Kiyomi came into the library in a gorgeous red velvet dress that hugged her slender curves.

She hadn't been much of a cook before coming here, surviving on whatever she could throw together with minimal effort that would give her some fuel. Since coming here, Marcus had taught her more than a few tricks in the kitchen, and she now cooked dinner for the three of them twice per week.

Making a full Christmas dinner with all the trimmings for a crowd this size, however, was a different matter.

"It's kind of like prepping for an op," she said. The planning. Gathering supplies. Prepping. Making contingency plans. And that was all before the actual cooking part happened.

Kiyomi laughed. "It feels exactly like that, minus the weapons. Unless you count the knives." She bounced her eyebrows, then looked past Ivy and pointed to the tree. "There's a little something tucked inside the branches there I wanted you to take a look at."

"What?" Ivy followed the direction Kiyomi indicated, stepped closer and saw the small package wrapped in shiny red foil paper. "Hey, Christmas isn't until next week," she protested.

"I know, but I couldn't wait. Go on, open it."

Secretly thrilled, Ivy pulled the present from the pretty blue-green spruce branches, biting her lip as she undid the paper. Corner by corner, afraid to tear the paper. Wanting to draw out the delicious anticipation and savor every second of opening her very first Christmas gift.

Lifting the lid of the box she unveiled, she gasped at what lay on the black satin bed. "Oh, its gorgeous."

"I ordered it special from Japan."

She took out the necklace, the delicate chain bearing a single jet bead decorated with any ivy leaf surrounded by a wreath of little cherry blossoms. The significance was impossible to miss.

"It represents you and me, and that I always have and always will hold you in my heart."

Ivy bit her lip, her eyes filling.

"Nooo, don't cry," Kiyomi begged, coming over to take it from her. "Here, let me put it on you."

Ivy half-turned, struggling not to cry as Kiyomi fastened it around her neck. The heavy black bead nestled perfectly in the little hollow between her collarbones. She put a hand to it, sniffed hard and blinked fast until the lights on the tree stopped blurring. "It's beautiful," she rasped out, overcome.

Kiyomi turned her around and pulled Ivy into a tight hug. "No crying. It's Christmas. Joy to the world and all of that."

She nodded, gave a watery laugh. "I know, but… Gah, you hit me in all my feels at once."

"That just means I made the right choice when I had it made for you." Kiyomi pulled back and put her hands on Ivy's shoulders. "Love you, forever friend."

She smiled back, her heart overflowing. There was nothing she wouldn't do for this woman. "Same. Thank you for this. It means so much."

"You're welcome. Glad you like it." Kiyomi stepped

back, looking pleased with herself. "I'm gonna head to the kitchen now and put my game face on to help Marcus so we can get dinner on the table at some point tonight."

"I'll be right there. Just need a few minutes to…" She gestured to her tearstained face and puffy eyes. She didn't want the others to see her until she was fully composed again, still uncomfortable with anyone but Kiyomi seeing any sign of weakness in her.

"Sure. Take all the time you need." Kiyomi breezed out of the room.

Ivy faced the tree again, examining the precious bead she held in her fingers. She hadn't expected anything like this. Not the gift, not being welcomed here so warmly.

Her life was completely unrecognizable from what it had been before. She no longer had to look over her shoulder everywhere she went, expecting someone to try and kill her at any moment.

She had a home, even if it was just temporary, and people who cared about her. Loved her, even. Her Valkyrie sisters and their significant others had become not just her family, but also her friends.

She looked up at the star glowing at the top of the tree. Marcus had insisted she place it there when they'd decorated it together last week, holding the ladder steady for her while she'd climbed to the top to put it in its position of honor. At first it had been hard to accept that this was real. That she wasn't going to be charged with anything or face jail time.

Rycroft had come through for her. Not only that, her clear record and shiny new US passport meant she was free to go wherever and do whatever she wanted.

She'd had a lot of time to think about what that was.

All the others were doing inspiring things, some of them raising a family.

Ivy didn't think that would ever happen for her, but she liked what Amber and Kiyomi were doing. In addition to helping them combat human trafficking and prevent orphans from being preyed upon like they had been, she wanted to set up a consulting business of her own and use her skills to help take down criminal networks across the globe.

She was free to pursue that now, and make a positive difference in the world on her terms. It was the most amazing gift anyone could ever have given her. Aside from the heartfelt symbol she wore around her neck.

A burst of laughter carried down the hall, breaking her from her thoughts. When she walked into the kitchen moments later, Marcus and Kiyomi looked up at her from the counter where they were finishing up several dishes at once.

Ivy rolled up her sleeves with a smile, happy to be part of the team. To finally feel like she belonged. "Right. Where do you want me to start?"

~

Once again the lovely old house was bursting with guests and filled with conversation and laughter. It looked and smelled amazing, the air perfumed with the smells of a full turkey dinner and spiced with the crisp notes of the evergreen garlands and bowls of orange pomanders studded with cloves.

Kiyomi sailed into the kitchen to grab more platters, smiling at Ivy, who was busy at the stove stirring a big pot of gravy, her new necklace clasped around her neck. Kiyomi liked having her around for company, and Ivy living in the gatehouse meant she and Marcus still had plenty of privacy.

The three of them had been prepping for the past two days to get everything ready for their guests. Yesterday they'd even brought in the cook, Mrs. Biddington, to lend an extra hand. Christmas was still a week off, but this date had worked for everyone, and with the whole Valkyrie family here to celebrate together, they needed all the help they could get.

The work was worth it. Apart from all of them being together under one roof again, the best part for Kiyomi was the relaxed, joyous atmosphere surrounding the celebration.

There was no threat to contend with this time. No mission to plan or work up to. Just all kinds of downtime to spend together visiting, sharing meals, doing various activities, or nothing at all.

Marcus stood at the granite counter taking another batch of Yorkshire puddings out of a pan, looking delicious in a cream cable knit sweater that emphasized the muscles in his chest and shoulders. She couldn't believe their first year anniversary was already days away. "Is this all?"

He raised an eyebrow. "That's four double batches. Why, do you think we'll need more?"

She snickered at the horrified look on his face. He'd done all of this for her, had opened up his ancestral home to all these people once again, because he knew how much it would mean to her. Just when she thought she couldn't possibly love him more than she already did, he went and did something that opened up a new depth of emotion inside her.

"Well, we're talking about Chloe, so…" She dropped a kiss on his cheek before taking the puddings out to the dining room. They'd opened the pocket doors separating it from the library, and placed three long tables end to end down the center of the combined rooms in order to seat everyone.

Sitting at the middle one next to Heath, who had fully recovered from his injuries except for some lingering concussion symptoms, Chloe's face lit up when she saw the puddings. "Yes! I knew he wouldn't forget."

"These six are for you, from Marcus. He says Merry Christmas."

"Tell him he's the best," she said, already loading them onto her plate.

A high-pitched squeal came from Kiyomi's right on the way back to the kitchen. She swiveled just in time to avoid impact with a running toddler.

Rosie was adorable in a little red velvet dress, her curls pulled up into a bow. Matt DeLuca swooped in to scoop his daughter up and blew a noisy raspberry on the side of her neck, making her squeal and belly laugh.

Kiyomi ruffled the toddler's soft hair on the way by and returned to the kitchen. Marcus was carving the second turkey now, his face set in serious lines as he worked. The way he took control in the kitchen was almost as hot as the way he took control in the bedroom, which now happened a lot more frequently since their interlude in the stables.

Ivy finished pouring another jug of gravy and wiped her hands on the dishtowel draped over her shoulder, smiling at Kiyomi when a burst of laughter came from the dining room. "So, this is what an actual Christmas feels like, huh?"

It was only her second one, but that was more than Ivy had experienced. "Yes." Noisy, chaotic, a whirlwind of activity and a lot of work over a short amount of time. But so worth it to celebrate with the ones she loved most.

Trinity and Briar came in to carry more dishes to the tables. Kiyomi took some mashed potatoes, and Marcus brought the second turkey.

She paused beside him at the head of the end table with a satisfied smile as she surveyed the scene before them. Everyone gathered together for this special meal, even Karas. The dog had strategically positioned herself under the table by Rosie's place, trying to evade the eager, grasping little hands that weren't always as gentle as they needed to be, yet still hopeful of something delicious dropping to the floor during the meal.

Marcus pulled out Kiyomi's chair for her, seated her, then reached for his glass and stood behind his place at the head, his weight equally balanced now that his hip had regained its previous level of comfort.

"A toast," he said, his deep voice carrying through the huge double room with ease while everyone watched him. "Kiyomi and I want to thank all of you for coming here to celebrate with us. Especially the new additions," he added, smiling at Rosie and four-month-old Rory, who watched him with curious, dark blue eyes from the security of Trinity's loving embrace. "Happy Christmas to all of you, and may this be only the first of many more we spend together. Cheers."

"Cheers," everyone chorused, and touched glasses.

"Cool, now can we do the Christmas crackers?" Chloe asked impatiently, shrugging at the looks she got. "I like how loud they snap when you do it right."

"Aye," Marcus said with a wry smile.

Everyone picked up their Christmas cracker from the top of their place setting, held one end in one hand, then crossed their arms and reached for the other half of the person's cracker next to them.

"On three," Kiyomi said when everybody was ready. "One. Two. Three!"

The resulting noise was a cacophony of snapping and cracking, sounding like muted fireworks around the tables. Chloe laughed and fished out her green paper crown, positioning it on her head like a queen before reading her joke aloud. It was terrible, making everyone groan, but that was part of the fun of it.

It was the best dinner Kiyomi had ever had. Roasted turkey, honey-glazed ham, roasted Brussel sprouts with bacon and onion and lemon zest, glazed carrots, corn, mashed potatoes, gravy, rolls, and of course, Yorkshire puddings. Everyone joked and talked as they ate, conversation flowing around and between all three tables.

After everyone had helped clear up the dishes, she and Marcus went back into the kitchen to get the desserts. She grabbed the bottle of brandy from the cupboard and liberally dosed both plum puddings she and Marcus had made using an old recipe from his family.

"You wanna light my fire now, or later?" she asked in a seductive tone.

His lips twitched, a wicked look heating his deep brown eyes. "Both. But especially later."

Anticipation kindled inside her. Much as she was

enjoying their guests, she was looking forward to being alone with him later tonight, in the private sanctuary of their bedroom while a fire blazed in the fireplace. Marcus was sexiest when he wore nothing but firelight on his skin.

He followed her to the kitchen doorway, dimmed the lights in the dining room/library, pulled out a lighter and flicked the switch, holding it near the pudding. The alcohol burst into beautiful purple and blue flames. Kiyomi carried it proudly through to the dining area.

"Oh, hell yeah, a dessert that's on *fire*," Chloe cried from halfway down the room, making everyone laugh.

Kiyomi grinned and set it in front of Chloe to admire, filled with blissful satisfaction. Ivy was right. This was what a real Christmas felt like. And it was hopefully just one of many more they would all share together.

—The End—

Dear reader,

Thank you for reading *Taking Vengeance*. If you'd like to stay in touch with me and be the first to learn about new releases you can:

Join my newsletter at:
http://kayleacross.com/v2/newsletter/
Find me on Facebook:
https://www.facebook.com/KayleaCrossAuthor/
Follow me on Twitter:
https://twitter.com/kayleacross
Follow me on Instagram:
https://www.instagram.com/kaylea_cross_author/

Also, please consider leaving a review at your favorite online book retailer. It helps other readers discover new books.

Happy reading,

Kaylea

Coming Up Next

Dangerous Survivor
Crimson Point Series, book #7

RELEASING JANUARY 2022

She's come back to face her demons.

Ember Thiessen is the sole survivor of a horrific attack that
killed her brother and blew her world apart. Months later
when she learns that his dog has been found, she returns to
Crimson Point, ready to confront the past and reclaim her
life. The last thing she expects is to recognize the hard,
reclusive man who rescued the pup—a man she has
crossed paths with before. He's everything she's come to
fear. Big. Hard. Deadly. Yet she's drawn to him on the
deepest level. But the danger isn't over yet. The killer
responsible for all her nightmares has escaped, and Ember
finds herself turning to this hardened soldier for protection.

He's the only man who can keep her safe.

After leaving his elite military career and its painful end
behind, Boyd Masterson retreated to a solitary life in the
hills above Crimson Point. All he wants is peace and quiet.
Then Ember suddenly appears on his doorstep, and everything changes. He knows what she went through. Knows
that she's still healing and trying to put her life back
together. He's a damaged warrior, the last thing she needs,
but she calls to a part of him that still yearns to protect and

defend. When the man responsible for killing her brother decides she's a loose end, Boyd doesn't hesitate to step up and protect her. But as the attraction between them builds and the killer moves in, Boyd realizes he's risking his heart as well as his life.

ABOUT THE AUTHOR

NY Times and USA Today Bestselling author Kaylea Cross writes edge-of-your-seat military romantic suspense. Her work has won many awards, including the Daphne du Maurier Award of Excellence, and has been nominated multiple times for the National Readers' Choice Awards. A Registered Massage Therapist by trade, Kaylea is also an avid gardener, artist, Civil War buff, Special Ops aficionado, belly dance enthusiast and former nationally-carded softball pitcher. She lives in Vancouver, BC with her husband and family.

You can visit Kaylea at www.kayleacross.com. If you would like to be notified of future releases, please join her newsletter at:

http://kayleacross.com/v2/newsletter/

Complete Booklist

<u>ROMANTIC SUSPENSE</u>

Kill Devil Hills Series
Undercurrent
Submerged
Adrift

Rifle Creek Series
Lethal Edge
Lethal Temptation
Lethal Protector

Vengeance Series
Stealing Vengeance
Covert Vengeance
Explosive Vengeance
Toxic Vengeance
Beautiful Vengeance
Taking Vengeance

Crimson Point Series
Fractured Honor
Buried Lies
Shattered Vows
Rocky Ground
Broken Bonds
Deadly Valor
Dangerous Survivor

DEA FAST Series
Falling Fast
Fast Kill
Stand Fast
Strike Fast
Fast Fury
Fast Justice
Fast Vengeance

Colebrook Siblings Trilogy
Brody's Vow
Wyatt's Stand
Easton's Claim

Hostage Rescue Team Series
Marked
Targeted
Hunted
Disavowed
Avenged
Exposed
Seized
Wanted
Betrayed
Reclaimed
Shattered
Guarded

Titanium Security Series
Ignited
Singed

Burned

Extinguished

Rekindled

Blindsided: A Titanium Christmas novella

Bagram Special Ops Series

Deadly Descent

Tactical Strike

Lethal Pursuit

Danger Close

Collateral Damage

Never Surrender (a MacKenzie Family novella)

Suspense Series

Out of Her League

Cover of Darkness

No Turning Back

Relentless

Absolution

Silent Night, Deadly Night

PARANORMAL ROMANCE

Empowered Series

Darkest Caress

Historical Romance

The Vacant Chair

EROTIC ROMANCE (writing as ***Callie Croix***)

Deacon's Touch

Manufactured by Amazon.ca
Acheson, AB